The Heartbreak Show

A BOUND BY RAVENS NOVEL

JESIKAH SUNDIN

Forest Tales PUBLISHING
Dystopian Fantasy and Faerie Tales

Text and Cover Design/Illustration
Bound by Ravens Copyright © 2023 Jesikah Sundin
All rights reserved.

ISBN-13: 978-1-954694-33-0
ISBN-10: 1-954694-33-4

Forest Tales Publishing, LLC
PO Box 84
Monroe, WA 98272
foresttalespublishing@gmail.com
jesikahsundin@gmail.com

All rights reserved. No part of this publication may be reproduced, stored in a retrieval system, or transmitted in any form or by any means – for example, electronic, mechanic, photocopy, recording or otherwise – without the prior written consent of the publisher. The only exception is brief quotations in printed reviews.

This book is a work of fiction. Names, characters, places, and incidents are the product of the author's imagination or are used fictitiously. Any resemblance to actual events, locales, or persons, living or dead, is coincidental.

Cover design by MoorBooks Design (@moorbooksdesign)

Hardcase art by Lauren Richelieu (@laurenrichelieuart) (@ghostinthegvarden)

Character illustrations by Lauren Richelieu, Alexandra Curte (@allexandraurte), and Chicklen Doodle (@chicklen.doodle)

Map by Elle Madison (@ellemadisonauthor)

Interior design by Forest Tales Publishing, LLC

To Raccoons and...

George, darlin', you stole gloves, our hearts, and nearly the last book's love story. Though I know one does not question the thieving ways of faerie raccoons, try not to steal Cian's and Glenna's spotlight too.

And to my Readers...

You wanted Cian's story and I couldn't resist you

And, thus, here is a low-stakes, romcom faerie tale as sunny and ridiculously chaotic as Cian, as sweet and spicy as Glenna, and as fluffy as George.

Stars above, especially the fluffy bit.

Lady of Man, bets...

...Gent of Fem, bets

Irish Pronunciations

Cian — [key-ahn]
Glenna — [Glen-uh]

Balor — [bawl-or]
Cillian — [kill-ee-ahn]
Carran — [Care-REN]
Crodh sìdh — [Crow she]
Dudeen — [Doo dean]
Eithne — [Eth-nuh]
Ferelith — [Feh-reh-lith]
Fomorians — [Fuh-more-ee-anns]
Gancanagh — [Gah-caw-nah]
Glas Gaibhnenn — [Gloss Ghav-lynn]
Lugh — [Loo]
Lughnasadh — [Loo-nah-suh]
Ogham — [Oh-em]
Seren — [seh-REN]
Tuatha Dé Danann — [Too-uh day dan-ann]
Tailtiu — [Tall-chew]

Seren

The Wild

PRIMRY GREEN

Bó Fi

STELLAR WINDS CASINO

PALAC STA

BEGGAR'S HOLE

CRESCENT STREET MARKET

FERRY DOCK

FERRY DOCK & TRAIN STATION

RHYLEN'S NIGHTMAR

RIVER DEORA CRANN

Kingdom of Carran

Fennel Marsh

Mineral Spring

Kilkerry Village

Fiddling Duck

Den Merrow

Witch's Cottage

Edona Wood

River Deora Crann

To the Eastern Cities

Prologue

The Tale of Cian from Irish Mythology

Once upon a time, there was a Fomorian king named Balor who could destroy entire armies when his one, evil eye opened. Many feared him, for good reason, including his enemy, the Tuatha Dé Danann. There was no way to defeat this monster except through a prophecy: he would one day die at the hands of his grandson.

Since he didn't have a grandchild, he didn't fear death.

He did have one child, though, a beautiful daughter named Eithne.

To safeguard himself, Balor imprisoned Eithne when she was very young in a tower made of glass, one built on an island that was reachable only by magic. Then he selected a staff of women to care for the princess's every need, but only if they agreed to his bargain first.

Eithne was never to know what a man was and, thus, they were *never* to speak to her of men.

As Eithne grew, she spent most of her time peering out to sea atop the glass tower. And, every night, she dreamed of a beautiful face unlike any she had ever known—one that first appeared to her as a woman. She dreamt of them so much, she ached to meet the person whose face bewitched her sleeping hours. But when she described this strangely beau-

The Heartbreak Show

tiful face to the women, they remained silent.

For every night, Eithne dreamed of a man's face.

Across the sea, in Ireland, dwelled a god from the Tuatha Dé Danann named Cian. He was a mighty warrior, born of the Great Physician and Danu the Mother Goddess. Despite his parentage and feats, he was best known throughout the clans for Glas Gaibhnenn, a magical cow of prosperity and fertility who appeared during times of famine and need.

A cow his brother, a blacksmith, once owned and bound to Cian through an enchanted bridle.

A faerie cow whose milk never ran dry.

Everyone desired to own Glas Gaibhnenn, none more so than Balor. The Fomorian king often followed Cian about in disguise, scheming how to steal this wondrous cow. But Cian was aware of Balor's plans and took every precaution to protect Glas Gaibhnenn from his enemy.

But not *every* precaution.

While Cian met with the very blacksmith brother who had bound him to Glas Gaibhnenn, he left the Cow of Plenty to another brother's care. An unfortunate mistake Cian would regret for the remaining days of his life.

Balor appeared as a redheaded boy to the brother overseeing Glas Gaibhnenn and shared that Cian planned to hoard all the new weapons for himself. Furious, the brother left the cow with the redheaded boy and stomped off toward the blacksmith's shop.

The evil king quickly absconded back to his land with the magical cow.

In a wild panic, Cian sought out a well-known druidess to help him steal back Glas Gaibhnenn.

It so happened this druidess knew of Balor's prophecy, though she didn't share the details with Cian. Instead, she declared that to retrieve his cow, he would need to kill Balor. But such a daring plan would re-

The Tale of Cian from Irish Mythology

quire Cian to first travel to a guarded island through the mists. Desperate, Cian readily agreed to her plan.

So, the druidess disguised him as a woman.

She then conjured a magical wind that blew both her and Cian across the sea, through the veil of mists, to the glass tower's very shores where Eithne lived.

The druidess knocked on the bolted door and shouted, "The Queen of the Faeries accompanies me! We seek shelter from the enemies who pursue her!"

The women opened the door and, as soon as the druidess entered, they fell under a short sleeping spell.

Cian climbed up the stairs in search of armed guards. Instead, he found a woman with long black hair who peered out over the sea. The moment his eyes locked onto her wistful form, his heart fell for her extraordinary beauty and sadness. And when Eithne looked upon him, she was astonished to see the face who had visited her dreams since she had blossomed into womanhood.

Cian married her with only the sea and stars as witness and then made love to her in the tower.

As the days stretched on, Eithne and Cian fell deeper in love. But the druidess grew increasingly afraid of Balor and announced they must leave. Cian begged the druidess to take Eithne back to Ireland with them, but she feared Balor would bring war to retrieve the princess. Before Cian could change her mind, the druidess conjured the magical wind and returned both her and Cian to the mainland, leaving Eithne behind.

And his magical cow.

Eithne was heartbroken and took to her bed. She grew more and more despondent when the face she loved more than any other didn't return for her, not even in her dreams. Her grief eased, however, when discovering that she carried Cian's child.

The Heartbreak Show

Months later, she gave birth to triplet boys.

Balor, learning of this, seized her sons in a rage and threw all three newborns into the unforgiving sea.

Eithne's keening wails shook the glass walls and filled the oceans.

The god of the sea was moved by her unending heartbreak, though, and rescued a single babe. A lad with hair as candescent and golden as the sun. To keep the boy safe from Balor, he personally delivered the child to Cian.

The very moment Cian gazed upon his son's bright, shining countenance, he fell in love and ensured the lad had the best training, leaving him to the earth goddess Tailtiu to foster, as was the practice of the Tuatha Dé Danann in that time.

He named the boy Lugh for his shining hair.

Lugh grew into great power and magic and, when a man, became both the God of the Sun and Light, Master of all Crafts, and King of the Tuatha Dé Danann—the very grandchild prophesized to end Balor's life.

Though Balor did eventually die at the hands of his grandson, Cian never did see his true love again.

Or his magical cow.

> "Gods and Fighting Men" by Lady Gregory, 1905, retold and abridged by Jesikah Sundin, a folktale adaptation of "The Fate of the Children of Tuireann (*Oidheadh Chloinne Tuireann*)," from "The Battle of Magh Tuireadh (*Cath Maige Tuired*) in The Book of Conquests (*Leabhar Gabhála Éireann*)," *The Mythological Cycle*, 11th century, Ireland.

"Beware the tunes that touch your heart. The Gancanagh will play the soul

Beware, sweet lass, don't crave his art. He'll pierce your heart and leave a hole."

– Unknown, Irish Origin –

Chapter One

CIAN MERRICK

Of all the fecking places for Owen to retch up the whiskey I nicked, it would be while on all fours next to the boarding docks.

The steam engine blared its horn. More like screamed to my fluthered head and I grimaced. People hurried past to board the eastbound train. I snorted at the open disgust in their upturned features. I wasn't sure if it was at seeing a lady man with a raccoon clutched to his dirt stained, blue skirts or a faerie losing the magical contents of his stomach—quite dramatically, too, the little shite.

I gathered Owen's long, decorated black hair away from his face when he heaved again. "I can't marry you now, lad," I slurred.

"But why, love bug?" Owen erupted into drunken laughter over my mam's nickname for me between bouts of sickness. "We're mad for each other."

"Because, my giant fae cock shifter"—I winked at a gent who strolled by—"I don't marry males who can't hold in their . . . *liquor*."

The mortal nearly choked and I grinned.

Most female birds, regardless of species, were called hens. And most male birds, including ravens, were called cocks, much to the mortification of wealthy mainlanders everywhere. Cock was such a delightful word too.

George patted Owen on the back.

"God—" Owen doubled over again before he could finish.

"Aye?" I knew he meant *gods*, but I was a shameless hussy. "Call me your god again, darlin'. You know it puffs my chest feathers when you do."

Owen started laughing once more.

Gods, I could use a cigarette. Not sure it was worth casing for one while piss drunk though. My world was spinning enough.

Since a wee thing, I had a seer's ability to notice what others tried to hide. Rhylen often teased that I missed nothing and . . . I really didn't— couldn't. My restless, racing mind craved the noise. Not just the noise, but the chaos of multiple thought strands at once.

Feck it. My gaze reluctantly lifted to hunt for a smoke and, immediately, the blurry pieces of settings and people rushed my tipsy brain at rapid fire.

A woman in a gaudy red silk gown and jewels pulled a single coin from her purse. Not enough for the train fare.

Was I even included in the exclamation "gods?" Could people pray to me, a demi?

An older man leaned against a column and lit a pipe to mask the unshed tears in his eyes.

As the great-grandson of the Mother, the most *rutting* fertile god of all the gods, obviously people were praying to me when—

The Heartbreak Show

A younger man escorted a woman off Seren's ferry platform, then peered over his shoulder. Shuffling behind them, a fae girl in a maid's uniform pressed a hand protectively to the barely showing bump of her stomach.

My eyes narrowed. *Obviously*, as the demi-god of a fertility goddess, the people praying "oh god!" during the throes of passion were praying to me.

Two lads around twelve or so shot marbles at the skirts of their mams. One spit into a small handful of dirt and painted a phallic symbol on the cream silk beside him while the other snickered.

The corners of my mouth hooked up at that. Wait. I narrowed my eyes again. Were the gods calling me a childish dick for pointing out the *obvious*?

George peered up at me and chittered.

"Well, Georgie Dirty Paws," I half-slurred, half-drawled—it was talent at this point, really. "Barry thinks everyone's a dick."

"Lady of Man . . ." Owen groaned, blindly reaching for me.

"If you call me a dick too, I swear by my heaving he-vage, our wedding is absolutely off."

He sputtered another laugh. "He-vage?"

"Male cleavage," I cooed and pet his head. "Now up, eejit." I dragged Owen to a wobbly stand.

A dandy gent who wore a hideous pair of red boots, brisked down the boardwalk on the way to Seren's ferry. A cigarette in his fingers.

Finally.

My hand shot out, plucked the cigarette from his mouth, then plopped it into mine. I dragged in deep and blew out slowly. The man skidded to a stop and gaped at me. A blush warmed his cheeks when I puckered my lips at him in a flirty kiss in thanks. Until, that is, we both noticed my glove-stealing faerie familiar caressing his red boots.

"George, no," I stage-whispered in horror.

The raccoon looked up at me with pleading eyes.

"You want me to . . . wrestle them off his feet?" I sucked another long draw, careful not to ruin my rouge-painted lips, and gestured at the dandy. "And scandalize this fine gent in front of everyone for *those*?"

George nodded his head.

The man straightened and lifted his chin. "How dare you insult me in an outdated gown from the Vanderbilt Leeson catalogue."

The hand holding the stolen cigarette paused mid-air.

There were catalogues . . . for *dresses*?

George scampered a couple steps away, apparently ashamed to be seen beside an outdated *catalogue* dress and proceeded to pet the red boots again, the wee traitorous bastard. The man, peering down his nose, spared me one last haughty glance, then doffed his hat at my bloody raccoon and strolled off.

Before I could holler a cracker reply, Owen stumbled against me, nearly knocking us both down. To steady himself, he nuzzled his face into my neck and patted my chest. "You do have nice he-vage."

I barked a laugh, making Owen fall into another fit himself.

"What are you two eejits doing?"

The voice registered in my scuttered brain, but I couldn't stop laughing. Especially with Owen's breathy wheezes tickling my neck.

I blinked back the growing blurriness in my vision and peered up to find Rhylen eyeing me, a scowl between his dark brows, Sean standing beside him. Corbin leaned around Owen and grimaced, placing a hand over his nose and mouth.

Cigarette ash fell on my fingers. "Feck," I hissed, shaking the embers

The Heartbreak Show

off.

"We're getting hitched, fellas," Owen sputtered out in Corbin's face, making the latter rear back in disgust. "For coin."

"For coin?" Rhylen repeated.

"Is my broody Raven jealous?" I meant to tap Rhylen's nose and poked his cheek instead. The scowl between Rhylen's eyes deepened. "Aye, coin."

I threw an arm around my best friend's shoulders, drawing him in close, Owen squeezed in along with him, and opened my mouth to speak. Except, I couldn't remember our plan. What was our stars damned plan? My mouth clamped shut. Let's see . . . I nicked an unopened bottle of whiskey from a bag. Owen found me. We talked about being poorer than felly poor, and—I remembered!

"A coin-beggar's show, darlin'."

My brother's lips dipped into a frown. "About getting married?"

"For gifts." I gestured at the station with my cigarette. "Mainlander wedding tradition."

With a sigh, Corbin eased Owen off me, who then patted Corbin's chest and murmured, "You have nice mleavage too."

I cracked a grin. Mleavage.

Warmth crept up Corbin's cheeks at Owen's petting.

"Lady of Man." The snap to Rhylen's voice sobered me up and my gaze whipped back to his. Despite the tired commanding tone, the feathered arse's lips twitched.

A small spot by his temple was rubbed raw. He blinked in a slow squint despite the evening sky. A tiny muscle by his left eye pulsed. His jaw was clenched, even with a half-smile.

I tossed the butt of my pinched cigarette to the ground and rubbed it out with the toe of my heeled shoe. If I weren't such an opportunistic strumpet, I would have saved the bottle for ol' Rhylee Lo here. Instead, I did the next best thing.

Facing my best friend, I squished his cheeks between the palms of my fingerless lace-gloved hands and pouted, "Tell me I'm pretty, Rhy-Rhy."

He breathed a laugh, a genuine one. The ache in my chest, however, the one I tried to drown with drink, began bleating for attention once more. We were broke. There was no real incoming revenue. Little to no food. A fever was sweeping through the mortals at camp. Winter would set in soon. Supplies to build our own Night Market wouldn't arrive until spring.

And Rhylen Lonan felt the hunger pains and desperation of every single person in his flock.

Goddess help me, but I would do *anything* to lessen this burden he carried.

Beneath my massaging fingers, the tension in his jaw relaxed; the worry wrinkling his forehead smoothed. Wells of exhaustion dulling his dark purple eyes brightened to amusement as we continued to hold each other's gaze. I waited . . . waited . . . and then his lips curved into a smooshed smirk I knew meant he felt sassy broody instead of stressed broody.

"Not as pretty as me," he tossed back.

I kissed his cheek, leaving a rouge mark, before releasing his face and grumbled, "Bloody Ravens."

His grin widened.

And dammit if I didn't swoon in brotherly affection—

A gasp left me. The pistons of my mind accelerated.

I knew the perfect coin-beggar's show.

Turning to Owen, I patted his upper arm. "Sorry to break your

The Heartbreak Show

heart, lad. But I can't marry you."

"For feck's sake," Corbin muttered.

I cocked a flirty smile and winked at the fellas before flouncing off in the direction of camp. I needed to find the Gent of Fem and make a bet.

One to spark that feisty, competitive nature of hers.

One that would save our new tribe.

Chapter Two

Glenna Lonan

Dusky afternoon light spilled into the wagon I shared with the eejit sprawled out in bed next to me. I gritted my teeth just thinking about his and Owen's idiocy. We could barely afford food let alone bail one of them from jail.

Last night, Cian had stumbled into camp, hollering my name like he was painfully dying and seeing my face was the only way he'd draw another breath. So loud, so very embarrassingly loud, people began gathering. His hips were swaying just as ridiculously as the rest of him. The pale blue dress he wore had slipped down his shoulders; the tattered hem of the skirt dragged in the mud. The dark red rouge on his lips had smeared onto his chin.

I had stayed beside Filena and Braelin, refusing to indulge the drunken gobshite and his dramatics. He found me though—he *always* found me. Grinning that rascally smile I could never resist, he pulled me into an embrace and I melted into a heart-sighing puddle, not that I'd let him know and feed his cocky ego.

Before I could ask why he was invoking my name to wake the dead, Cian laughed into my neck while mumbling nonsense about not marrying Owen.

Marry . . . Owen?

Then he passed out.

He was trying to kiss me one second and, the next, his body went boneless. The lad dragged me down with him as he fell, too.

Rhylen had to carry Cian inside.

The arse had been sleeping ever since and I . . . I was melting into a puddle once more at the sight of him undressed, at peace, tangled in our blankets. Well, melting since his mam, who slept on the pullout bench, left to keep Gran company.

My fingers trailed through Cian's wavy locks. The constant disheveled, just bedded look of those silky strands blushed hot in my veins, even when I was pissed at him. Stars, I craved preening his hair every second of every day. And when those rich, sunny strands fell over his gray eyes? When he peered at me through those very same fallen, mussed locks?

I became moonstruck.

He was a kind of beautiful that defied convention. With a masculine beauty in form and a feminine beauty of face, his soul possessing the aspects of both. Now that I knew he was part fae—not just any fae either, but a demi-god descended from a powerful triple goddess line—his strange, indescribable Otherworldliness made sense.

His insatiable carnality too.

And oh how he openly indulged in his sexuality.

For as long as I had known Cian Merrick, people of all races and genders had eagerly hung off his arms, kissed him behind the tents. When older, they took him to their rooms in the villages we rolled through or visited his and Rhylen's wagon instead.

Not that I was any better. I had a trail of dalliances too. My appetite for casual seductions couldn't rival his, though. Not in this lifetime. Not in two lifetimes. The lad was as sensually charged as he was chaotically restless.

The pad of my finger brushed over the soft curve of his full lips, ones no longer stained with rouge. It made my pulse race when they were, though. When they left their marks on my skin too.

For seven years, since I was thirteen and he sixteen, I had dreamed of those lips tasting mine.

Yet, despite my growing fledgling feelings clear through maturity, despite Cian always noticing every little thing around him, he acted unaware and would tease me, like he did Filena. Include me in his escapades, also like Filena. I was nothing more than the pesky, bossy little sister of his best friend and the granddaughter of the faerie who owned him.

Until, that is, our tribe's Winter Solstice celebration four years ago.

While hiding behind another's wagon, drinking wine a village boy had bought me, Cian found me. Just walked up as if he knew exactly where I was. Like usual, he didn't peer directly my way. Instead, he fell against the wagon beside me, staring up into the night sky as we passed the bottle back and forth.

We were sixteen and nineteen and he was just so beautiful, I couldn't help stealing moonlit glances at him. The night had dusted his lashes in silver and painted the sweep of his cheekbones in pale light. And his lips, full, lush, often tipped in mischief, were flushed with desire. Confused, my gaze had drifted upward and . . . he was looking at me—truly looking at me. Not as a sister or friend, but as something *other*. As something that could be *more*.

And what we wanted was forbidden.

But I didn't care.

Right before Cian's lips met mine, my brother had called his name. Panic had flashed across Cian's eyes for the faintest heartbeat. Panic fol-

The Heartbreak Show

lowed by an emotion I couldn't decipher. He hollered "here" and walked backward, flashed me one of his trademark boyish, up-to-no-good grins . . . and left.

After that night, he avoided looking my way again.

And my pining soul began withering to dust.

I slowly blinked and dragged my fingers from his lips to caress the delicious lines of his abdomen.

We had co-existed in a strange, shapeless place the four years since. But a month before the tent fire, the one that destroyed part of West Tribe, our relationship had materialized into something breathless and intentional. And it was us, only us. Our siblings were not involved, like in the past. I had been drowning in loneliness. I missed Filena. I missed my brother too. Our work and social schedules constantly conflicted. And when we weren't working, we took turns caring for Gran.

Cian began dropping by the confectionary wagon to check in on me before meeting up with the lads. He made a point to also sit beside me around the cook pot as well as riddle me while doing chores. Well, more like sparking my competitive ire. He had this knack for winding me up.

But suns above, I had needed him. I had needed a fight too, to give my grief fists.

Cian acted the fool—*was* a fool—but he had this uncanny ability to show up when one needed him most. He knew exactly what was needed too.

Cian just always . . . *knew*.

The pad of my finger began tracing the curves of Cian's chest and I bit back a dreamy sigh.

"Glenna . . ."

My fingers stilled.

His sleep-roughed voice shivered down my body.

Gray eyes slowly squinted open. "Keep worshiping me, darlin', and—"

I flicked his forehead.

"Ow!" He pushed up on his elbows, every muscle taut. "What the feck was that for?"

I shoved open the curtains and his face twisted into a grimace. "Need another hint?"

Groaning, Cian shut the curtain as he fell back onto the pillows, then draped an arm over his eyes. "Sadistic witch."

"Preening harlot."

He snorted.

I waited a second, then gritted out, "You could have been arrested!" Public drunkenness was legal at licensed markets, fairs, and pubs. *Not* train stations. He knew this too. I could throttle him, I was so upset.

"You know why drunkards never stop drinking?"

"You're a reveler, eejit. Not your da."

Cian rolled over onto his side to face me. "Pain," he answered quietly—seriously. "We're not cut out to handle pain." He glared at me. "Including hangovers."

"Next time, *darlin'*, drink the bottle at camp." I rested a hand on his bicep and softly added, "Lean on me, Cian. Whatever pain you face, I'm always here." Then squeezed. "At. Camp."

A rascally corner of his mouth lifted for half a heartbeat before his features tightened. His eyes were suddenly sharp and studied my face with an intensity that pebbled my skin. "What happened?" He brushed the tip of his finger in the barest caress over a small scrape on my upper cheek.

"An accident." My eyes darted to the window above our heads. "Nothing to fuss about." If he knew it was from hitting the ground last night . . .

Cian gently pinched my chin between his thumb and forefinger and

The Heartbreak Show

forced me to look at him. "What happened, Glenna?" The wildness building in his eyes combined with the lower, deadlier tone of his voice pooled liquid heat low in my belly—and dread. When I didn't answer right away, the protectiveness in his gaze shattered. "Oh gods, I did . . . I did this . . ."

"No," I quickly reassured him. Falling stars, my heart. "You would *never* intentionally hurt me, Cian Merrick, drunk or sober."

"Intentionally?" He laughed bitterly. "Does it matter?"

I blew out a slow breath. "You passed out and I wasn't strong enough to hold you up." To lighten the moment, I smirked. "You were trying to kiss me, eejit, and while telling me you ended your fake wedding with Owen."

The paleness of his face grew more bloodless. "I was forcing myself on you."

"Gods, no, Cian." I rolled him to his back to straddle his hips, then cupped his face. "You are *not* him."

"If I ever—"

"You'll not finish that sentence, mate."

His eyes widened, same as mine. We had never called each other mates. We hadn't called ourselves . . . anything. But the word slipped out. I had loved him for years. Pined for him to the point of only taking blond-haired, blue-eyed mortal lads to my bed. Creepy, probably, a Raven collecting trait absolutely, but my stricken heart didn't know how else to indulge in what was forbidden.

Now my fantasy was reality and I would *not* let him fear a real relationship—fear me.

I pressed my mouth to his in a soft kiss.

His chest rose and fell with a deep, trembling sigh. I could feel his panic rising. This was a man who didn't settle easily, with a body that was always on the move, a mind that spun faster than a spinning wheel.

A man who had drifted from lover to lover, not caring if he knew their name or if they knew his.

I scraped my small canine along his bottom lip, gently bit down, and ground my hips against his.

"Glenna, darlin'..." His voice cracked.

With a wicked little grin, I tugged on his lip, satisfied when he released a breathy moan.

"Be a good boy, promise to never get drunk at the train station again," I teased, though I was quite serious, "and I'll give you another treat."

Cian's smile was slow. "Know where else you can bite me?"

"You'd enjoy that too much, *darlin'*." I yanked the curtain open again.

"Fecking hell," he hissed, scrunching up his face. "Cake hag."

"Gaudy tart."

He grabbed the curtain, snorting back a laugh, and I smacked his hand. "Promise me." I opened the curtain more.

"Aye," he groaned, covering his eyes. "I won't get drunk at the train station while we don't have bail money."

"*Be* drunk," I corrected. "You won't *get* or *be* drunk at the docks, period."

"Gent of Fem," he drolled, voice flat, "we'll live hundreds of years. Don't be a dryshite." He peeked at me from beneath his arm just so I could see his eye roll.

I let out a loud sigh. "Fiiiine." I pulled his hands from his eyes. "Swear in the blinding sunlight that you won't get drunk in *any* unlicensed public place while we can't bail your shiny, sparkly arse from jail."

Squinting a glare, he drawled, "I promise that my *sexy*, sparkly arse you want to bite and kiss"—he suggestively bit down on his bottom lip and my traitorous thighs clenched—"won't intentionally get drunk in any unlicensed public place while you can't spring me from jail."

I shut the curtain and his body deflated in relief. With the motion,

The Heartbreak Show

loose curls from my still-pinned up hair spilled around his face and he softly blinked. The appreciative daze didn't linger long, though, and was quickly replaced with a devious slant to his lips.

"While worshiping me in my sleep, as you should," Cian lilted, "the reverent motion of your fingers seemed insultingly distracted." My brow arched in a silent scoff. The lad was so full of himself. "What was your pretty head thinking about?"

"Honestly?"

"Obviously."

"Why did you ignore me for years?"

His eyes sharpened onto mine again. "You were thinking about the Winter Solstice revel?"

I nodded, not surprised that he knew what I asked without much information.

His hands slid up my thighs, tugging my cotton nightgown higher and higher with the possessive touch. "Because," he whispered against my mouth, "I only know how to obsess and you would ruin me."

"For others?"

"If I got too close . . ." His fingers curved around my bare arse and dragged me across his hardened length and gods, my eyes fluttered closed. "If I kissed you that night or any night, I would have died of a broken heart."

My eyes opened and found his. Our breaths heavy. Our bodies moving in a lazy, teasing rhythm.

"I would have pined for you until I wasted away to nothing."

The fingers gripping my arse dug into my soft flesh, a bite of pain that was all pleasure, and I gasped.

"You are my *gean cánach*, Glenna Lonan. My Love-Talker."

His mouth crushed mine in a bruising kiss right as he spun me to my back. And Holy Mother of Stars did this man kiss with his whole body.

I had promised him another treat for agreeing to behave, but now he was worshiping me. Fire raced just beneath my burning skin. The muscles of his arms and chest danced as he hovered above me. I sank my fingers into his bed-mussed locks. The searing heat of his hands pushed up my nightgown—

And stilled.

His entire body froze.

"That wee bastard."

I angled on the pillow to track his gaze and wrinkled my nose when spotting the hideous red boot. Aye, it was a horrible crime against fashion and . . . *everything*.

An instant mood killer.

"George left that abomination here last night, then ran off with Barry."

Cian groaned a few choice words and slipped from the blankets. He groaned again while straightening, this time from the throb in his hungover head. Not that it stopped him when seducing me. But that arsehole would attempt seductions while rattling his final, dying breaths.

No, *he* was the legendary *gean cánach*, a Love-Talker . . . what the eastern city mainlanders called a gancanagh, a male faerie who seduced mortals and fed off their lust and pining. Just one touch of his skin and she would grow instantly addicted to him, never to recover, the poor lass fated to die of a broken heart in a lovesick frenzy or by refusing to eat when, after taking his fill of her, he left.

Such a creature didn't exist. At least, not anymore. It was a tale to warn about the dangers of becoming elf struck by male faeries with honeyed tongues who abused their predatory beauty and coercion magic to the social shame of mortal girls.

Beware of faerie boy smiles . . . as the saying went.

No warning mortal lads about faerie girls, though, thank the wish-

The Heartbreak Show

less falling stars. Half my wardrobe came from elf struck village boys. My favorite feathered hat too.

Oh fine, maybe I was a gancanagh too.

We both were.

"Glennie Lo," Cian murmured while pulling on a pair of pants. "I need you to break my heart in a coin—"

I didn't hesitate. "Pink-toned rouge is entirely the wrong color for your complexion."

Cian's mouth fell open. "That was unnecessarily cruel."

"Cry on Owen's shoulder." I leaned back on my elbows, shaking the loose curls from *my* shoulders for extra dramatic effect.

"Jealousy doesn't become you, darlin'."

Cian pulled a shirt over his head and I could weep. Those muscles, that body that almost owned mine until a single, ghastly red boot ruined everything. Why? Who really knew with Cian Merrick.

Cocking his head, he grabbed said romance-ending ugly boot and pointed it at me, a trickster's gleam in his eye as he did so.

"Owen's heartbreak over being my fake ex-mate-to-be still counts."

Now I did scoff. "*Darlin'*," I tossed back, "fake breaking Owen's drunk heart does *not* count."

"He was sick with anguish."

"Villagers, Cian, not a Traveler lad."

"What about a mainlander *traveling* lad? Or lass?" He flashed me that up-to-no-good grin of his and I hesitated.

Was he suggesting we seduce strangers like before we—well, before whatever we were? I wanted to wipe that smug grin off his irritating, way-too-pretty face. But I wanted to crow in victory over his defeat even more.

Rolling my eyes, I slid to my feet and fisted my hands on my hips. "I'd still *fake* break more of their hearts than you, *darlin'*."

"My feisty Love-Talker..." he caged me against the bed, the revolting red boot pressing into my hip. "My gorgeous Gent of Fem."

Cian swooped in and kissed me, a hungry, demanding kiss I felt clear down to my curling toes. I could eternally die to the feel of his lips on mine every single time. A thousand suns were setting in my tightening skin. My entire body was floating in his arms when the arse backed away, grinning the smile of a boy who knew he was magic. Then he left me pressed to our bed, in a rucked-up nightgown and panting for him.

As if he had already won our bet.

But I would destroy him at his own game.

Chapter Three

CIAN MERRICK

Barry's yellow eyes slid to the repugnant boot I gripped as I approached the community fire pit. Catching my glare, the lad chuffed a low laugh. I ignored the fox and plopped down onto an empty stump, my brows pinched and my hair a finger-combed mess. The fellas, my sister, Braelin, Mam, and Gran eyed the red leather cradled in my arms but said nothing. It wasn't the weirdest thing I'd carried to a gathering. Definitely the ugliest, though.

Last night, I was too drunk to truly register what it was, only that my blurry vision found it revolting. This afternoon, though? I should throw this atrocity into the fire. Or stake it as a ward against evil fashion puns sported by arrogant dandies who believed themselves witty.

It was a cock boot.

A bloody *cock boot*.

Red, dome-shaped, with a rooster stitched on both sides.

Gods above . . .

The throbbing in my hungover head didn't give a dying star's arse how I destroyed this boot, though. But it needed to be somewhere George would never find it again.

Since I offered no explanation, or greeting, people returned to their conversations. Filena, however, was practically giddy over my suffering. After kicking her ankle a few weeks back, I deserved her mockery—and more. In my defense, though, my magic hadn't picked up, at any point, that the Fiachnas knew Filena was both a *fáidhbhean* and a *cailleach*. I had only wanted to stage the illusion that the collector had attacked her . . . instead of the reverse.

Still, when Rhylen looked away, I shot Filena a rude gesture and she snickered. That same moment, to my sister's eternal joy, the clouds parted in a dramatic reveal of the lowering sun and my smirk twisted into a pained grimace.

Gods, the fecking light was a constant dull, stabbing knife in my eyes. Worth it, though, to leave Glenna aroused and breathless to piss off her competitive nature. And damn every handsome freckle on my pretty face, did I crave being the target of her verbal talons and crowing grins.

Especially the past two weeks.

Glenna's creative mind had little to do since resting our wagon wheels beneath Seren. Supplies were low, our pooled coin laughable. Carran's government had yet to approve our Market and Fair License request. Fortune telling, unfortunately, fell within the license's business perimeters too.

But not music or plays, so long as we didn't charge for admittance.

The songbirds we threw at the station's travelers earned us little. Buskers were ten a penny in every poor village let alone in the sprawling cities east of Caledona Wood. We were shaking a copper in a tin can at their deaf purses.

No . . . our coin beggar's show would need to be clever, bawdy, and over-the-top. Whatever low-class but high-brow dramatics it took to legally glamour the eastern mainlanders out of their money while also giving Glenna an occupation to keep her from slipping into the shadows.

She did that—often.

There were many times over the years I had wanted to knock Rhylen's and Filena's heads together for failing to notice Glenna's struggles. Aye, I had abilities others didn't. My frustrations didn't care. I had *seen* visions of the future, like Filena, though only a few times. But unlike Filena, my seer magic primarily *saw* clues in the buried past as well as *saw* what was hidden in the present.

I could *see* through the mask Glenna glued tight to her face.

Sometimes I thought I was the only person who truly saw the real Glenna Lonan.

"I'll search for more wild apples today," Filena volunteered, cutting through my thoughts. "Mushrooms, berries, and nuts too."

"Need company?" Braelin asked.

A few others nearby offered to join as well.

"When a wee hennie..." Gran began and the small gathering hushed for the beloved Brenna Meadows to continue. "Me mam and nan added birch bark flour to spread out our rye and wheat stores."

Tree bark flour? As if a termite? I arched a brow at that. No one would argue with an ancient, though. Caravan fae were still connected to their wild origins when she was younger. Across from me, Filena wrinkled her nose at that suggestion and I almost snorted.

Rhylen slowly nodded his head in reluctant agreement. Stars above, the lad needed a drink. Perhaps the whole bottle. But, like the reveling tosspot I was, I saved none for him.

"We do need more firewood," Rhylen conceded a second later.

Owen slid me a disbelieving side-glance. I loathed his full-fae magic this afternoon. Not a lick hungover despite his retching last night, the lucky arse.

Gran patted Rhylen's knee. "Mixed the bark flour with faerie cattle milk, we did."

"Magic cows?" a formal mortal indentured asked her.

"Nae, lad. I don't speak of that type of *crodh sidh.*" Gran chuckled. "The faerie cattle herded in The Wilds."

Corbin choked and Sean patted him on the back, harder than necessary.

Rhylen's body, however, went deathly still. "You're suggesting we milk . . . *deer*?"

"Aye, the wee ones need milk, Rhylee Lo."

The slight horror on Rhylen's face fed my hungover soul. I opened my mouth to request the first sip of deer milk, provided by the gentle stroke of his skilled hands, when Glenna stepped from the woods and all breath left my lungs.

Sweet goddess . . .

The same sun I cursed I now reverently blessed. Silky afternoon light caressed the soft feathers of Glenna's large wings in iridescent purples and blues. The dusky plum hue of her favorite gown—and mine—hugged her mouth-watering curves and pushed up her breasts. Artfully fallen, obsidian ringlet curls bounced to her swaying steps and I had to bite back a groan.

Win by tempting me into an early grave it was then.

Excellent strategy.

Since we first kissed three weeks ago, since we'd done far more than kiss, I could think of nothing else but her. She had already been in my veins, my breath for years. I wasn't joking when I confessed that I only knew how to obsess. She was going to ruin me.

The word "mate" terrified me, though.

I locked onto the small scrape on her upper cheek. Shame heated my skin and I blinked back the panic building in my pulse. It sickened me to look at the wound, as minor as it might be. But it also sickened me to not fixate on the consequences of my recklessness.

The Heartbreak Show

Glenna sidled up Mam, who spoke in quiet tones while gently touching the injury. It was imperceptible, but Glenna flinched, and my heart cracked—

I sat in a rickety chair, watching my bruised knuckles twist a fraying ribbon, gritting back the furious tears. I had hit him back. Knocked him square in the jaw. The power, the pleasure that filled me was indescribable. It was a fleeting feeling, though, quickly replaced with familiar, sharp pain. At thirteen, I could fight back, but I refused to cry, no matter how much I wanted to. I wouldn't give that vile man any other reasons to call me a filthy Molly.

Mam dabbed a cool cloth on a bleeding wound on my cheek. I was still wearing an old, tattered dress of hers, refusing to take it off, despite Da's threats to sell me if I didn't.

"Not all heroes wear armor, Cillian," she had whispered. "Cian, the warrior god who fathered Lugh, wore a dress when he left his known world to chase after his birthright. He met and married his true love in a dress, too, he did."

My eyes lifted and I swallowed thickly.

Mam lowered the cloth and cupped my face with the barest touch. "It's time to chase after yer birthright, my wee Cian."

My mind snapped back to reality.

I was struggling to keep my breathing calm.

Everyone warming themselves at the fire probably saw Glenna fall when she couldn't keep my eejit arse up. I didn't beat her in a drunken rage, like Hamish did us, but what if I did one day? What if I lost control of myself? Because of a darker magic I may possess? Like Filena's actual ability to curse and transmute an object into another?

I jumped up from the stump when Glenna caught my eye. A saucy smile softened her lips—one meant *only* for me. Her gaze dipped to the deplorable heeled, stitched leather I clutched in my arms and that smirk turned impish.

That smile, those lips, *feck* that gorgeous mouth . . .

"Cian, lad," Gran spoke over the fire, "why do ye have *one* boot?"

I tore my gaze from Glenna's rouge-painted lips to wink at Gran. "To right an ancient wrong with a bloody raccoon."

Barry chuffed again.

I narrowed my eyes at the fox. "Remember, Barry Berry Muffin Moo Lonan Merrick"—I pointed the boot at him—"I'm with the lass who makes your treats."

Corbin tilted his head. "Is that a—"

"A cock boot, aye," Owen finished for him with a grimace. "George was caressing them last night."

Filena burst into a loud cackle. "While on a man's foot?"

"He wanted Cian to wrestle them off the gent's feet," Owen confirmed.

Gran wiped away tears. "Tell me ye didn't . . ."

My jaw slackened. "You actually believe I would assault a dandy for his sh—" I didn't finish. Why would anyone naturally conclude George did this? I blinked. How *did* George steal this heinous boot? No, not important right now. Shifting on my feet, I pointed at Mam, then Edna, Mam's red cardinal who perched on her shoulder, followed by Gran in mock-outrage. "You didn't raise a hussy."

Filena snorted. I slid her a glare—one she knew was all for show.

Gran wheezed another laugh, laughing louder when Rhylen cut in. "You're just mad that George stroked the gent's *large* boot first."

"Feck you, former best friend."

Corbin shrugged. "It *is* something you would wear."

Sean and Owen both nodded their heads in vigorous agreement, their faces contorting with the effort to not giggle like fledgling girls.

The Heartbreak Show

Feathered bastards.

Aye, I was a gaudy tart, as Glenna liked to call me, and I did tease and riddle the word cock, as the fellas knew, but even I had fashion standards. This was a mockery of all that was holy and good and right with the world.

The stitching was mustard gold.

Mustard.

I opened my mouth to reply when Glenna moved toward me. "Cian," she sighed, "your hair is the real horror story."

With a tsk, she reached for the wild strands falling over my eyes.

I flashed her a smirk and gently caught her wrist mid-reach. When her jaw adorably clenched, I then leaned down until my lips brushed her ear.

"Glenna," I whispered, low and rough, "grab my hair while moaning my name in the woods. I'll leave now. Just say the word." Her body stilled. I could feel the building steam ready to blow in that blushing head of hers. Satisfied, I angled back and added, "But don't scandalize the children." I gestured my head at the boys, who replied with playful insults in return.

Glenna lifted her chin, a flirty smile tilting her lips in an invitation to verbally tumble. My answering grin replied *feck yes*. The glittering dark gaze holding mine thundered back *your loss, your wake*. Gods above, my heating blood rushed straight to my groin with that one single look.

This was the opening I was waiting for, too.

A public performance to riddle her into another.

Slowly, I released her wrist. "Glennie Lo," I drawled, "I need your dress."

The lads cheered and whistled, including Rhylen. Others at the fire pit clapped. This was how I opened every flirty fight between me and Glenna.

"You almost ruined the blue one, *darlin'*." A single black brow arched.

"Next time be more patient when *undressing* me, Gent of Fem." Laughter erupted around us and I bit down on my lower lip. "So unladylike."

Glenna pointed at Owen. "Your ex-mate-to-be wept in relief. The poor lad feared marrying a man who wore *that* boot while in *that* outdated catalogue dress."

My brows shot up. I told her about the dandy's comment? Intuition flooded my gut; my mind replayed images and snippets of conversation faster than a storm-raged river—no, not me. I side-eyed Owen and mouthed, "pecker," and he grinned.

Glenna stepped closer and I leaned in like I was going to kiss her but stopped short. Her gaze touched mine and . . . my whirring thoughts stilled for a stuttering beat of my heart. How I loved her starless night eyes. They soothed the chaos in me.

But not yet.

"I need your dress," I repeated with a pout.

"Lady of Man, bark up another skirt."

The fire pit broke into more cheers and laughter.

And here it was. The moment I would change our fates. Hopefully, our new flock's too.

Leaning in closer, I stage-whispered, "How else will I earn more gifts at the train station than you?"

Glenna reared back. "The cock boot hit your head, *darlin'*?"

She didn't understand. I knew she wouldn't. I also knew she wouldn't admit to being in the dark about my nonsensical comment. But I had unwittingly planted the seed in the wagon. Sometimes I was bloody brilliant without meaning to be.

"Gifts to the Love-Talkers," I sashayed in our verbal dance, slowly, emphatically,

Her mouth slightly parted. Then her eyes brightened. A slow grin kicked up the corners of my mouth. I softly winked for her to take control.

Without missing a beat, Glenna flicked my forehead.

"Ow!" I snapped. Feck, I knew it was coming. I consented for her to do this—unlike most times. And she never flicked hard enough to inflect pain despite my dramatic reactions to feed her crowing glee. But the throbbing in my head increased tenfold for a few rapid breaths.

"Wear my dress all you like, but I'll still get more broken heart bargains than you."

"Aye, I'll wear your dress." I tossed her a sensual grin. "Your corset and drawers too."

Glenna snatched Rhylen's top hat off his head and angled it low on her brow. The fire pit erupted into hoots, suggestive cheers, and laughter.

My gancanagh placed her hand onto the unbuttoned part of my upper shirt, the skin of her fingers touching the skin of my chest. I was already addicted to her. Already wasting away in endless want and had been for years. But when she said the four words that *always* made me swoon, I fell for her all over again.

"Lady of Man, bets."

Chapter Five

CIAN MERRICK

"The rules"—Cian leaned me against a tree, kissing down my throat while unbuttoning his shirt—"no coercion magic."

We had disappeared into Caledona Wood to swap clothes. Filena and Braelin led a party in the opposite direction to find more fruit and nuts before the sun set.

I slid the cotton shirt off his shoulders and tossed it onto a bush while answering, "No kissing others." Followed by, "What about touching?"

He grinned against my racing pulse and possessively cupped my breasts. Clearly, I wasn't talking about us. I started to roll my eyes, but the feel of his hot breath on my neck, just beneath my ear, set my skin on fire.

"I want to kiss the rouge from your lips until it stains mine," he murmured.

Gods . . .

I had been with a fair share of males and females the past couple of years. No one talked much during sex. Not really. But Cian? I could orgasm just from the erotic things that came out of that man's mouth.

"Touching others, eejit," I redirected and he nipped my earlobe.

The Heartbreak Show

"Faces and arms only." He quickly began unfastening my bodice. "What genders?"

"Males for you, Lady of Man. Females for me." I would suggest others, but mortal society didn't tolerate anything different. Also, flirting with our same sex would lead to less mixed signals.

He slid the bodice down my arms and hung it off a low-hanging branch. A familiar twinge of shame crept up my neck at the dirty, fraying state of my corset, camisole, and petticoats. Cian didn't care. His clothing was in poor shape too. But my vanity struggled. Aye, I liked pretty things and to feel pretty in those pretty things. It wasn't my fault Caravan pecking order decided I should be poor because of who raised me.

This past year, I had let a couple elf struck village lads buy me one used hat as well as two used dresses tailored for larger women that I then modified for my non-mortal size, but no underthings. Males, regardless of race, grew possessive over the strangest things. A frilly strip of cotton covering a lady's unmentionables might as well spell "my property."

A cool evening breeze danced around us, pebbling my bare arms. But it was the intensity of Cian's hawk-eyed stare that lifted the hairs on the back of my neck.

For years, I believed the nosey arse had trained his trickster ways to read people. But he had a familiar. Strangely, one that hadn't appeared in his life until recently—one whose magic remained a mystery to all. Moira, his mam, speculated that Barry had protected Cian's magic while Cian protected Filena until the Sisters Three set her and Rhylen's fates into motion.

I longed to ask Cian about his magic, but this was his secret to share. Unlike mortals, we fae didn't see secrets as offenses. We lived by the rules of magic, bargains, tricks, and curses. Secrets were our power over others as well as our downfall—our luck, good or bad.

Still, it didn't take much to conclude that Cian had intuitive magic, like Filena. It was the only explanation as to why the gobshite always *knew* things.

My brows wrinkled.

And why he didn't truly look at me before we were . . . what in the feck were we? Lovers, aye. Friends in lust reveling in what was no longer forbidden? Also, true. We couldn't keep our hands and lips off one another—touching fed an addiction, seductions our game long before we turned them on each other.

Stars, I would sacrifice all my dresses for him to choose me as his mate the way I chose him.

But he wasn't ready.

He loved me. I knew this without question. I just wasn't convinced it was romantic love despite his confession that I was his ruination. Cian Merrick *was* truly honey-tongued, like the Love-Talkers of legend—

"Glenna," Cian spoke softly and I blinked back my whirling thoughts. The barest tip of his finger traced the swells of my breasts. "One day," he whispered, his voice rough, "I'll buy you a corset from the finest shop in Den Merrow."

Tears blurred my vision. Once again, he *knew*.

Just like he *knew* I'd been struggling without my cake witch sisters, who had remained in West Tribe. Filena and I also no longer shared a bed. Holding my best friend all day while we slept soothed the loneliness. It made our conflicting schedules more bearable. Now we had all the time in the world to spend with each other, but she was my brother's bonded mate and I no longer shared a wagon with her.

". . . silk stockings, satin-tied drawers too . . ." Cian's silky voice pulled me from my grief and I loosed a shaky breath. "I'll buy you whatever you want."

The ache in my chest sharpened. Why did he have to be so romantic at times? I couldn't fall harder for Cian Merrick, not if I wanted to hold

The Heartbreak Show

onto any future happiness. I meant what I had promised him two weeks ago: I would *never* break his heart, but he . . . he could break mine.

I loved him. I loved him so much I accepted every part of his nature, including the part that was too chaotically restless to settle down with one mate. He'd had enough people attempt to fit him into their narrow-minded cage. I refused to let him become something he wasn't for me—or anyone.

Aye, my tongue had slipped and called him "mate" in a moment of weakness.

But I wouldn't again.

Shite, tears pricked my eyes once more. If I started crying, I wouldn't stop. Nor did I want Cian to read too deeply into my emotions. Flirting and playful bickering would have to remain my shield.

"Ci-Ci," I drawled, straightening my shoulders, "you're too much of a strumpet to buy *me* a corset."

He pretended to gasp. "Insolent hen."

Playing up the sass, my eyes swooped to the deft fingers quickly unhooking my corset—the one *he* planned to wear.

The lad's face tightened with the effort to hold back a laugh. "No wings."

I scoffed. "Then no cigarettes."

Cian's lips now parted in true horror. "My one vice? No bargain."

"*One* vice?!" I laughed.

A corner of his mouth tilted in a dangerous, sensual smile and I nearly groaned.

"Don't you dare seduce your way out of—"

"Be a good girl." My face fell flat right before his thumbs teased the hardened peaks of my nipples beneath my thin camisole. My traitorous core clenched and the sensual curve of his smile grew. The bastard knew. "Help me into *your* corset, Glenna darlin'"—he lowered that deliciously wicked mouth of his to my ear and whispered—"and I'll remind you of my *other* vice."

"Not if you feather ban me, you won't."

The heat of his lips trailed along my jaw, "Where are my wings?"

"The gods knew you'd already be too pretty, eejit." I pushed him back. "Now, *darlin'*, make that big mortal head of yours focus." He smirked—again—and I tapped his head. "*This* head."

Leaning away with a breathy laugh, he wrapped my corset around his torso. I circled to his back to loosen the ties as he reclasped the front. The graceful way his muscles moved in the dusky light while the same bewitched twilight caressed the elegant lines of his face made my mutinous body react all over again. Cian's halfling beauty and duality was utterly mesmerizing to me.

He wasn't as tall or as large-bodied as a Raven Folk male. I was larger than mortal women too. Apparently, the size of a tall, well-toned man and why Cian could wear my dresses.

"Hands on the tree," I ordered.

Obeying, he leaned onto the mossy oak and I pulled to tighten the laces. More like yanked, as if I were holding reins, and he shot me a playful glare over his shoulder.

Flashing him a smug grin, I asked, "The bet?"

"We break hearts in a nightly show"—his voice caught when I tugged—"for one week. We 'curse' them to a lovesick heart." He grunted with another pull. "Gifts break the spell."

I tied the ribbons into a bow, then angled toward his front. "Any gift?"

"For our bet, aye. But let's direct to our tribe's needs as much as possible." Cian ran a hand through the silky waves of his golden hair before turning and the air caught in my lungs.

Those disheveled locks would be my downfall one day. And I swore he did it on purpose just to torture my Raven urge to preen my mate.

Mate . . .

My heart stumbled a beat.

Before I could stop myself, I reached out and brushed a few strands from his beautiful gray eyes and . . . his gaze caught on the scrape on my upper cheek. Fear paled across his face for a mere second. He blinked rapidly and looked away.

Oh no, he wouldn't retreat over an accident.

He was *nothing* like Hamish MacCullough.

I understood his fear, though. Well, not personally. But I didn't need intuition magic to *see* how my injury triggered his trauma. If that despicable mortal wasn't rotting in jail right now, I would peck at his mind by any means possible until he broke the way he had tried to break his family.

I lowered my hand from Cian's hair to straighten the front of the corset. To snap him out of his self-loathing, I pretended to push up his breasts and his lips twitched.

"Owen is right," I said. "You do have nice he-vage."

"I'm offended you needed Owen to point out something so obvious." Cian unbuttoned his pants. "Also, pink rouge *is* an excellent choice for my complexion."

"Pink doesn't convey 'I'm-an-upstaging-hoyden.'" I stepped out of the skirt and petticoats I'd untied from around my waist and handed them to him. "Red does—"

"Feck. Me," Cian moaned. His lids lowered in a heady look that fluttered the muscles of my stomach. "I might go feral over this." His fingers caressed a pink garter ribbon around my white-stockinged thigh. "Is this new?"

It wasn't. I had nicked the decorative underpinning from a dalliance a couple of years ago and wore it only when I meant business. Like beating Cian at his own game.

"Oh aye." Schooling my face, I took his pants from his hands and tossed them beside his shirt on the bush next me. "A gift from George last night, it is."

His gaze darted to the phallus boot of nightmares perched on the ground beside us then back to my ribbon- and rosette-festooned garter. "That wee traitorous bastard."

I shrugged. "George has a list—"

"A list?!"

"Aye, he can read."

The betrayed shock on Cian's face was so comical I burst into laughter.

"One . . ." I sputtered out, "does not question . . . the thieving ways of . . . a faerie raccoon." I was laughing so hard, I could barely throw Cian's words to me two weeks ago back at his wide-eyed, slack-jawed face.

But you couldn't lie to Cian Merrick. Not for long, at least.

Mischief darkened his smiling eyes. I took a single step back, sputtering another laugh. Cian pounced before I could shift and I squealed, dashing out of his grasp. To crow taunts from an upper branch would be the icing on the cake. The bite of happiness I craved. He wrapped his arm around my waist and spun me to face him.

"The punishments I have planned for you . . ." he teased across my lips. "But not in the woods so close to camp."

"Remember who gives you treats."

He grinned, a boyish, rascally kind, and excitement shivered in my roaring veins. "Treats or *treats*?"

Rather than answer in words, I brushed my mouth against his. "Our bet," I murmured, trailing my hand down his chest, lower, lower, stopping to grip his hipbone. "If I win—"

The Heartbreak Show

"Aye?" His quickened breaths pulsed against my lips. Very little separated our bodies. I was in only a camisole, drawers, and stockings. He was in my corset and his drawers. "If you win . . . ?"

"George is mine to direct for an entire month."

"Two weeks," Cian quickly countered. "For fashion only."

My brows shot up. "What other talents does George possess?"

"George moves in mysterious ways, Glennie Lo."

With a roll of my eyes, I started to pull away. "No more treats for you."

Cian tightened his hold on me. "Three weeks, you minx."

"Deal," I practically chirped in victory.

"When I win"— Cian grinned that up-to-no-good smile again— "you'll call me your sex god during—"

I grimaced. "Full-blooded gods save me from this half-blooded eejit."

"They didn't save you from worshiping me when you thought I was sleeping."

He arched a brow.

I arched mine back.

Wait.

"Thought?" My eyes thinned. "How long were you awake?"

"From the moment you touched my lips." He tapped my nose with a wink. "You'll call me your sex god a minimum of three times when I win—"

"If."

"No, darlin', *when*."

I made a sound somewhere between a scoff and a taunting laugh. "One time."

"Two times."

"One time, Cian." I stepped back to ensure he got the full measure of my flirty ire. "One. Time."

"You'll make it loud, too."

"Are you asking me to fake an orgasm for you?"

A devilish corner of his mouth lifted. "So, they've all been real?"

I threw my head back in a laugh so loud, the forest momentarily quieted. The arse already knew the truth and was riddling me into proving how he was clearly a god in bed *before* winning that confession from my lips.

"You're shameless."

"You forgot the hussy part."

"And pet your ego?"

He heaved a dramatic sigh. "One time," he drew out, lifting my leg to his hip. "And," he added, caressing my thigh, "I get to wear your garter ribbon tonight."

"That's my lucky battle ribbon, so no, lad."

"*Battle* ribbon?"

"Aye, accept defeat."

"I'll surrender to you"— Cian caged me against the oak tree with one arm—"only on my back while you cry out, 'Cian, my sex god—'"

To shut the man up, I crushed my mouth to his. He was so infuriating. But sweet moons, his lips were blessed by the gods. The fingers wrapped around my thigh splayed. Strands of his wavy hair draped down my face and I was quickly forgetting my irritation with his riddling ways. Just to rest in his arms, to hear his beautiful heart sing to mine, to know the reverent touch of his laughing soul . . . was a completeness incomparable to *anything*.

Cian smiled into our kiss for a mere second, then he grabbed my other thigh, hoisting me up. I wrapped my legs around his waist as we fell against the tree at my back.

"You're a craving I never want sated," he whispered. The hands gripping my hips ground me against his hardened cock and my breath caught on a soft moan. "My gorgeous Gent of Fem . . ."

That honeyed tongue of his teased my bottom lip. Then his mouth was on mine once more and this kiss . . . *this* kiss, it devoured me. The hungry way his lips feasted on mine, the sensual dance of his body moving to our pounding heartbeats, I was quickly unraveling.

Let him win every argument.

Every competition, so long as—

Cian's entire body went rigid. Our kiss froze. My heart stopped with the sudden intensity rippling down his muscles.

"What is it?"

"That wee bastard," he swore under his breath.

My head fell against the tree in a quiet groan. Twice today, that wee bastard had murdered the mood. Not only that, but Cian had the attention span of a bee drunk on nectar, buzzing and bumbling from one flower to another.

With a sigh, I rolled my head to peer where Cian was looking.

There, beside the vomitous red boot, was its equally as nauseating mate.

. . . How?

For as sweet as George was, in this moment, he was a tad terrifying.

Cian lowered me to the ground. In two strides, he snatched the boots and circled in place, his gaze furiously sweeping across the forest.

A soft chuff sounded nearby, one too quiet for Cian's mortal ears to pick up.

Barry.

I cracked a smile. I couldn't help it.

Cian halted his circling a few seconds later, narrowed his eyes, and pointed a boot into the woods past my head. "George, I see you."

The raccoon chittered.

Cian straightened. "You did *what*?"

I peered around the tree, but I couldn't find the thieving lad.

"Don't you dare run off!" A split second later, Cian gasped, then kicked into a run. "Come back here, you fluffy, cuddly arse!"

I caught a glimpse of George and Barry dashing into the underbrush, Cian hot on their trail.

I blew a wisp of hair from my eyes, holding back a giggle, and studied the lowering sun to gauge the hour. A dewy chill was falling over the autumn-blushed woods. I rubbed at my prickling arms.

No point in remaining in my undergarments for a man who would rather chase a raccoon than my racing pulse. Turning back to our clothes, I whistled a tune to myself and grabbed his shirt, suspenders, and trousers, and quickly dressed. The final touch? Rhylen's top hat. My brother was gracious enough to let me borrow it for the night.

Cian shouted again and, this time, I full-on laughed.

Those two heroes deserved a dozen frosted cookies each for their mischief.

And I would join them.

Snatching my bodice and skirts, I jogged back toward camp, unable to stop my laughter.

Chapter Five

CIAN MERRICK

I slowed my steps, my chest heaving. Dying stars, I couldn't breathe. Clenching my teeth, I dropped the boots and unclasped the corset partway. My head was oscillating between swimming and pounding. I flopped against a tree and ran a hand through my messy strands.

George had drugged the dandy.

Drugged.

Or hypnotized him.

I couldn't figure out exactly which it was. The only time Raccoon was clear to whatever magic tethered us together was when I was drunk. Sober, though? My translation was spotty. I rolled to my shoulder, to better scan the underbrush for that banded thief, when the forest began spinning around me.

Feck.

I dug my nails into the tree.

A discordant noise suddenly buzzed in my head. Trees whipped by my vision, growing faster and faster. I sucked in a sharp breath and grit my teeth.

Feck.

Feck.

Feck.

I hadn't felt so intensely tipsy on magic since The Wild Hunt. The moment I looked into the constable's eyes, I *knew* Bram had him in a bargain. Frantic, I had run off the trail through Caledona Wood to escape the authorities and find Rhylen, but the ground had rolled beneath my feet and slowed my steps.

Like now.

The world was flipping upside down all around me. But to my reveling chaos, it had never looked more level and balanced despite the many thought threads intersecting all at once. Thoughts of insights past. Revelations of information I hadn't yet processed.

Voices were speaking—gods, the voices—each one growing louder. I grimaced back the slowly building pain.

To focus my spiraling cognitive control, I peered up through the carouseling canopy of bare, clawing limbs to the faint whisper of stars flecking the twilight sky. My gaze sharpened and settled onto one star.

One star.

One star.

Only think of one star.

. . . just one star . . .

"Not all heroes wear armor, Cillian."

I winced at the warbly echo of Mam's words.
Did George possibly mean . . . *coerce*?

"It's time to chase after yer birthright, my wee Cian."

We couldn't herd deer to milk. That was absurd. We needed a cow.

The Heartbreak Show

I don't speak of the crodh sìdh.
Yer birthright . . .

If coercion, hopefully George glamoured the man's mind to forget he had been robbed—

Did anyone ask Filena if she wanted to have *many* childr—

—The Donnely mam was secretly hoarding herbs used to relieve the spreading sickness at ca—

What if I had accidentally married Owen last night?

"He met and married his true love in a dress."

No legal authority would believe that a raccoon could take down a grown man and thieve the boots right off his feet.

One star.

Just one star.

Cian, Ancient One . . .

My eyes shot to the woods.

Shadows swayed around me. Dead leaves lifted in a breeze and churned in the air.

Cian, Enduring One . . .

I pushed off the tree, the boots nearly forgotten, and took a few wobbly steps forward. Keeping my body grounded, despite the spinning world, I hunted the forest with a slow sweep of my gaze.

Magic crawled across my skin and continued to swirl in my head.

"Great Niece-Nephew."

I whirled toward the sound, my heart in my throat.

A shaft of rosy sunlight illuminated an elven female with long, silky auburn hair and moon pale skin beneath a flowering hawthorn tree.

In autumn—a hawthorn was flowering *in autumn*. I blinked.

Niece-Nephew?

I blinked again.

My mind, it was suddenly, unsettlingly calm. The chaos had silenced and . . . my eyes rounded.

Holy fecking stars in a falling sky, I was standing before the Maiden.

The.

Maiden.

My great aunt.

And while wearing only a corset and drawers and nothing else. I dug my bare toes into the forest substrate and grit my teeth.

"Cían of the Tuatha Dé Danann," the Maiden greeted, "it is time."

Tuatha Dé Danann, the fae gods.

I continued to stare wide-eyed like an eejit. She appeared so much like Filena, it was hard not to gape.

"Your magic has been born many times, Cían," the Maiden mused softly, a kind smile on her Otherworldly beautiful face. "This is my favorite re-souling of you, though."

That snapped me out of my daze and tossed me into a completely new one.

I held up a hand. I needed a moment. Maybe a hundre—

Re-souling?

Was she suggesting I was actually Cían, the legendary warrior god?

A scowl pinched between my brows.

I blinked yet again.

Then it hit me.

Mam knew.

She bloody *knew*.

The story she had shared the day before Filena and I fled to West Tribe wasn't just to piece back together my personhood, but to confirm this future moment.

There were so many questions slamming into me at once. So, so many. But my bewildered, eejit brain fixated on the most ridiculous one of them all. "How old is George?"

I cringed.

I didn't mean to speak that aloud. I was thinking about if I were re-souled, then . . . I loosed a tight breath. Had I spoken the other questions blurring past my mind aloud too? I sounded like a wee bairn.

My great aunt laughed and the airy sound was like a frolicking breeze in a meadow of wildflowers. "He, too, is ancient."

Ancient faerie raccoons. The horror.

"All familiars gifted to the Children of the Gods are immortal."

Immortal?

Starless skies, Barry wasn't even twelve years old and already he was a grumpy, old ancient.

I drew in a breath and exhaled slowly. "Why am I reborn?"

"You, Great Niece-Nephew—"

"Nephew is fine."

She paused. "Is it, truly?"

I shrugged. "Call me a she or him. I like both. But"—my lips twisted into a wry smile—"Niece-Nephew is a wee bit of a mouthful, aye?" The Maiden tilted her head and studied me with a keenness I recognized. "I always feel like a lad, even in a corset and dress," I added with a wink. "But sometimes also a lass. The intensity of my female gender fluctuates."

"Great Nephew," she said with a dip of her head. Then, "It is time for you to claim your birthright."

My heart lodged firmly in my throat.

How many times had I claimed this birthright?

Or had I never and was this why I was reborn?

And how many times had I been reborn?

Was Filena reborn too—

"The cow *Glas Gaibhnenn*."

My wildly galloping thoughts skidded to a complete stop.

"A *cow*?"

"Aye, Enduring One."

The Maiden lifted a hand toward me and made a show of curling her fingers into a fist. I bit the inside of my cheek. Dramatics clearly ran in the family.

Trying not to laugh or weep—maybe both simultaneously—I repeated, "My birthright is a fecking cow?"

The Maiden turned her wrist toward the sky. "A Cow of Plenty."

"Is this a real cow or a metaphorical cow?"

Instead of answering, she unfurled her hand. My brows shot up. On her palm lay a dudeen—an ornate clay tobacco pipe.

Did I trip and fall and accidentally ingest blue mushrooms? Nothing was making sense and everything *always* made sense to me. It was more disorienting than a spinning forest.

My aunt placed the strange pipe into my hands. I turned the dudeen in my fingers, then met her piercing emerald stare. "And," I began, wary, "where do I find this magical faerie cow?"

"By following a trail of broken hearts."

Chapter Six

CIAN MERRICK

"Filena!" I shouted. Dirt kicked up into the air as I wended down the trail. I had no idea if I was running in the right direction, but I had to find my sister. Ducking under a limb, I once again yelled, "Filena!"

Running in a corset was not for the weak, dear gods.

"Filena!"

"Cian?" my sister stepped out from behind a tall berry bush just up ahead.

Around her, the small group she wandered into the woods with turned and gaped at my frantic approach. I barely noticed them, so intent on my sister, until Braelin and Sean stepped beside Filena.

Shite, I didn't know Sean had joined the hunter-gatherers.

Never mind. I'd swear him to secrecy later. Rhylen had enough on his plate. He didn't need my weird life colliding into his any more than it already had. But more than anything, I . . . I wasn't ready for Glenna to know.

I slid to a stop before my sister, my chest heaving, my eyes wild. I couldn't hide my shaking.

Filena grabbed my face, her own eyes growing wide. "What happened? Where's Glenna?"

"I need to speak to you."

Sean peered over my shoulder, his gaze darting from one object to another.

"Glenna's fine," I rushed out and Sean's tightened shoulders lowered. Filena's body relaxed just a tiny drop too. I knew I looked a sight in a partially unbuttoned corset, in my drawers, feet dirty and face flushed. "Sean, let no one follow." When he nodded, I gently took Filena by the wrist and tugged her down the path until we were well out of earshot.

"Brother dear?" The pale hue of her skin turned sickly. Tears began gathering on her lashes.

I locked onto her emotional struggle and . . . I could kick myself. "Gran, Mam, and Rhylen are fine too."

She blew out a slow breath then cupped my face again. "What's ailing you?" Her thumb caressed my cheek in a comforting stroke.

"The Maiden—" I stopped and swept a quick gaze around the woods, dropping my voice. "Our great aunt appeared to me just now and—"

"You spoke with the Maiden?"

"—and I have to find a fecking Cow of Plenty."

Filena's eyes narrowed slightly. "A cow?"

"Aye, *Glas Gaibhnenn* of the Tuatha Dé Danann."

"A green . . . cow . . . of the blacksmith?" That translation made me sound even more insane. My sister studied me. "Did you eat mushrooms?"

"I wish." Taking her hands from my cheeks, I placed the dudeen in her palm. "She gave me this."

The Heartbreak Show

"A . . . clay pipe?" Filena tilted her head. "Brother—"

"I know I sound mad."

"Sound? You look *and* sound unhinged."

I snorted and she rolled her eyes. When did I not appear as if unhinged?

"Darlin', I believe you," she said, handing the pipe back. "Start from the beginning."

Drawing in a trembling breath, I told her about all the events leading up to encountering the Maiden—well, all but how my magic spiraled out of control. Filena didn't know the depth of my abilities. No one did. Most believed George was connected to my resourcefulness. I preferred it this way. If those I cared about knew I could *see* into the private areas of their life? Well, that would make things awkward and fast.

My sister's brows scrunched together. "The Maiden said you are Cian of the Tuatha Dé Danann?"

"Aye. Or I have his magic. I didn't quite understand." I ran a hand through my messy hair, my fingers still shaking. The Maiden's story after her cryptic trail-of-broken-hearts answer swirled in the whirlpool of my mind. "Apparently, Cian is re-souled every few hundred years until he is united with his ridiculous Cow of Plenty and . . ." My words trailed off.

And . . . until he burned for a love brighter than he had for his first.

Glenna's black-as-night eyes filled my mind. I could feel the press of her mouth whisper, "Mate," across mine, and building terror twisted in my gut anew.

I wanted her more than my next breath. I had for years.

But if I hurt her? If I destroyed her perfection with my dysfunction?

I had lost myself in others for so long. She was never a part of my future. She never could be, not without destroying our families. But now...

Clearing my throat, I continued. "Two things broke Cian's heart. Losing his beloved cow and being forever separated from his wife."

Filena sighed. "How romantical."

"No."

"Yes."

"Filena—"

"Poor Cian," my sister drawled with a large grin, "forced to wander for the broken pieces of his heart until he finds them."

Break my heart, Cian Merrick. But I will never break yours...

The knot in my gut tightened. "Only for the damn cow."

My fecking birthright.

Her lips twitched and my eyes squinted. "How do you find this faerie Cow of Plenty?"

I heaved a dramatic sigh. "The Maiden said I needed boots cobbled by a leprechaun, thieved by a Master of Disguise."

She burst into a cackling laugh. Aye, it was utterly, embarrassingly outrageous.

My lips pressed together. "A ribbon from a Wishing Tree."

"Ohhh..."

I flashed my sister a rude gesture, who only cackled louder. "And a *gifted* Lughnasadh's Day straw hat."

Filena winked. "With the largest fruit to decorate any Lughnasadh's Day straw hat in all three kingdoms, aye?"

"Obviously."

My sister brushed at a tear on her cheek. "Brother, only *you* would be possessed by a dead god to find a faerie cow and require new shoes, ribbons, and a hat to do it."

I yanked her into an embrace and wrapped my arms around her, the pipe clutched in my fist. "You're an imp."

"Ew, you're sweaty!"

I tightened my hold around her. "You laughed at my beloved cow."

"If you don't release me—"

"Don't release you?" I pressed my cheek to the top of her head. "I enjoy snuggling with you too."

"Cian Merrick!"

"Filena Lonan, only if you promise not tell Rhylen or Glenna or anyone about my cow heist or seeing the Maiden."

She shoved at my chest and I released my hold a little. "A heist?"

I arched a brow. "Someone has *Glas Gaibhnenn*."

"True."

"Promise me, sister dear."

She searched my eyes. "Aye, I promise you. Your romantical cow heist tale is your own to share. Now release me or I'll tell George to thieve every pair of cock boots in Carran for you. The gods' will."

I dropped my hands as my mouth parted in a loud gasp. "How dare you lie to George about the gods. May he never bring you mismatched socks again if you do."

"Is it a lie, though?" She schooled her face.

"Imp," I punctuated with a pop of my lips.

My sister wrinkled her nose in a teasing smile and I melted. I loved her wit and feistiness. She had a knack for bringing calm to my constant storm. I couldn't imagine my life without her. We were a pair, she and I.

I kissed her forehead. "Thank you, darlin'."

"You can always tell me anything," she replied softly.

"Aye." I smiled sweetly at her. "Keeper of gossip and secrets."

"I'm jealous you saw the Maiden, though."

"You look just like her," I whispered, unable to hide the awe from my voice. "The resemblance was uncanny."

Filena's face sobered. "Ravenna Blackwing said the same before we parted with West Tribe."

I kissed her forehead again. "I need to find George and—"

Another gasp left me, a genuine one this time.

The cock boots!

I left them back where I had spoken to our great aunt!

I could laugh as a thousand thoughts collided into a central one that cleared in the mud of my churning head. And I knew. I just knew.

Those hideous shoes were cobbled by leprechauns. They were full of faerie mischief. Probably glamoured to the dandy who had worn them to appear as something else, perhaps even a different color. But to everyone else? We could see them for the awful, tasteless things they were.

And George's obsession with fashion and thieving clothing—he must be the Master of Disguise. Was that part of his faerie-touched magic?

"See you at camp," I rushed out to Filena and spun on my heel. Took three steps and halted.

Cow!

Glenna needed milk to bake. For the first time in this strange, mind-bending evening, I felt a spark of hope. I would hunt down a hundred faerie cows if that was what it took for my heart to revive her creative pulse. Perform in an eternity of coin beggar shows, for

The Heartbreak Show

her to buy all the baking supplies she needed too.

Sorry, Gran. No deer milk for the wee ones . . . or the rest of us, thank the wishless falling stars.

With a smile forming, I started up again—and stopped.

Sean!

Pivoting, I ran past my sister toward the group who pretended to be busy. "Fruit pickers," I hollered while slowing. "You never saw me nor was I ever in a panic, agree?"

People mumbled agreement or looked to others in question. Mostly everyone in Rhylen's tribe had grown familiar with my random, nonsensical ways by now.

Though, my actions rarely were.

"All together," I said, lifting my hands as if orchestrating a band. "I agree . . ."

"I agree," they repeated.

"That I never saw Cian in the woods or Cian in a panic just now."

They echoed my words and Sean's brow kicked up when finished. I winked at him, followed by a puckered kiss as I stuck my arse out in a sexy pose. Filena groaned from behind. Sean, however, tossed a berry at me while biting back a laugh. A berry I caught in my mouth. The small gathering cheered and clapped.

With a dramatic bow, I spun on my heel once more and tracked back to where I left the boots. Then dashed back to Glenna—but she wasn't there. Or her bodice and skirts.

"The minx," I muttered under my breath.

A few minutes later, I marched into camp wearing her corset and my drawers, the dandy's cockblocking cock boots in my arms, the dudeen gift in my fingers, a taunting grin on my pretty face. And George at my heel.

Wait. *George?*

My raccoon peered up at me, a fellow man on a mission. Well, I couldn't be mad at the lad now. Not when he was acting on the Maiden's mischief. Straightening, I continued on my war path into camp.

The smug slant of my lips curved higher when Glenna caught my triumphant return.

Oh aye, she would pay.

And she knew it, immediately shifting into a raven to caw her laughter from a branch.

Gran wiped tears from her eyes. "Me sunshine boy," she wheezed beside Mam who was also in a fit of laughter.

Ignoring Glennie, I scanned the wagons for Rhylen. When I couldn't spot him, or Corbin, I pointed at Owen with the clay pipe. "Grab your banjo. We're hustling the train station."

Gran's eyes flew wide. "A gancanagh's dudeen."

The strange, ornate pipe? It was a gancanagh's?

Of course, a Love-Talker smoked—

I blinked.

My great aunt couldn't be suggesting . . .

The Maiden *did* give me this pipe with no explanation.

And the Mother was a fertility goddess—*No*.

I wouldn't dissect that possibility. Not right now, at least.

"Did you meet a Love-Talker in the woods, lad?" Gran examined my face. "Did you touch him?"

My gaze slowly lifted to Glenna's raven form and I smirked. "The Gent of Fem better get down from the branches before I break more hearts than her."

And with that threat, I snatched her skirt and bodice, then twirled toward the train station, making sure I swung my hips in a

The Heartbreak Show

rhythm that playfully shouted, "feck you!"
    Glenna flew ahead of me with a loud caw.
    Oh aye, she would definitely pay.

Chapter Seven

GLENNA LONAN

Owen gently plucked a common Traveler melody on his banjo. Patterned shadows fell across part of his lantern-lit face from the wrought iron and stained glass vaulted overhang. The worn toe of his brown boot tapped in line to the reveling beat.

The strange fae dudeen rested in my palm. One does not just happen upon the famed faerie pipe of a Love-Talker. Nor does one take a show prop that just magically appeared in Caledona Wood.

Cian was too clever to fall for such obvious faerie tricks.

Do mortal women truly find a male who smokes a pipe like an older gent seductive? Or was this an old-fashioned notion?

"Final boarding call for the 7:45 train for Ballykiln," a signalman with a loudhailer announced from a central platform. "All aboard!"

A kaleidoscope of passengers rushed by where we stood. Men in sharp suits, women in rags, children in silks, Fair Folk in traditional or mortal attires.

The signalman lifted a clipboard, checked his stopwatch, then made a mark on his time roster with a piece of lead.

"The 8 o'clock ferry to Seren boards in five!"

The Heartbreak Show

Steam hissed from the train's stack and banked the station in a thick fog. A few seconds later, the boiler steam mechanics that lifted the ferry from the docks to the floating island of Seren released a vaporous cloud that, unlike the train's, shimmered beneath the gas lamps.

Odd. Though, given that Seren was run by the Carrion Crime Syndicate and stayed afloat by steam mechanics *and* magic, perhaps the illusion of enchantments wasn't terribly surprising.

Owen met my nervously ticking eyes and arched a brow. Where was Cian? He had disappeared around the train shed's wall for "preparations." I started to turn away when Owen chuffed a quiet laugh and shook his head. George was scampering by him with a black ribbon in one paw and a small white parasol in the other.

Stars above, that man's vanity was worse than mine.

I blew out a slow breath and wrapped an arm around my middle. I didn't perform publicly. Not even music despite my songbird line. I preferred to work with my hands, creating confections, not live in the spotlight. But I had agreed to Cian's bet—no, *riddled* into Cian's bet.

I was an eejit.

The train whistled a long call and I jumped. The next second, the engine jolted forward and another cloud billowed over the station.

Gritting my teeth, I twisted toward where Cian disappeared. I would drag that arse out by his rounded ears to get this show started, if he didn't hurry up—

A parasol opened around the overhang's ornate wrought iron wall.

Finally!

Waves of disheveled blond hair fluttered in a light autumn breeze as he lifted his head and . . . and . . .

. . . *Áine's suns* . . .

A dizzy rush tickled down my body.

There was truly no creature alive as beautiful as Cian Merrick.

Ash was smudged around his steely moonlit eyes, as if he were a Raven Folk male. Dark red rouge lined his lips. The black ribbon George had pilfered was now tied around the side of his neck in a flirty bow. He wore my strapless corset, no bodice. And my skirt and petticoats were hiked up on the side to reveal a scandalous flash of a stockinged calf.

Holy Mother of Stars, I was dying on agonizing repeat.

Cian slowed before me and twirled the parasol behind his head.

My skin, it was too tight. My pulse was pounding too hard, too fast.

Not quite looking at me, he gripped the edge of Rhylen's top hat and tilted it more on an angle and lower over my brow. "A proper saucy gent," he said with a wink. "The pipe?"

I uncurled my fingers, not even aware I was doing so at first.

George handed Cian a large maple leaf that same moment, then scurried off.

"I'll warm the crowd up first." Using the leaf, he pointed to the mortals moving through the various gates around the platform. "Burlesque humor, aye? We're a classy but bawdy song and dance."

Could an elf be mortal struck? Halfling struck?

Lovestruck.

I was lovestruck.

"Keep looking at me like that, Gent of Fem," Cian murmured, still not quite meeting my eyes, "and you'll be screaming 'Cian, you're a sex god' loud enough for all to hear instead of breaking hearts for ol' Rhylee Lo."

That snapped me out of my spell. "Rhylen?"

"We need revenue."

"The 8 o'clock ferry is now departing for Seren," the signalman announced. "Last ferry of the night in forty-five minutes."

The ferry undocked in a glimmering whoosh of fog and began rising above the mainland on a steam-powered track.

The Heartbreak Show

Cian lifted my chin with a forefinger. "Ready to be heroes?"

"All of this is for the tribe?"

"And for bets." He leaned in close. "Darlin', your battle ribbon is no match for mine." He brushed a tail of black satin over his shoulder and I scoffed. "Now," he lilted, leaning back. He placed the maple leaf into my free hand. "Illusion this into a sign that reads 'Sacrifices to the Love-Talkers,' and lean it up against the cock boots of nightmares." He gestured with his head to where George was now dragging one of the red leather monstrosities in front of a grimacing Owen.

I burst into laughter; I couldn't help it.

"Our pot for gold," he said with a smug grin. "Cobbled by a leprechaun, it is."

My eyes shot back to the boot. I hadn't seen a leprechaun since I was a wee hennie. But I could see what Cian suggested now. It had all the markings of being faerie made. I would bet all my petticoats that the knots in the stitched rooster were spelled.

A chill prickled my skin. "How do we know these bring good luck?"

Cian reared back. "You dare question the thieving ways of Georgie Dirty Paws?" The raccoon waited for me to notice his "innocent" dark eyes. I huffed a quiet laugh. If I had a cookie, I'd give him a chunk, the adorable wee thing.

My shoulders sagged a notch.

Stars how I missed baking . . .

Well, better get this show on the road or—what did we say now that our wheels no longer roamed? Sighing, I focused on the leaf. A warm trickle of magic traveled down my fingers and whirled in my head. The leaf illusioned into a small painted wooden sign, similar to the kinds I'd seen in village storefronts. George appeared at my side and lifted his paws. I handed him the illusioned leaf. Industrious fella. That raccoon always appeared right when he was needed . . . like Cian.

My brows pushed together.

Speaking of the pretty eejit, Cian twirled the parasol again while studying the mortal travelers.

A man slowed as he passed, a scowl between his brows as he took in Cian with equal parts disgust and curiosity. Cian flashed his ash-lined eyes to him, a flirty smile teasing the corners of his mouth as he made a show of taking the mortal in from head to toe and back up. Then, in an equally as dramatic fashion, Cian's silver gaze swung back to mine and intensified.

Was he reading me? To see if I was jealous over his come-hither interaction? I wanted to glare at that judgy stranger. But Cian might think I was pissed for reasons other than his defense.

"I'm not jealous," I said instead.

Cian smiled that boyish, rascally up-to-no-good grin of his. "You are a little."

"Do you want him? Or do you want me?"

"Gent of Fem," he whispered roughly, stepping close. "The ways I want you . . . to lose."

I chuckled low under my breath. "Owen," I hollered and he lifted his chin in acknowledgement. "A song to kick his mortal arse to!"

The tune he plucked on the banjo kicked up to a livelier melody.

Cian snorted. "Pastry shrew."

"Tawdry Trollop."

Barely had the words left my lips, when he skip-stepped back and shouted, "Ladies and gents," in a slightly higher-pitched, sultry voice. "Beware of faerie boy smiles for *he* will break your heart."

Those coming and going slowed.

"Beware mortals," he called out again, moving by the travelers to the rhythm of the music, his hips in full swing. "Do not fall for *his* confessions of love!"

The Heartbreak Show

Nerves violently buzzed in my middle. *Showtime...*

Lifting the gancanagh pipe to my mouth, I stuck a trembling hand in my pocket and strutted toward where Cian stood near Owen.

"You there"—Cian pointed to a couple, then pointed at me—"resist his honeyed tongue or you'll grow sick with want."

"My tongue isn't the only thing that's sweet," I bantered in a flirty tone to a group of girls around my age. They giggled and whispered to each other behind gloved hands.

A much older woman behind them gasped. "You ought to be ashamed."

"Owen." The music abruptly stopped. With the quiet now brighter than a spotlight, I placed a still-trembling hand beside my mouth, as if sharing a secret, then pretended to gesture to Cian on the sly. "The only shameless hussy here is the Lady of Man."

The dramatic arse threw an exaggerated, suggestive wink to the crowd. Owen strummed a well-known bawdy pub song to add to the humor. People laughed in reply.

The older woman harrumphed and stomped off toward the carriage platforms, probably to hail a ride to a fancy inn nearby. A few others followed in her wake, but their moral grandstanding only served to bring more curious spectators our way. There was nothing else to do while waiting for the last ferry of the night anyway—

My mouth parted.

That lad was fecking brilliant.

Cian, already on the prowl again, bit his lip at a young man in a fine tailored suit and silk top hat. "You, sir," he simpered, placing a hand on the gent's bicep. "Beware..."

The mortal blinked bashfully. Cian leaned in closer and the crowd around them hushed. A half-dozen more passersby stopped to see what was going on.

Trailing his fingers down the mortal's arm, Cian heaved a breath to draw attention to his chest, then stage-whispered, "Your heart will break unless you have him and *only* him."

I removed Cian's hand from the man's arm. "Has *me*, the Love-Talker." With a tap of the pipe on Cian's nose, I added, "Not *you*."

Shite, I meant to use my finger.

Cian's lips twitched.

Before he could make a joke, I quipped, "Most ladies swoon when I show them my . . . *large pipe*."

Owen switched to the bawdy pub song he played earlier and the crowd erupted into laughter once more. Late evening Seren travelers were a rowdier bunch. A tad on the younger side too—which Cian *knew*.

"Gent of Fem," Cian practically purred. Owen paused his playing. "I don't need to flash my *large pipe* to make the lads swoon. Every part of me is *divine*."

If he uttered one more I'm-a-demi-god joke, I might flick his forehead with both hands.

"Only half of you is, darlin'." I made a grand sweep of my arm before Cian and Owen began fingerpicking a reeling tune again. "Ladies and gents, beware of halfling faerie girl smiles, she'll—"

"She'll break more hearts than you." Cian twirled the parasol behind him and blew a kiss to the gathering, who ate it up.

"That so?" I slid the mortal girls a smirk. "If a lady touches my arm, she'll pine for my *honeyed* tongue."

"If a gent touches my hair, he'll ache for my *throbbing* confessions of love."

His *hair*?

He was asking strangers to preen *his hair*? My fingers started to curl into fists. "That wasn't in our rules," I whispered low enough so only he could hear.

The Heartbreak Show

"Head, face . . ." Mischief glittered in his laughing eyes. "The first punishment." The crowing delight in those three words ignited a fire just beneath my skin. "Jealousy doesn't become you, Glennie Lo." The words he said to me about his fake engagement to Owen.

Oh the lad would be weeping into his pillow later.

"Lady of Man," I cooed, "bets."

"Gent of Fem, bets."

Swishing his skirts for the crowd to glimpse his calf, he pranced over to where a group a men had gathered to watch. He pointed at the males as if counting them, then stopped on one. Cian placed his finger under the gent's chin and lifted his face toward his, as if he were going to kiss him. The man's eyes grew wide and he stepped back. The friend beside him reached out and patted Cian's hair, making the group laugh.

"Darlin'," Cian said to the friend, "I confess to love head"—he paused a comedic beat—"on a stout ale."

The men grinned, appreciating the lewd joke.

Cian threaded through the gathering, interacting with as many males who would let him.

Taking his lead, I angled into the crowd. I barely had to say anything and girls were reaching out and touching my arm—the poor wee elf struck mortals. It was almost too easy sometimes.

"Your long, silky hair is luscious," I murmured to one.

I caressed the blushing cheek of another and stage-whispered, "The dark wine of your lips brings the sky out in your blue eyes."

"The fit of your pink gown is sweeter than decadent cake."

With each brush of fingers, I gave a honeyed compliment.

A couple of girls touched the gancanagh's pipe instead of my arm, erupting into giggles, and I threw them a seductive wink.

"Last ferry to Seren begins boarding in ten!"

Cian and I locked eyes through the gathering.

"Ladies and gents," he sing-songed, then sashayed his way back toward Owen. "There is only one cure to ease your breaking heart as we part ways. Aye, only one way to reverse our faerie bargain." When an anticipatory hush settled, he continued. "Sacrifices to the Love-Talkers." He pointed to the cock boots and the crowd, once more, erupted into laughter. "Coins, jewels, sacks of flour, barrels of sugar..."

I sucked in a quiet breath.

He was asking for baking ingredients?

A crack fissured across the furiously pounding organ in my chest.

"...bottles of whiskey. A ribbon from a Wishing Tree will do too."

My brows shot up. Was the man so vain he now needed a Wishing Tree's ribbon to battle me?

Cian gestured to our pots for gold once more. "Left boot for the Lady of Man and right boot for the Gent of Fem."

No one moved.

But no one left either.

My pulse pounded loudly in my ears. Perhaps we had misjudged the younger crowd. They may come from money but that didn't mean they brought enough to spare if traveling to Seren.

I tucked the dudeen into my pocket, looking anywhere but at our audience—and stilled. George capered through the travelers to the shadows, where he scampered behind Owen and around the wrought iron wall, a bottle of tooth powder and a lady's bathing cap in his paws.

Well, someone had been busy.

"Glenna..." Cian whispered and I lifted my gaze.

The girls I had flirted with most were dashing over, purses in their hands. They dropped a few coins into my boot. One removed a silver hairpin from her curls to sacrifice. When finished, they walked arm-in-arm toward the ferry. Others came forward with offerings immediately after.

The Heartbreak Show

I was so stunned at first, I almost missed how Cian was grinning at me.

It worked.

Cian's coin beggar show actually worked!

Tears pricked the back of my eyes. My brother would have wages to buy food for his flock.

And maybe, if we did well again tomorrow, I could start baking again too.

Chapter Eight

Cian Merrick

I tipped the bottle of *sacrificed* aged whiskey to my mouth and drank, heavily, before passing it off to Rhylen. For the first time in weeks, we were alone. Not too far from where we sat on the edge of camp, the hum of pixie wings serenaded the night. An owl hooted in the distance. And above us, bare tree limbs swayed.

Everything was swaying in my vision, though. We had imbibed in a different bottle of sacrificed whiskey with the fellas first. Before Corbin dared me to steal Bryok from storage and take the skunked pecker for a walk. I pet the former prince's adorably vile, whiskered head, making Rhylen snort. We all wanted to snap his neck. The girls would snap ours if we did, though.

Alas, pranks would have to do.

George materialized at my side from the night's shadows. The shape of him was a wee blurry to my blinking eyes. His little paws dropped a silver case through the flower crown in my lap, the one I had attempted to weave in my tipsy state for Mam. Snorting a quiet laugh, I placed the simple wreath of wild purple asters atop my head, then grabbed the . . . cigarette case? I popped the lid and nearly moaned at the sight of a half-dozen shop-rolled sticks. I opened my mouth to thank the fluffy lad, but he was gone.

Rhylen lifted a book of matches with a crooked smile. He didn't have to say a word. George nicked those too, gods bless him.

I placed a cigarette between my lips and Rhylen struck a match. Leaning forward, I dragged on the smoke until it lit—and sighed. A cigarette and a bottle of whiskey—perfect.

Well, almost perfect.

I fell back in a graceful arch until my head rested in Rhylen's lap. My fingers sought his and knotted them together with mine across my stomach.

Now it was perfect.

Rhylen chuckled under his breath. I was still trussed up from tonight. The fall of skirts around my legs was like a blanket. It was a pleasant, comforting feeling. Though now I wore Glenna's bodice. It was too fecking cold near dawn to wander around camp sleeveless.

"Talk to me," I murmured.

I knew he wouldn't thank me for tonight's revenue—not directly. The fae didn't use mortal expressions of thanks. The words bound them in a bargain to owe a future favor. And while Rhylen trusted me, it just wasn't a faerie's way.

"I'm . . . I'm overwhelmed." My brother imbibed another sip of whiskey, then leaned his head back against a tree and peered up at the stars. "I was so bent on burning the Fiachna's empire to the ground, I didn't fully consider the logistics of starting a new tribe from the ashes of my fury."

He hadn't named his tribe yet either.

Images of Raven Folk at camp rushed through my mind at breakneck speeds. The hems of their emotions and inner thoughts ripped at the seams before me and . . . I quickly understood what Rhylen was too afraid to speak aloud.

"Don't confuse fighting the shame forced on us to feel all our lives as shame for following you." I caressed my thumb over his fingers. "Your flock lowers their eyes and looks away out of conditioning."

Rhylen's throat bobbed. "That shame," he whispered, "is a different fire still burning in me."

"Aye." I twisted to flick the cigarette's ashes away from us, considering Bryok's dead stare for a second. "Most here are still afraid to meet the eyes of Braelin and other former middle-ranks. It's not you, *chieftain*."

He rolled his bottom lip into his mouth for a second. "What you and Glennie did tonight—" his voice caught and he blinked his eyes. "I don't just want to feed the camp. I ache to see those former fellys and slaves feast every fecking day. I . . ." He swallowed thickly again. "The memory of our fellas wolfing down food in the groom's tent, like the starved dogs we were, remains a white-hot flame in my veins." A tear slipped down his cheek. "Not providing food makes me feel like I'm no different than those govs."

I *knew* he felt this. I had *seen* it on him since the first full day of camp set-up—the very moment he realized we literally had nothing to survive on. He discussed flying to Seren to call in a bargain owed for cows, chickens, pigs, and farming supplies. But the fellas decided to wait and see if busking could bring in enough coin to purchase livestock and feed first. Once our license was approved, Filena could begin reading fortunes.

The Kingdom of Carran, however, was slower than a snail on sharp gravel.

Rhylen continued to smile and interacted with everyone in that playful, teasing way of his. He led with the same patience and kind directness he had with the set-up and break down crew. But that shame, that fear of becoming what he had despised marked every tense muscle in his body.

Bryok the Skunk

I intimately knew that overwhelming fear, that sickening shame . . .

The scrape on Glenna's cheek filled my vision and I shoved at my da's blistering voice in my head. Hamish deserved no part of my life, not even my self-loathing.

Another tear slid down Rhylen's cheek.

"Your coin beggar's show," he said with a gentle squeeze of his hand, "will restore people's dignity. We'll be beggars no more."

Well, shite, now my eyes misted.

I rolled my head to fully see him and the forest tilted a little. "I'll shake my arse and flash my ankles as much as it takes to not eat termite flour bread."

Rhylen threw his head back in a loud laugh.

And damn, I could melt into a puddle at the sight.

"Milk a deer for me, though, Rhy-Rhy." I bit my bottom lip and he laughed again.

The crunch of leaves sounded nearby and Rhylen's head whipped to the side. "Glenna and Filena," he whispered.

I would never not be amused by how our sisters' names rhymed.

Nor would I never not irritate Glenna as payback for her pranks.

Dangling the cigarette between my lips, I twisted to grab the whiskey from Rhylen's hand and settled it against me. Then I took that same hand and combed his fingers into my hair, above the flower crown. "Play with the strands, lover."

He sputtered another laugh but obeyed.

The girls slowed before us. I blew out a stream of smoke and lifted innocent eyes.

My sister's lips quirked to the side. "Gossiping and braiding each other's hair, are you?" Her gray eyes slid to the taxidermized-ish skunk. "Braiding his too?"

Glenna considered my and Rhylen's knotted hands on my stomach,

The Heartbreak Show

then how he was preening the longer locks of my hair.

"Rhylee Lo loves to braid my hair," I half-slurred, "while telling me all his darkest birdie secrets."

Glenna remained fixated on the rhythm of Rhylen's fingers, her jaw moving back and forth.

"Cian's hair is so silky," Rhylen murmured. "Makes the secrets spill out of me, it does." Our eyes locked and my brother lost it. He could never keep a straight face. The whiskey didn't help.

Glenna snatched the cigarette from my mouth and placed it in hers.

I drew in a scandalized breath. "Pie harpy!"

"Dowdy wench," she shot back.

Smirking that competitive smile of hers, she bent to thieve the whiskey next and I grabbed the bottle. Glenna batted at my hand and I snorted, gripping the neck of the bottle tighter.

Her slender brow peaked.

I narrowed my eyes—

Ash fell from the cigarette balancing between her lips. I dodged it just in time, pushing into Rhylen, who grunted with the impact. Orange embers winked out in the grass where I had been laying. Glenna's eyes widened in horror only for a slight second. Then they slid to the whiskey.

The corked bottle was tipped on its side.

We both dove for it, but her sober arse was quicker.

My sister's cackling filled the forest around us, but Glenna's crowing howls were louder.

With a growl, I pushed up from Rhylen's lap to stand.

"Shite," she breathed, then grasped Filena's hand and tugged her into a run.

I was too sloshed to give a proper chase. But dammit all. A few seconds later, the girls disappeared into the dark surroundings.

I slumped against the tree beside Rhylen.

"Bloody Ravens," I grumbled.

A corner of his mouth hitched up. "She didn't wing whip you this time."

"That whiskey was my happy cake." Possibly the best bottle I'd ever had.

Rhylen climbed to his feet with a groan, then offered me his hand. "Let's see what other happy trouble we can find."

I grabbed his hand and he yanked me up into an embrace.

"I love you, brother," he said softly.

I rested my head on his shoulder and he tightened his hold. "You're *nothing* like those govs, Rhy."

"Hungry bellies don't care."

"Your flock knows the difference."

He was quiet for several seconds. "Aye, maybe."

I pulled away and cupped his face. "They do, chieftain." Our eyes met and . . . for once, my mind didn't spin with information. Did I now know everything he tried to hide? Warmth bloomed in my chest and I leaned my forehead against his. "Love you too, brother."

We walked into camp a few minutes later, Bryok cradled in one arm, my other looped through Rhylen's until he broke away to sit beside Filena. The girls, including Braelin, were passing the whiskey back and forth, and I cracked a smile. My sister didn't let herself drink often enough.

Glenna glanced at me over her shoulder and my heart stuttered a beat. Firelight kissed her skin and flickered along her midnight hair. She won tonight. There were more women in the audience than men. Or men willing to laugh off their buttoned-up, mortal notions of masculinity to sacrifice coin to someone like me.

Others around camp eyed Bryok in my arms. But only for a second.

Lugging around a cursed taxidermized Raven prince was *still* not

The Heartbreak Show

the weirdest thing I'd brought to a gathering.

I set said skunk down to remove the aster flower crown from my head and walked a few unsteady steps to Mam. "For you," I murmured and placed the droopy wreath atop her wavy blonde hair, then kissed her cheek. "Our Faerie Queen this night."

Edna, her red cardinal, chirped from her shoulder in approval and gently tugged at a tiny petal.

She smiled sweetly at me. "Yer too kind, love bug."

Love . . .

My mind snagged on that one word. I twirled to Gran. "How many Love-Talker pipes have you seen in your young life?"

Gran laughed. "My fair share." She ended with a wink and I grinned. Dirty old hen.

Lifting my skirts, I lowered onto the stump beside her and Mam, picked up the skunk, and started to pet his cute, disgusting head when George appeared at my side. "Aye, you too." The lad climbed up into my lap and wrapped his arms around my neck first before cuddling up against Bryok. May the smothering snuggles of Georgie Dirty Paws cause him eternal suffering.

Returning my attention onto Gran, I asked, "The gancanagh were real, then? Not a faerie tale?"

"Oh aye, they're real," she said and patted my knee.

A scowl pinched between my brows. They *are* real, not were. Well, feck. She and Mam exchanged a quick look, one my fluthered head didn't miss, and my stomach dropped. "And they always smoke . . . a pipe?"

"Smoking adds to his dangerous, reckless beauty, aye. Cigarettes are new, lad. A mortal invention."

Mam was staring at me so intensely, the hairs on my arms lifted. "Not all gancanagh are predatory, love bug. Or cause death by breaking hearts. Some speak love and light to those they touch."

The scowl between my brows deepened. "Came across the pipe in the woods."

Gran patted my leg again. "A perfect prop fer yer coin beggar's show, it is."

Mam's eyes remained riveted on me. She knew I wasn't telling the entire truth. Or maybe being around a drunk man, especially one with Hamish's blood in his veins, kept her on high alert. Beneath lowered lashes, I studied the scrape on Glenna's beautiful face and bit the inside of my cheek.

Should I leave and give Mam space?

Would she feel safer if I weren't around?

I could use my seer's ability to find out but if I *saw* her disgust, her terror...

Nausea fisted in my gut.

George nuzzled into my chest with a soft, comforting sigh. I leaned my cheek on his head and loosed a shaky breath of my own.

"Asters are me favorite," Mam spoke quietly, knotting her fingers with mine.

I lifted my head and whispered, "I remembered."

Our cottage had little, but she brightened the space with the asters she had dried from autumn bouquets she picked each year. When Hamish would disappear for a couple of days, she'd weave the flowers into her long, golden braid and tie off both her hair and flowers with an old, ratty blue satin ribbon. The ribbon she had packed into Filena's runaway sack.

"Asters," Mam said, handing one to me and another to Filena, "grow where wishing stars fall. The blooms hold one last wish, they do."

"What do ye wish fer?" Filena asked, twirling the flower in her little fingers.

The Heartbreak Show

"*Fer me bairns to find the truest love.*" Tears glossed her eyes. "*Fer ye both to capture happiness and to dance with shiny ribbons in yer hair and new shoes on yer feet.*"

"*I wish fer three bowls of berries,*" Filena shared with a grin. "*And a dragonfly friend.*" My sister turned to me. "*Cillian?*"

The pad of my thumb brushed over the soft, pointy purple petals. "*To never be him.*"

Mam set her bouquet on the table and cupped my face. "*Asters are the flowers of wisdom, valor, and . . . love. And ye, me son, have a strong, wise heart made to speak only love.*" She leaned in close and whispered, "*Ye'll never be him.*"

The memory ended and I drew in a shaky breath.

Beside me, Mam plucked a flower from the crown. Edna alighted from her shoulder with the movement to peck for bugs and seeds on the ground. Leaning forward, Mam gently tucked the purple blossom behind my ear, then kissed my cheek. "I *wish* fer ye to stay with me awhile."

My eyes flicked to hers and stilled.

Apparently, I wasn't the only one who could divine what others tried to hide.

Apparently, I needed to follow my own advice too.

Your flock knows the difference . . .

The tribe didn't see corrupted govs when they looked at Rhylen.

My mother didn't see Hamish when she looked at her drunk son.

A corner of my mouth tipped up. "I *wish* for you to dance with shiny ribbons in your hair and new shoes on your feet."

I tugged on the black satin ribbon around my neck. Seeing this, George climbed off my lap and into Gran's so I could slip the ribbon beneath Mam's long, beautiful tresses. Tears warmed her green eyes, her lips trembling into a smile while I looped the satin into a bow. No one deserved a battle ribbon more than Moira Merrick.

No one.

Taking Mam's hand, I pulled her to stand while simultaneously setting the skunk onto my stump.

"Music!" I shouted, hoping someone had an instrument nearby. "The Faerie Queen wants to dance!" A few seconds later, a fiddle started up. Then a bodhrán drum. I wrapped an arm around my mam's waist and held her hand in the air. "Ready to capture happiness?"

The camp spun and tilted as we stepped to the beat.

Our smiles wide, our singing loud.

Perhaps it was my fae blood, perhaps it was a toast to all the broken hearts who survived to beat another day, but I craved dancing around a bonfire with my friends and family until the rising sun brightened the sky.

I reeled with Mam. Jigged with Rhylen. Then Sean. Drank more with Filena. Stole kisses from Glenna whenever I passed her while draped on Owen's and Corbin's arms.

And when the sky feathered into light, I fell into bed beside my heart's obsession, the one I would no longer be afraid to call mine, laughing until it hurt to smile.

Chapter Nine

Glenna Lonan

A bright wedge of sunlight beamed onto the pillow where I lay. My eyes squinted open and blinked. The room was blurry in my fuzzy exhaustion.

Our third Heartbreak Show was last night. The revenue was twice that of the previous nights combined—a king's ransom. The cock boot coins clinked in song the entire walk home. Cian couldn't stop stealing victory kisses from me, each one growing more and more passionate as we changed back into our normal work clothes.

The eejit then left me panting to chop firewood in the forest with the fellas, smirking as he sauntered off. That up-to-no-good grin of his would flash my way whenever he returned to stack the wood . . . until he tugged me back to our wagon at sunrise.

Dark skies above, that man had way too much energy.

With a tired sigh, my lids slid closed a second later.

I had dreamed of decorating trays of tiny cakes in candied flowers and berries before waking. The warm memory of cinnamon and vanilla still lingered in my nose. Angling my face into my pillow, I begged the gods to return me to that familiar place where I not only had beloved, predictable tasks each day but busyness from a job that fed my magic. Even if just in dreams—

A paw tapped my cheek.

My eyes flew open to find a pair of dark brown ones watching me intently. I groaned, placing a hand up to shield against the late afternoon light. From his position on the pillow beside me, George patted my cheek again.

I yawned. "Does your master demand I attend him?"

George made a cooing chittering sound.

I hadn't the faintest idea of what he was saying, not without Cian.

Wait... where was Cian? I pushed up and studied our small wagon. He was gone. So was Moira.

In the three weeks we had lived together, Cian had not once awakened before me. The gobshite slept like the dead and needed to be dragged from the bed each day.

George snuggled up to my stomach, then grabbed my nightgown and tugged on me to lie back down. A giggle slipped past my lips. I moved the fluffy lad closer and George sighed. I started to relax again when something coarser moved against me and I pushed away, eyes wide. Sheila rolled to her back and stretched.

"George," I asked slowly, "why is wee Sheila in my bed?"

The raccoon pulled Sheila to him, like she was a child's well-loved doll. The hedgehog's nose snuffled out from where his paw cupped her face and I giggled again.

"Does Filena know you stole her pocket of happiness?" Poor Lena, I hoped she hadn't been searching for her hedgehog since whenever George ended up in the wagon. "Let's return her, lad."

I slipped my feet to the floor and stood. From a drawer beneath the bed, I pulled out my corset, stockings, petticoats, and a threadbare day dress. I promised to help Gran wildcraft medicinal plants for the mortals still recovering from the fever moving between the families. Thankfully, it hadn't proven to be dire and was finally slowing down.

I quickly dressed, with George handing me each article of clothing in turn when not hugging Sheila to him. The wee lass didn't seem to mind, licking one of his whiskers.

A knock sounded on the door. I turned just as Filena popped her head inside. "Oh good, you're awake."

I arched a brow. "Missing something, darlin'?"

She shut the door behind her. "Cian asked to borrow Sheila."

"Cian?"

"Aye." Mischief glimmered in my sister's gray eyes. "A wee *slice* of happy magic."

I twisted to peer at the little hedgehog and . . . burst into laughter. The darling rested on my pillow with my battle ribbon around her neck, as if a ruffled collar.

Filena snatched my hand and yanked me to the bed to lie down across the short side, her back to my pillows. Snuggling closer, we wrapped our arms around each other until we were nose-to-nose, grinning. I missed this. I missed our gossip sessions of all our ridiculous moments during the night before falling asleep each morning. Our witty back-and-forths too.

"Tell me something deliciously scandalous," Lena whispered. "My soul needs cheering, it does."

"You do look ghastly," I teased, a concerned pinch to my brows. "Primal male problems, is it?"

"So growly."

"The growliest."

We sputtered a laugh.

George crawled over Filena and plopped Sheila between us, the garter ribbon still around her neck. He pet Lena's hair while disappearing behind her once more.

Sheila

"George is taking his job very seriously," I said.

Filena's eyes sparkled again and I narrowed mine in reply. "Gossip, pet?" She stroked Sheila's back. "If I don't find joy in another's misery soon, I might create drama to satisfy my dark soul."

"Niamh Beirne"—a former West Tribe felly in our new tribe—"stole Meira's love charm—"

"The rusty key?"

"Aye." My smile was slow. "She drops it in Meira's path and illusions it into horse shite right before the lass steps on it."

"Nooooo." Filena started cackling. "Is this over Fadam?"

"All your fault, darlin'." I poked her in the side.

Filena wrinkled her nose. "If Rhylen asks me to read apple peels on Áine's Day, I'll curse all the fruit to—"

"Ah-ah," I chastised, placing a finger to lips. "Don't spoil it for me."

Filena's grin was equal parts delighted and wicked. "Believing a key will unlock a lad's heart *is* horse shite."

It was but the fae were superstitious to a fault.

A slight furrow appeared between Filena's brow. "Where did you get this garter?"

"Nicked it from a mortal dalliance up north."

My sister gently pulled the pink satin off Sheila and turned it in her hand. "This is the Ogham rune hÚath."

I propped my head up onto my palm and studied the stitched ancient language of the trees. I could read the mortal common tongue, but not the ancient fae one. Runes here and there I recognized, aye—like hÚath. All faeries knew this one specifically. Many mortals did too. I just hadn't noticed the stitching on the garter until now.

"Hawthorn," I murmured.

The faerie tree. Or what mortals called a Wishing Tree. There were a few dotted around Carran and what inspired the Caravan tradition of

Beltane and Samhain ribbons on our Truth Telling Trees. The ribbons represented different desires and mortals believed if they tied one to a hawthorn branch, faeries would grant them the wishes of their hearts.

Faeries didn't *grant* wishes.

No, we tricked and bargained and Wishing Trees were a clever trap—

My pulse kicked into a gallop.

Cian . . . he had asked for a mortal to sacrifice a ribbon from a Wishing Tree to break our Love-Talker curse. Did he know my battle ribbon was one? Or was this part of his scheme he believed I didn't see him spinning?

No, he knew I could scent a trail of Cian-made chaos. There was no hiding much from the lad.

"That mortal lass," Filena continued, "either nicked the garter herself or took back her Wishing Tree ribbon to craft into a love charm."

"Well," I drawled with a wink, "it worked."

"A memorable night, was it?"

"I might have granted a wish or two." I plucked my battle ribbon from Filena's fingers.

She snorted. "Then you broke her heart."

"Aye, I broke—" I shut my mouth.

I might go feral over this . . .

Did the ribbon call to Cian? As a demi-god, could he feel the wish?

I considered the embroidered rune on my garter. "Can Cian read Ogham?"

Filena considered me a couple of seconds. "We both read Ogham before we could read the common tongue." Her eyes narrowed. "Why?"

I ignored her question and rolled to a stand. "Where's the eejit?"

George pulled Sheila to him before Filena scooped up the wee hedgie. After a hug, he gently put Sheila into Filena's skirt pocket and my

The Heartbreak Show

sister giggled.

"You really do like cuddling," she cooed to the raccoon who cooed back. "Muffin Moo needs some Georgie snuggles too, aye? Go cheer up that fluffy red raincloud."

Cian's familiar climbed down the bed and scampered to the door, and Filena quietly cackled under her breath.

"After you, Mistress of Chaos," I said to my sister.

She curtsied, "Raven Folk temptress."

Filena wove her fingers with mine and led me outside. At the bottom of the steps, I looped my arm with hers. We wove through the mossy trees and tumbling fall leaves, a light tune on my lips. My sister glanced my way. The mischief in her gray eyes practically danced in glee.

What was going on?

Why did Cian really borrow Sheila and deliver the little lass through George?

A wee slice of happy magic . . .

Before I could think more on that man's seemingly nonsensical schemes, we ambled into camp and those cooking meager, watered-down meals, working on chores, caring for children immediately stopped to watch as I moved toward the central fire pit.

A chill prickled down my spine.

Chapter Ten

Glenna Lonan

The sudden hush was so intense, I was almost afraid to take another step. My gaze flitted from face to face; my fingers curled tight around the garter ribbon. Stars, I needed help fighting my erratic pulse.

I spotted the fellas, who grinned at me. Braelin too.

A chicken clucked and I halted. We had a . . . *chicken*? I spun toward the sound. Gran held a laying hen. No, we had two chickens. Moira cradled another.

I gaped, a million questions flying through my mind.

Rhylen stepped forward and I almost flinched, not sure if I should prepare for the worst or for a reaction everyone around me seemed to anticipate. The love shining in my brother's eyes plucked at the forming knot in my throat. He gestured with his head. I released Filena's arm and twisted to where he indicated—and gasped.

A polished table stood behind the fire pit, one hewn from maple and topped with several ceramic bowls, measuring spoons and cups. Beside the table was a cart filled with—

I clapped a hand over my mouth.

Tears lined my lashes.

The Heartbreak Show

Two hefty burlap sacks of flour leaned against an equally large sack of sugar. Enough flour to last our camp two weeks, even if I made a dozen loaves per day. Even if I made a couple of cakes or mounds of cookies after the loaves. Balanced around crates of vegetables and eggs were several crocks of lard, bins of salt, smaller jars of other baking ingredients, and . . . a half-dozen cake and loaf tins.

Tears streamed down my cheeks and I hiccupped a disbelieving laugh.

Then I saw him.

Cian's stormy eyes were steeled onto me from the shadows of a nearby oak he leaned against. A hawk-eyed stare that soaked up every emotion. Clutching the love charm in my fist, I moved toward my heart's wish, my soul's one desire. His lips tipped up, a bashful smile that alighted my thrumming pulse into flight. Cian was many things, but never shy.

I considered the table as I slowed before him. "You chopped up more than firewood, darlin'."

"My skilled hands know how to work wood, Glennie Lo," he said with a wink.

My lips trembled into a smile at the riddled innuendo. He tilted his head closer and locks of sunlight-limned hair fell down to his upper cheek. But not before I caught the dark circles under his eyes.

"Did you sleep at all today?"

"No," he whispered and cupped my face. His thumbs brushed at the tears. "Took the early morning train to Den Merrow after you fell asleep."

Another tear-choked laugh left my tight lungs. Aye, he purchased these supplies for the tribe, to support Rhylen. Most villages refused to trade with Raven Folk. But the entire camp knew he really did this for me, no matter how much it benefited everyone else.

A faint blush crept up his neck. He *knew* I understood this too and .

. . and . . .

He had nothing and gave me *everything*.

Falling stars, my heart, it was blissfully breaking beneath the heady romance of his gesture. And those shattering pieces of laughter and longing? They ached inside me with a love so fierce, so exquisite, I hoped to remain in beautiful ruins at his feet for all eternity.

"You know," I said through my tears, "most boys gift a girl jewelry or a hair adornment when courting."

"And let you upstage me?"

"True, a locket with our initials doesn't shout 'pea*cocking* doxy' loud enough."

An impish corner of his mouth kicked up. "Kitchen witches demand the unborn children of clucking fowl, the oils of sacrificed bovines, and the ground seed of golden grass before one can declare their intentions, aye?"

"And what are your intentions, Cian Merrick?"

"To eat the first slice of cake infused with a bite of happiness before my sister, obviously."

"Naturally."

"Glenna," he whispered in my ear, all humor gone, "I hunger for you."

Sweet goddess . . .

"Ravenous," he practically moaned. "Starved."

"Devour me," I whispered back. "I want to be consumed by you."

"That's my *intention*." His tongue teased my bottom lip, his fingers sliding down my neck, around my breasts, and I shivered.

"This is a family show!" Owen shouted from the now cheering and whistling crowd.

Cian smirked over my head. "Fecking voyeurs!"

I turned to mock-glare at everyone just as Owen covered Corbin's

The Heartbreak Show

eyes. "The lad had peep show virgin eyes. You ruined his innocence."

"Corbie's officially a grown cock now," Cian teased back. "You're welcome, lad."

Corbin tried to elbow Owen, who jumped out of the way with a crowing laugh. Tracking the troublemaker's movements, Corbin flashed Owen a smug grin, one that was all sharpened edges. The next blink, he pounced and tackled Owen to the ground.

"Bets!" Sean called out, not missing a beat.

The tribe gathered around Sean and lifted beads, rocks, and other wagers as Owen and Corbin continued to tussle in-between bouts of fake insults and laughter.

My brother hung back, grinning. The next breath, he was doubled over in laughter when Corbin illusioned something into a snake and Owen swore, scrabbling back on hands and knees. Laughing harder the moment Owen realized it was a trick, mock-growled at Corbin, then leapt back onto him.

While everyone was distracted, I lifted my battle ribbon before Cian's face. "I have a sacrifice for the Love-Talker."

His sleepy eyes rounded. "You're surrendering?"

I scoffed and pointed to the stitched Ogham letter and his eyes rounded even more. "I didn't know it was a Wishing Tree ribbon until Filena noticed this rune. George put the garter on Sheila like a collar."

The fluffy lad probably knew of its origins and wanted Filena to see the stitching.

George, like Cian, also seemed to always *know*.

Taking Cian's hand in mine, I knotted the ruched pink ribbon and cream lace around his wrist.

"Tying me up?" He flashed me a lip-biting smile.

I tapped the ribbon. "You *wish*, darlin'."

Cian snorted.

I waited for him to explain why he needed a Wishing Tree ribbon so badly, as well as a Lughnasadh's Day straw hat, or how he knew those hideous pots for gold boots were cobbled by a leprechaun—which, interestingly, also involved George.

But an explanation never came.

Instead, Cian gathered me close and gently brushed his lips across mine. "I need to sleep before our Heartbreak Show."

"Aye," I kissed back against his mouth. "Or we can skip tonight?"

"The only way I'll accept defeat—"

"—is when I win," I finished for him. "Now shoo!" I stepped back and fluttered my hand in the air, as if I were a Caravan gov.

Cian's grin was sensual, rascally so. Even sleep deprived, he was far too pretty. I would look too haggard for polite *and* impolite society. Lowering his lashes, he moved his head until strands of his golden hair fell over his half-lidded eyes. Gods, liquid heat pooled low in my belly. That look disarmed me each time and the arse *knew*. He wanted to watch me suffer—for more punishment? To prove that he'd win?

I shifted on my feet and resisted the urge to brush the fallen strands from his eyes.

I would *not* preen the eejit.

Be strong, lass.

My fingers twitched.

Be strong . . .

I was one cursed breath away from caving when Cian kissed the garter around his wrist and began slowly walking backward, his heavy, tired eyes fastened to mine. Then he whispered, "Devour me too," and spun on his heel, taking my thundering heart with him.

Dying suns, how that man made it hard to breathe. To think intelligently. To stay calm for more than two seconds. To resist pushing him against a wall, to touch and lick and kiss him until he moaned every last

The Heartbreak Show

breath he stole from my panting lungs first.

He pecked Rhylen's cheek as he passed by, then playfully shoved my brother's face to the side while moving on.

Sean lifted Corbin's arm up into the air. "Winner!"

The laughing crowd circled into small pockets to deliver lost bets.

Cian continued angling through the tribe—smiling, winking, jesting—and slowed only to smack Owen's arse. Another round of teasing and laughter erupted around the gathering, my brother's laugh loud when Owen shot a rude gesture at Cian and Cian replied by blowing Owen a suggestive kiss that he then caught and slapped to his own arse.

"Oh that's a proper challenge, it is," Sean said.

Owen grinned. "Run, mortal."

"Ruin my pretty face, Owen Delaney," Cian drawled, "and"—Owen pretended to charge—"Shite!" Cian hissed and took off toward the wooded trail.

I snickered.

The pranks and games between Raven Folk males never failed to entertain me. And when they teased Cian? Frosting on the cake!

Which sounded divinely delicious right now.

I leaned over the cart and took in all the supplies, pressing two fingers to my lips.

A cake I could make, but not one infused with a bite of happiness. For that, I would need to bargain with a green witch for rare spellcraft ingredients to brew into an elixir.

A basket was wedged in a corner of the cart, one large enough for gathering supplies. Cian thought of nearly everything and my heart fluttered. Fighting a smile, I grabbed a crock of lard, a dozen eggs, several apples, a bottle labeled vanilla, and a jar with cinnamon scrolled across the front in fancy lettering, then moved toward my new baking table.

Gran scooted to stand beside me and unfolded an apron in her hand—*her* apron. One she gently tied around me and I blinked back tears. My fingers slid down the old, worn cotton. My apron was in West Tribe's confectionary wagon.

"Sean, lad," Gran hollered and waved for him to join us.

"Aye, Gran?" he asked, jogging over.

"Ask five families to ready their wagon stoves fer apple pudding." She considered me. "Do ye need more stoves, lass?"

"Five is plenty."

He dipped his head and jogged back into the gathering.

Gran squeezed my hand, both our smiles large, then we busied ourselves with making the apple cakes to celebrate our happy future.

We would survive—

"Need help?" Filena asked.

Maybe not.

I lowered my voice into a stage whisper. "Who are you wanting to kill off?"

"That was *one* time." Filena snatched a spoon she then pointed in my face. "One. Time, Glenna Lonan. And he wasn't really dead."

Moira and Braelin sidled up next to me, grabbed apples, knives, and began peeling.

Lloyd scurried down Filena's shoulder to creep close to Braelin, who offered him a tiny slice of the fruit. The squirrel was smitten with two lasses: wee Sheila and Braelin.

Not wanting to be left out, Edna chirped from Moira's shoulder. Braelin nicked off a sliver of apple and held it up to the red cardinal, who happily pecked it off her hand.

Filena scowled at Braelin, who playfully ignored her. "Just because *she* hasn't fake-murdered a mortal by accidentally adding a sleeping draft to the batter instead of water doesn't mean she won't one day."

Braelin continued to pretend as if Filena wasn't ready to fake-curse her arse.

"You may peel one apple, Filena Lonan." I held the poor, beautiful sacrificial fruit out to her. "But only if you peel it in one continuous curl—"

"This is what my love means to you, does it?"

"—then toss it over your shoulder—"

"I helped you bury Cory Reily's favorite baby tooth into Ríona Cairn's pillow."

Braelin glanced up. "Her last name was *Cairn*?"

Filena tipped the spoon at her. "Gravediggers. The whole family."

Braelin's face scrunched in a mild grimace. "You *buried* a tooth in a gravedigger's wagon?" She blinked. "A faerie's tooth?"

"Aye, for this ungrateful cow." Filena tossed me a smug grin. "A bad omen, it is, pet," she continued in a melodramatically mysterious voice, the one she used to dazzle her customers. "For a leprechaun to collect your fallen tooth and return it to your pillow the next day. Seven years bad luck."

Gran chuckled and I smirked at her.

It was a clever trick. Ríona Cairn was my inseparable since birth, middle-rank friend, before my parents died. I was only five. But her family refused to let us remain friends when Gran took us in. Brenna Meadows was a felly and, therefore, Rhylen and I lost pecking order. For the next seven years, Ríona ensured no one believed us friends.

Filena decided the lass had crowed her rank long enough.

Faeries lose their last baby tooth around age twelve, same as mortals. But unlike mortals, our final baby tooth holds magic. We leave that nibble of magic for the Wee Folk to collect and, as a favor owed, they gift us faerie children with good luck.

Unless they return your tooth.

I cracked an egg into a bowl. "Ríona was a nasty horsefly when we were fledglings."

"Poured spoiled milk on Glennie Lo's head, she did." Filena reached for the cinnamon.

"And so," I drawled, smacking her hand, "you fake-cursed her with bad luck. People feared being near her at first."

Filena lifted her chin for a dramatic beat. "She dug her own grave."

Gran barked a laugh. Moira and Braelin grinned.

Barry, however, groaned and stepped away.

"It was funny," she shot back. Barry, not convinced, closed his eyes and lifted his snout—similar to what Filena had just done to me. "Muffin Moo," she cooed in a syrupy voice, "George is looking for you, darlin'." The fox's eyes snapped open and narrowed. "Be a good a lad and cuddle with your best forest friend." Barry's gaze slid to mine and I shook my head. He, like Ríona, had dug his own grave. With a huff and a flick of his tail, he trotted off.

Lloyd climbed down the table and scampered after Barry and Barry began moving faster.

Filena quietly cackled.

Braelin set the partially peeled apple down on the table. "How did you know which one was that boy's favorite baby tooth?"

"Cian," Filena and I said at the same time.

I cracked another egg. "Cory Reily was—"

"A creepy child." Filena shuddered.

"He collected teeth," I explained to Braelin. "Still does. Mostly mortal teeth. Favors the baby ones most."

Braelin's nose pinched. "And Cian knew exactly—"

"Aye," I interjected. "Cian always *knows*." I paused, then added, "Everything."

"It's why he's an eejit," Filena drolled.

"The man is a punch bowl of gossip—" I swatted at the hand sneaking around Braelin's waist. "Sean Byrnes, get out of my kitchen!"

He snatched two apple slices with a grin and plopped them in his mouth. "The ovens are warming for you," he said while chewing.

Oh.

I had forgotten.

"One more slice," I offered in gratitude.

Sean plucked another piece of apple from the table, pressed a soft, lingering kiss to the back of Braelin's neck, then sauntered over to the lads.

"A bit of ancient wisdom fer ye, Braelin Byrnes," Gran said with the beginnings of an impish smile. "Cook yer lad a wagon meal in only yer apron when ye need to bargain with him."

"Gran!" I chastised around Filena's raucous laughter and only for the poor girl's sake.

Braelin blushed but her eyes slid to where Sean stood beside Rhylen, talking.

"I have ancient wisdom fer ye too, Glennie Lo," Gran teased.

"And ruin Filena's appetite before she can dip the spoon she's clutching to death into the batter?"

I *loved* Gran's advice about boys, girls, and sex.

Gran's impish smile grew. She knew I was playing a part for Braelin, who was raised to have modesty like a mortal lass. "Foreplay for boys who fantasize about kissin'—"

"STOP." I pointed at Filena. "She *will* curse this cake."

Filena's grin was wicked. She knew too. "Fantasize about kissing *what*, Gran?"

"Kissin' the rouge from a girl's lips." The ancient's dark purple eyes twinkled. "He'd sacrifice his favorite dress to paint her mouth the color he wants stainin' his own."

Wait . . . that was what Cian had confessed in the woods a few days back. Well, all but sacrificing his favorite dress.

How in the stars blasted skies would I now concentrate on anything but satisfying *that* fantasy?

"Offer him yer rouge," Gran added with a wink, and I understood her deeper meaning. *Offer him this in thanks, as your courting gift to him.* "But offer it to him only when ye need to subdue the mischief-making lad fer five focused seconds."

We all burst into laughter. Even Moira smiled.

Gratitude flushed across my warming chest. This . . . I had missed *this*. Needed *this*.

The delicious banter between sisters in the kitchen while baking together was the bite of happiness I had ached to have again since departing West Tribe.

I cracked another egg into the bowl. My singing heart was soaring so high above the sunlit clouds, I didn't know if I could land anymore. Or wanted to.

Oh aye, I'd offer Cian rouge to paint my lips so I could then stain his. Anytime he desired.

Chapter Eleven

CIAN MERRICK

Until this evening, I hadn't felt territorial... about anything.

Tearing my gaze from Glenna, I focused on the mainlander coin purses captivated by our Heartbreak Show. Particularly one young gent who watched me sashay toward him to the melody of Owen's banjo and with an intensity that flushed his neck.

"Beware, darlin'," I simpered loud enough for all to hear. "He'll make you fall in love with him." Squeezing the man's bicep, I bit my bottom lip and... moved on to the next lad, tossing over my shoulder, "Then he'll leave you."

Until three weeks ago, I owned nothing. Not even my life, which was always on the line to be beaten to death, traded away, or sold. My only possessions were moments I could claim to their fullest.

Friends. Music. Drink. Sex.

> *A man locked onto Glenna's seductive movements beneath lowered lashes while pretending to check his pocket watch. The pulse fluttering in his throat accelerated. He licked his lips. A woman at his side leaned in to speak. The man snapped shut his*

watch and smiled politely at her.

The breath in my lungs flamed hot. Mortals were easily elf struck. Aye, Glenna could take care of herself and didn't need me growling at every person who lusted after her while putting on a coin beggar's show to make people do just *that*. Still... the Raven Folk feminine urge to peck a man's mind to insanity was a new feeling to me.

For the past two years, I had refused to feel a single drop of jealousy over her dalliances. That was unfair to her and me. She could never be mine. I could never be hers. And my sister had to remain my entire world.

If I knew the details of Glenna's trysts?

Or paid much attention to the ones in front of me?

It would have eaten me alive. I would have obsessed to the point of self-destruction. Aye, hypocritical considering all the lovers I'd indulged in—far more than her. Yet, the very moment my weak, desperate soul learned she only kissed blond-haired, blue eyed mortal lads, I caved and looked her right in the eyes.

Feck, I *knew* what I would *see* and still I wasn't prepared.

> *Hidden behind the folds of her skirt, a young woman inched her hand closer to a girl of similar age beside her. Their fingers touched. Both blinked back shyness. The initiator blushed. The pursued bit back an excited smile. Their concealed fingers wove together as they continued to watch our show, eyes straight ahead.*

She was obsessed with me, like I was her. Loved me, pined for me, fantasized about me. Gods above, the force of her emotions mirrored my own.

And I panicked.

The Heartbreak Show

And started losing all my self-control.

And began drinking more to drown out the pain bleating in my chest.

The fear that I wouldn't be able to stop myself and risk my sister's safety consumed me. The terror that I would cause Glenna's banishment if I pursued her—destroying Rhylen in the process—haunted every beat of my breaking heart. West Tribe would have sold me to Seren, if her banishment happened, and I would have been forever separated from Filena.

> *A tree spirit around my age slid into the lower-lit shadows on the fringe of the gathering. His fingers moved like a lover's whisper. In a matter of seconds, he had unclasped a bracelet from a woman's wrist. He winked at George, who was gaping at him, before disappearing into the thicker crowd.*

"Beware," I purred to a hazel-eyed lad in a flat cap. "He'll squeeze every drop of fevered blood from your lovesick body." I caressed his cheek with a single finger and twirled away to find my next sacrifice.

I should have reveled with abandon in being able to openly love Glenna in Rhylen's new tribe. But the self-hate over being Hamish's son painted my life in the deepest shame.

My new family, my friends saw that fecking piece of shite. Witnessed the food matted on his clothing, his greasy, unkempt hair and beard, his drunken rages. They were there when I brought Mam to my wagon, covered in bruises and dressed in warm clothing George found for her to wear over the thin scrap of fabric barely covering her body.

After all Mam had endured, knowing Moira Merrick didn't fear me when I was slurring and stumbling on whiskey ... changed *everything*.

Knowing that I could provide for the girl I wanted to make my life partner ... was *transcendent*.

Cian Merrick

I plucked a cigarette from a young man's fingers and placed it between my red-stained lips. Winking at him, I sucked on the smoke in a suggestive draw. He and his friends laughed at my lascivious joke.

"Beware," I said while blowing out smoke—

"She'll *pet* more than your ego," Glenna quipped, "and leave you forever unsatisfied."

I gasped, then leaned toward a gent in a newly tailored black suit and stage-whispered, "I always *finish* what I start, sir."

He cracked a smile. "I would hope so, *miss*."

I blew him a kiss and dragged on the cigarette again.

Damn, his suit was a finely cut masterpiece.

I had never bought a brand new anything in my entire life.

But I bought, with coin I earned, factory new cake and loaf tins for Glenna. Mixing bowls, spoons, and cups she was the first to use too.

Stars above, *I bought food*. And chickens! Why was buying chickens empowering? It wasn't the first time Rhylen found me with two girls on my arms. But when he met me at the train station, I had swallowed my pride and disembarked in the gods-awful cock boots, strutting toward him with a hen cradled in each arm. My brother laughed to tears.

Making Rhylen laugh was a full-time job I took very, *very* seriously.

Making Glenna laugh too.

Two days had passed since that day, but the unfettered joy on my heart's face, the magic thrumming in my love's veins still danced wildly in my aching pulse. A humbling feeling.

> *An older man opened a locket dangling in his fingers and stared wistfully at a faded image of a woman. Tears reddened his eyes. With a tiny, trembling smile, he kissed the illustration and tucked the necklace into an inner pocket of his suit vest.*

The Heartbreak Show

Maybe I was the metaphorical Cow of Plenty and the quest for three items was an annoying adventure of self-discovery. That would be my shite luck.

If true, that muffin hag would call me a brassy cow or . . . brazen heifer.

Feck, brazen heifer was fantastic. I needed to call myself that first.

"Beware of halfling faerie girl smiles," Glenna said from the other end of our makeshift stage. The word *halfling* always made the mortals look at me with hyper-curiosity.

Round and round we went, flinging challenges and insults while flirting with the crowd. When the boarding call was announced, we pointed to the red eyesores with our usual tale about sacrificing to the Love-Talkers to prevent a broken heart in our separation.

I glanced at Glenna to smile and—

Feck.

Me.

A woman strolled by in a dainty fruit-patterned dress and . . . wearing a Lughnasadh's Day straw hat tied in a stylish bow beneath her chin.

Why was she wearing that hat to Seren? In winter? Lughnasadh's Day was a summer festival for first harvests our sun god created to memorialize his foster mother.

My son.

Wait.

Where did *that* thought come from?—

Holy Mother of Stars! If I were a re-souled Cian, then the sun god was my fecking son.

No, I'd unknot that mind-blowing mess of weirdness later.

First, I needed this hat—

My mouth fell open. Three more ladies in fruit decorated straw hats and orchard-themed dresses skirted around the dispersing crowd toward the ferry docks.

"Gent of Fem!" I pointed, eyes wide, a goofy smile pulling at my lips. "Go!"

Her dark eyes narrowed. "And do what?"

"Whatever is necessary," I said low so others couldn't hear. "Play up your natural compelling allure. Trade a kiss for a hat. Coerce one of them."

Glenna placed a fist on the hip she popped out, her head tilting the opposite direction. "Coercion is against the rules *and* against the law."

Shite. I forgot the hat had to be *gifted* too.

"Fine, no coercion. But—"

"I'm not seducing an ugly hat from a woman to rival those hideous pair of boots. Not without telling me why."

I pouted.

"No."

I pouted some more.

"Cian Merrick"—an accusatory brow arched—"kissing is also against our rules."

A corner of my mouth tipped up. "I'm only allowed to flirt with males, Gent of Fem."

"Why do you *need* this hat?"

I heaved a frustrated sigh. "To get a cow."

"A . . . *cow*? You need a tacky arse hat, a Wishing Tree ribbon, and repulsive boots cobbled by leprechauns for a *cow*?"

I shrugged.

"Full-blooded gods save me." Glenna rolled her eyes.

"And sexy demi-god before you, but your arse in my pants distracts me to—"

She shooed her hands at me. "Go get your hideous fruit bowl hat, eejit."

The Heartbreak Show

"How dare you insult my son's fashion tastes." Grinning, I kissed her forehead, the one wrinkling in confusion over my next nonsensical comment, then dashed off toward the group of ladies, who now numbered a dozen.

And skidded to a halt halfway to my mark.

The tree spirit, the one I saw sliding between shadows, stepped into my path. His dark forest green hair was shaved close on the sides and around the back of his head with longer strands tied up into a messy knot. Loose tresses fell over pale green eyes. The rascally tilt to the elf's lips grew wider.

"Cian Merrick," the familiar voice said. "Been awhile, yeah?"

The thumping organ in my chest stopped.

"Finn Brannon?"

Chapter Twelve

CIAN MERRICK

"Ten fecking years," I said on a laugh, the orchard ladies completely forgotten. "Damn lad, thought I'd never see your pretty mug again."

A gorgeous water spirit male shifted on his feet beside Finn. Beneath lowered lashes, I quickly took in his ruffled mid-ear length blue hair, gold hoops up his pointed ears, and . . . the skirted wrap favored by the wild fae fastened around his waist, draping down to just above his knees. My gaze rested on the tattoos trailing down one arm.

He was once an archer.

The water spirits who trained with long bows tattooed their draw arm in runes and symbols for luck in aim, battle, and bravery . . . and left the other bare, according to the wild fae orphans I'd met over the years. They began training as children.

"Rhylen has a new tribe, yeah?" Finn asked.

"A tribe of misfits." I combed my fingers through my tresses. "Mostly fellys and a handful of middle-ranks along with their former slaves, and from all four tribes."

"My best mate here was fostered in North Tribe."

"Oh aye?"

The Heartbreak Show

A muscle along the elf's jaw pulsed, his brows low over dark blue eyes—the pupils slightly slitted from the male's water dragon heritage. It wasn't an angry look. Or a broody one. Not the intensity of a male attracted to another either. The lad was studying me and . . . strategizing.

Good. Perfect timing.

A man walking toward us lit a fresh cigarette. Eastern city gents were walking chimneys, much to my light-fingered delight. If I couldn't drink at a train station, I'd indulge in other vices. And so, per my usual trick, I reached out and plucked the cigarette right out of the mortal's hand and immediately placed the smoke between my lips and sucked long, slow. The man froze. They always froze.

I puckered my rouge-stained lips at the gent. "Thank you, darlin'."

The water spirit sputtered a laugh when the mortal harumphed and strode on.

Finn gave his friend a light shove, then pointed to the makeshift stage. "The Heartbreak Show?"

"I'm a professional Love-Talker, lads," I said with a mock-flirty wink at the blue-haired elf, who began eyeing me anew, as if to see if I were an actual gancanagh.

The feck if I knew...

But behind me, where Finn had pointed, was a simple stage frame the fellas had built that could be broken down to fit into a cart. Red and gold designs covered the entire structure, made from flour paint Glenna prepared with wildcrafted plants. And draped along the sides were old, quilted blankets for curtains.

"A coin beggar's burlesque show," I continued, "until the Kingdom of Carran approves Rhylen's Fair and Market license."

An older woman strolled by with a disapproving glare my way. I adjusted my corset, then blew her a kiss as smoke left my red-painted mouth.

The rascally slant of Finn's lips deepened.

The blue-haired elf at his side quietly groaned. At first, I thought it was because of me until he muttered, "Shite, not *them*."

Finn followed where his friend looked and quickly schooled his features. The familiar calculating mischief was written all over him, though. Stars how I had missed that troublemaker.

The water elf's eyes narrowed. "Finn Brannon, I'll knock that smug grin off your devilish face."

"But you love their blessing ceremonies, Kalen Kelly." Finn grinned now. "Brings you endless joy, it does."

Kelly ... that wasn't a water spirit name or a Caravan one. Probably a surname assigned by the Thieves' Guild on Seren.

"Those mortals?" I pointed to the women in the fruit-decorated hats, the ones now boarding the ferry to Seren, begging the gods it was indeed them.

"The Ladies of Lugh," Kalen answered with a slight shudder. My pulse kicked into a gallop and I studied the women closer. "They visit Seren each winter to worship Lugh while blessing the waning sun."

Kalen's voice still carried the heavy lilt of the wild fae but with a touch of a Seren street accent—a Caledona dialect, similar to the Caravan fae, but drizzled with an eastern cities flavor. Based on still present intensity of his wild fae brogue, he must have been older when sold to North Tribe. Must not have lived with them long either.

"To hunt *sky* fae to bless," Finn continued. "Kalen here is twice blessed. Smelled like rancid pie for a week."

"The bastard pushed me into their circle while I was following Guild Master's orders to thieve their jewelry. Two years in a row."

"Aye," Finn said with a serious nod, "and still not lucky with the lasses, are you, mate?"

Kalen chuffed a quiet laugh. "You're shite luck, that's why."

The Heartbreak Show

Chills prickled down my arms and torso. What were the chances Finn Brannon would show the exact moment I needed to thieve or riddle a Lughnasadh's Day straw hat into my possession? From the Ladies of *Lugh*.

I locked eyes with my childhood friend and focused my magic.

A tiny smile ghosted Finn's mouth.

Images flitted through my mind.

> *Finn naked in a river.*
> *Finn naked in the forest.*
> *Finn naked—*

I barked a laugh. "Arse."

"Most mortals thank me for the fine view."

"How did you shield?" Goosebumps flushed down my bare arms. He knew I had the Sight.

Finn tugged me close and whispered, "You know how, mate."

The blood rapidly drained from my head.

The only seer *I knew*, outside my Mam and Filena, was the Maiden.

How in the fecking dark skies above did he know my great aunt?

Did he know I was also related to her?

My gaze darted to the Ladies of Lugh, then to Glenna, who was breaking down the stage with Owen, to George who sat at Finn's feet, gaping like an elf struck mortal, and then back to Finn. Grabbing Finn's arm, I yanked him to the edge of the platform, closer to the forest and away from milling travelers.

"How do you know the Maiden?" I whispered.

He shrugged. "I work for her."

I needed a fainting couch.

And smelling salts.

And for the handsome Gent of Fem to wipe my sudden clammy-fevered brow because . . . *what*?!

I puffed on the cigarette.

My rapidly-racing mind was moving in and out of focus.

"Darlin'," I finally managed, "tell me in ten words or less how you ended up working for the Maiden." The spinning, tilting equilibrium in my head accelerated.

"A bargain."

"That's two words, damn."

"That's all you need to know right now, love."

I smiled at the street slang Seren boys used when talking to girls. The momentary warmth in my chest at his gesture faded in the next breath. I dragged on the cigarette again. My fingers were starting to tremble, in shock, in excitement. I side-eyed Glenna, who glanced over and thinned her eyes on Finn, then Kalen.

Stepping in closer, I lowered my voice further. "Glenna will be over in a few seconds."

"Wee Glennie Lo?" Finn asked.

I ignored him. "The Maiden told me to find a magical faerie cow."

"A . . . *cow*?" Finn asked, all traces of humor leaving him. "What kind of faerie cow?"

I waved my cigarette in the air. "A Cow of Plenty."

He stiffened.

"Named Glas Gaibhnenn. Apparently, my birthright."

Kalen's mouth parted. "Cian Merrick," he said under his breath. "Powerful Ancient Enduring One." He translated my first and surname, turning to Finn. "Cian of the Tuatha Dé Danann, warrior god and father of Lugh."

Finn's eyes flashed back to mine. "*That* cow."

"My birthright, aye," I emphasized *again*.

The Heartbreak Show

"Are you . . ." Kalen scrutinized me *again*.

I peered toward the stage and—*shite*. "Glenna and Owen are coming. Need to make this quick. The Maiden charged me with finding red boots cobbled by a leprechaun"—Kalen's brows shot up—"A ribbon from a Wishing Tree"—I lifted my wrist—"A Lughnasadh's Day straw hat."

Finn's head fell back on his shoulders as he muttered, "Feck. Me."

Kalen burst into laughter.

"How did that cow survive?" Finn asked Kalen, who was practically doubling over in wicked humor.

"You've seen my cow?"

"Seen it?" Kalen sputtered between laughter. "Should have burned down with Stellar Winds Casino."

"It's unnatural." Finn's face paled a little. "Told you, mate." He pointed to the garter ribbon on my wrist. "Still weeping . . ."

Kalen's laughter grew louder.

My stomach leapt to my throat. "The Cow of Plenty was at Ren Cormac's casino?"

"Aye," Finn said with a slight shudder. "The cash cow—"

Finn straightened, elbowing his friend, and flashed a crooked grin at Glenna.

Who barely acknowledged him.

"The cash cow?" her brow arched, still annoyed with me.

Picking up on this, Finn added with a twist of his lips, "Aye, love. The cash cow of his heart."

I puffed on my cigarette, to hide my snort.

"You need an ugly hat for a cow of . . . *your heart*?" She threw her hands into the air. "Cian Merrick, what is that eejit brain of yours scheming?"

"How dare you slight the cow of my heart in front of George, Gent of Fem."

Finn winked at my raccoon, who pet his leg and cooed. My face scrunched, eyes widened at George. A what-the-hell-was-wrong-with-you look. My familiar was banjaxed.

"Not wee," Kalen whispered to Finn and dragged his gaze down Glenna's curvy form in my clothing and Rhylen's top hat.

My Glenna.

I flicked the cigarette's ashes and, in such a way, they flung toward Kalen. He reared back, swearing under his breath. The lad shot me a scowl. But sobered when catching the bladed edge of my warning smile. Kalen dipped his head.

That's right. She was *mine*.

"Finn Brannon!" Owen said with a delighted laugh and clapped him on the shoulder. "I almost didn't recognize you, lad."

Glenna gasped.

"Owen Delaney," Finn returned with a large grin.

"Heading somewhere?" Owen asked, even though all the trains and ferries were done for the day.

"Looking for Rhylen. My best mate, Kalen"—he pointed to the water spirit—"is in need of a Raven Folk male to hire."

"That so?" Owen said to Kalen. "For what?"

"Bargaining agent," Kalen answered and I locked eyes with him.

My already swirling mind picked up speed as intuition gripped me. Snippets of conversation echoed in my ears. Plans about buying a boat. The voices were cut off. Then images flashed through my mind's eye.

> *A water spirit lad was running through the forest, a bow gripped in his hands. Screams and gunfire trailed him. Tears streamed down his face. "Anlinn!" he shouted. "Anlinn! Cá bhfuil tú?"*

"Bargaining agent for the Carrion Crime Syndicate?" Owen asked.

Kalen pulled his gaze from mine. "Yeah, mate. Caravans too."

Finn watched me closely. He knew I *saw* something.

I tossed the cigarette to the ground and rubbed it out with my shoe.

To break the tension, I said to Finn, "Rhy will molt a feather when he sees you," then gestured with my head to follow and stepped off the platform in a flurry of skirts.

Owen, taking my cue, grabbed the cart handles and began pushing toward camp. "Kalen," he said over his shoulder, "walk with me, lad."

Glenna wove her fingers with mine and I lifted her hand to my mouth and pressed a kiss as we ambled toward camp. She was frustrated with me still. Not over having a secret, but for dangling it so obviously in front of her. I didn't blame her. I should have explained myself far sooner. She deserved answers, even if I was afraid to reveal what I possibly was to her. Even if I didn't fully understand what was going on.

Of all the fecking people on Carran's green earth who knew my cow, it was Finnan Ó Brannon.

My *unnatural* cow, apparently.

Of course, a creepy arse cow would be my birthright.

Speaking of the rascal, Finn jogged up to me and Glenna, George right on his heel, and threw an arm around my shoulders with a wink at Glenna. Then he whispered in my ear, "I was tasked to help *you*." I gave a quick nod and continued to peer forward. "Rhylen was an excuse to not tip off me best mate."

Another shiver wended down my spine.

"Kalen's going to the Greenwood," I whispered, knowing Glenna could hear me. But she'd learn once we got to camp.

"Aye."

Anlinn! Where are you?

Chapter Thirteen

Glenna Lonan

"One article of clothing for each secret," Cian spoke against my cheek.

My hands slid up the corset strings along his back. I sighed at his earthy scent.

We snuck away from the gathering the moment Finn and Kalen bunked up in a supply wagon the tribe had partially emptied. Unlike us, they were on a daytime schedule.

Cian and I couldn't leave fast enough, either.

The sexual tension between us had been building and building...

It had been *days*.

Expressing our fears, our vulnerabilities wasn't something neither he nor I did easily. We laughed off those darker emotions. But when he touched me, when I kissed him, our souls understood without words.

I *needed* him.

He *needed* me right now too.

This man had orchestrated everything since stumbling home drunk from the train station, to help Rhylen and to restore my world—to give me the sweet bite of happiness I had craved for weeks. Aye, I had been

The Heartbreak Show

annoyed earlier. He chose to share details with an old friend about a cow he hunted objects for before sharing with me. Objects I had unwittingly participated in retrieving for him through our Heartbreak Show.

A smile tugged on my mouth.

Only Cian would need shoes, a garter ribbon, and a hat for a cow.

A *cow*.

But his brewing insecurities began days, no *weeks*, before his public courting gift.

With those gaudy boots of nightmares in Owen's care, Moira busy with Gran, and George locked out, our hearts could finally speak, our bodies comfort, our souls intertwine.

"If you have more secrets than the clothing we wear?" I asked him.

"Only enough secrets to undress *you*."

"How do I then undress you?"

"You won't," he murmured in my ear. "I'll remove one article of clothing for each desire I confess."

I would enjoy every second of watching him strip for me too. But I wasn't sure I'd survive his honeyed-tongued confessions. Already my pulse was racing from how he planned to undress us both.

Unfastening the top button of my shirt—*his* shirt—he dragged his mouth to mine in a sparking trail of fire. The warm press of his lips was sweet, almost chaste. But the sensual way his excited breaths tangled with mine ignited my blood into flame.

And I was burning . . .

Always burning for this man.

"The Maiden," he whispered, "she appeared to me in the woods the night of our first coin beggar's show." I sucked in a quiet gasp. Cian ignored my reaction and pushed the now unbuttoned shirt down my shoulders, letting it drop to the floor.

"She told me," he continued with the next secret, "it was time to claim my birthright. A faerie cow named Glas Gaibhnenn."

Green Cow of the Smith? A *green* cow?

Cian gripped the hem of my camisole and pulled it over my head. My black curls fell down my arms and to mid-back.

I would laugh at the absurdity of a cow being one's birthright—a faerie cow, no less. But the seriousness of his tone sobered me. It was so unlike his sunny personality, a knot of dread tightened in my gut.

"Feck, you're gorgeous," he moaned under his breath.

Biting a corner of my lip, I leaned back onto my elbows across our messy blankets and shook the loose strands from my shoulders to give him a better view of my breasts. Anything to cheer the lad. It was the least I could do.

Like a moth to flame, he caged me in, his hands on either side of my hips, and devoured me in a hungry kiss. A quiet sound of pleasure loosed from the back of my throat. Dark skies, his tongue, his lips, the delicious feel of his hair brushing my face . . . I was melting into the covers.

There was a desperation in the sweep of his mouth dancing across mine, though. As if he were kissing me for courage before battle. Or to reassure himself that I wanted *him*. Truly wanted *him*.

The muscles in my stomach tightened again.

Protecting his sister had been his purpose until her and Rhylen's mate bond. Before The Wild Hunt, his entire identity was that of a mortal life too. Despite possessing magic since birth, he didn't receive a familiar until right before the Autumn Night Market either—unlike Filena.

My fingers brushed along his wrist.

Freedom . . . he now owned his life, and for the first time in his twenty-three years.

Gods above, my heart began breaking for him all over again.

Our kiss slowed and he quietly groaned, a sound of pleasure I felt

The Heartbreak Show

clear down to the tips of my toes.

"My obsession," he spoke across my lips before pulling away.

With a gentle nudge, he encouraged me to straighten and scoot up to our pillows. Then he dipped onto the bed, lips flushed, eyes bright.

"Three more secrets."

"I only wear trousers and drawers."

"A bonus secret, darlin'." I snorted as he started unfastening my pants. "I was told to fetch three items and follow a trail of broken hearts to find Glas Gaibhnenn."

A trail of . . . my mouth fell open. "Seren?" Those who chose not to sacrifice to the Love-Talkers traveled "brokenhearted" to the City of Stars. "The faerie cow is on *Seren*?"

Cian pulled his trousers down my hips, down my legs, and dropped them to the wooden floor. "Finn said Ren Cormac hid my Cow of Plenty inside Stellar Winds Casino."

My *cow*? He was already claiming this faerie cow as his actual birthright?

Why would Ren Cormac hide a faerie cow?

What if it burned down with the casino? Feck, I hoped not. Poor cow.

No, the Sisters Three wouldn't send Cian on a doomed mission. At least, I didn't think so.

Cian crawled up my body then sat back on his knees. Pools of blue satin rippled around us as he straddled my hips in an old skirt—the one he wore at our coin beggar's show this evening. The pensive pinch between his brows returned. He blew out a shaky breath. And my body stilled.

I took his hand in mine and he studied our lacing fingers.

"The Maiden gifted me the gancanagh's pipe with no explanation." He visibly swallowed. "I was too overwhelmed to ask. My magic it—"

Cian's face quickly drained of blood. He squeezed his eyes shut in a long, panicking blink and hissed, "Shite!"

This was the first time I had heard him mention *his* magic. It was no mystery Cian was magical—he was related to the Sisters Three and had a familiar. But he continually riddled around the topic when it was brought up.

"You have the Sight, aye?" The question spilled from me before I could stop myself. Still, I asked, even more softly, "Like Filena?"

"Filena doesn't know how deep my magic runs," he rushed out, a thread of fear in his voice. "Only that I've *seen* a handful of futures. Mam suspects, but I've told no one, Glenna. I don't want people to know what I *see* or that I can."

I lifted our joined hands to my mouth and kissed his fingers. "I promise I will never tell a soul you have the Sight, Cian Merrick. I make this bargain with you." His body relaxed. "You never have to tell me how your magic works either. I shouldn't have asked you."

Cian considered me for several long beats without meeting my eyes. "I *see* what others try to hide," he whispered. "Their fears, their secrets, their desires, their shame. I *see* their past; I *see* their present. Sometimes, though rarely, I *see* their future."

If he looked in their eyes, that is. The portals to a person's inner-being. He didn't need to say that part aloud, though—

Oh...

The thundering pulse in my chest stilled.

If I got too close, I would have died of a broken heart.

His confession hit me with sudden clarity: for years, he had suspected that I loved him and had protected us both by refusing to truly look at me.

I only know how to obsess and you would ruin me.

And we would have destroyed our families like Rhylen and Filena almost had.

I would have pined for you until I wasted away to nothing.

After his courting gesture, I no longer questioned if his love was romantic or if it was just friends reaching for one another.

But I was dying to know how long he had actually *loved* me.

A muscle worked in his jaw. "I don't know why the Maiden gave me that pipe and it's driving me fecking mad."

I snapped out of my thoughts. "You believe you could be a *gean cánach*?"

"What if I am?"

"What if all the legends are wrong?" I tossed back. "What if being a Love-Talker is about intention?"

Fae and witchling magic were heavily based in intention. If I fae marked Cian, I could make him my thrall. Or I could mark him as mates did, with a piece of me for him to carry always. The ritual and the magic were the same. The intention, however? A gancanagh with good intentions may speak actual words of love and not for any manipulative or malevolent reasons.

Cian's chest heaved a heavy sigh. "That wouldn't frighten you?"

"No," I whispered. "Nothing about you frightens me, Cian Merrick."

"Next secret." He visibly swallowed.

"You haven't removed my drawers."

A strained smile was my only reply. "The Maiden claims that I'm a re-souling of Cian of the Tuatha Dé Danann."

The warrior god?

My eyes rounded. "You're the actual god . . . Cian?"

He looked away with a small shrug, as if embarrassed. "Part of me is, I guess. Another part of me is the Sisters Three. And . . . and the son of a mortal monster." His voice cracked on the last words.

I sat up and cradled his cheek. But he refused to look at me. "Cian—"

"I'm not ashamed of who I am," he interjected quickly, his voice faint. "I never stopped being . . . *me*." He gritted his teeth. "Not even when my own da wanted to beat those sacred parts of myself from my soul. Not when Kilkerry accused me of being possessed. Not when West Tribe owned my life and could trade and sell me at a moment's whim." Tears rimmed his lashes. "Cillian . . . 'bright headed,'" he angrily whispered one translation for his birth name. "Cillian . . . 'from the temple,'" he translated the other. "Hamish named me."

He gestured to his bright-headed tresses. The color of Lugh's sunny locks. The Mother's golden-wheat hued strands too. "Did he know the son who wore dresses was divine?" The question came out in a choked whisper. "Did he know who I was before I was born?"

Stars above, my heart . . .

Those beautiful silver-blue eyes of his traced my cheek where the scratch was mostly healed. Blinking back the anger, he leaned into the fingers holding his face, and my thumb traced the corner of his mouth.

"I didn't tell you these secrets"—he drew in a trembling breath—"because . . . for the first time in my life, I'm afraid of what I am and . . ." His eyes snapped to mine. "And you are perfection."

Chapter Fourteen

Glenna Lonan

He thought me ... perfect?

A blush crept up my neck and warmed my cheeks.

"I've been so scared," he continued, "that I might hurt you."

While not his actual words, I understood what he feared—that his magic might one day suddenly manifest a darker side like Filena's had and ... become the violence shown him. Or become a dangerous drunk instead of a happy reveler.

But Cian was a lover. It wasn't in his nature to harm others. Not even those who reviled him. He winked and blew kisses instead of returning their unkindness. Filena would fake-curse their arses and hoped they trembled in fear days after.

I brushed my nose along Cian's, teasing his lips in lingering, yearning kisses. "Lady of Man, the gods gave you powerful gifts of magic because of *who you are*." He started to speak and I lightly shook my head for him to wait. "Aye, you're a shameless hussy"—I could feel a corner of his mouth lift a tiny fraction—"but *never* to draw attention to how you care for others. And sexy demi-god before me, do I swoon over your kind, giving soul." The pad of my thumb caressed his cheek. "Cian Merrick, you are sunshine and laughter and chaos and cleverness and beauty and strength." I softly kissed him again and whispered, "And I still think pink rouge is the wrong color for your complexion."

"You promised to never break my heart, Glennie Lo."

"For a demi-god who *knows* so much," I quipped back, "your utter lack of cosmetic nuance is adorable." I dropped my hands from his face and pointed to a small drawer by the bed. Cocking a brow, he opened it, well aware of the contents. "Be a good boy and pick out a tin."

"Even pink?"

"Whatever color you stain my lips, will also stain yours."

He quietly moaned.

I flashed him a flirty grin and leaned back on my hands.

He twisted to rummage around the drawer and began opening tins to consider each color in the low candlelight. I shook curls from my shoulders to fall down my back.

"Blood red." He shut the drawer and repositioned himself across my middle.

His muscles flexed in an excited shiver. Removing the lid, he dipped the tip of his finger into the rouge. The breath pulsing on my skin quickened. He watched the stroke of his finger with a molten gaze that seared me.

"You're every fantasy I possess."

The hoarseness of his voice shot heat straight through me. I could orgasm just from the intensity of arousal softening his face.

He dipped his finger into the rouge again, then set the tin aside.

"Shouldn't you remove an article of clothing with that confession?"

"I still have a bonus secret."

Circling an arm around my waist, anchoring my hips to his, Cian dragged the last dip of rouge across my bottom lip to the slow rhythm of his grinding thrust. Fire exploded down my already flaming body. Dark

The Heartbreak Show

skies, he was going to be merciless. Desperate for more friction, more of him, I rolled my hips as he lifted his, refusing me with a wicked smile.

Oh the bet was on. When he was done with this little game he was playing, I would play back.

"The Maiden," he said, scooting down my legs, "shared that Cian's soul would finally rest when he was reunited with his cow *and* . . ." Cian's fingers caressed the contoured planes of my stomach in reverence. A soft, trembling sigh left me. He then grabbed my drawers and slipped them off to the floor.

"And?" I asked.

"And," he repeated, lifting a leg to drape over his shoulder.

The seductive heat of his mouth kissed along the thigh pressed to his face. He really did plan to make me suffer. My hands curled into the covers in anticipation. The fingers sensually feathering across my stomach once more slid to my hipbone and gently dug into my flesh.

Just one curling flick of his tongue and, gods, I was ash and smoke. My fingers relaxed and clasped the covers again. Breath, hot and teasing, pulsed over my clit. I could feel his impish smile even though he wasn't touching me anymore.

"And?" I prompted again, getting too worked up to remain patient.

"And . . ."

I clutched his disheveled strands and lifted my head to glare at his attempt to hear me beg. "Cian Merrick, I swear—"

Oh sweet goddess . . .

My head fell back to the pillow.

His tongue dragged over my clit before pulling me into the warmth of his mouth. The hand just holding my hip wrapped around my thigh and pushed my legs wider. Then his tongue was on me again, licking in long, torturous sweeps.

Cian moaned. The carnal sound of his pleasure while pleasuring me bordered on animalistic.

I arched into him.

The fingers I wove through his disheveled strands gripped tighter.

Cian tugged me closer, adding more pressure to each swirling flick and savoring lap of his tongue.

Every part of me was electric.

"Cian . . ." I whispered in a plea—more, I craved more, more, more.

I swore he grinned at the sound of his name forming the breaths heaving from my lungs. I couldn't stop, either. Songbirds were vocal during sex.

"More," I begged. Aye, I *begged*. At this moment, I didn't care about bets and games.

In answer, he rocked me against his mouth, faster, faster.

I writhed in the blankets.

My muscles were clenching. My skin tightening.

When I didn't think I would last another second, he lowered my leg from his shoulder and began kissing up my stomach. I wanted to weep. But Cian had only just begun and he . . . fiery suns help me, he was an exceptional lover.

And a stars damned edging tease.

One who still hadn't touched the breasts I kept putting on display for him.

Or kissed the lips he had painted.

Noticing my narrowed eyes, he slowly straightened, a flirty smirk on that far too pretty face of his. Oh aye, there would be paybacks.

"You didn't *finish* telling me your bonus secret, pet." I playfully huffed.

His gaze caressed the shape of my breasts, the dip of my waist. "I desire every line and curve of your body to know my surrender," he confessed.

The Heartbreak Show

My eyes fluttered shut in a languid blink. The heat rippling through me with that one confession was a thousand suns setting in my pulse. Was that his magic possibly as a true Love-Talker?

Cian began unhooking my corset around his torso and I drank in the reveal of skin, inch-by-inch. The low candlelight traced the mesmerizing dance of his muscles with his graceful movements. He tossed the undergarment to the floor beside my discarded clothes.

I lifted a hand to his chest and trailed my fingers between his pectorals; down, along the ridges of his abdomen; lower, over the hem of the skirt, to the hardened cock slowly grinding into my palm. At my touch, he loosed a shaky breath, his eyelids lowered.

"I want to die between your thighs," he confessed next, breathless.

Dark skies above, I wasn't going to last.

If I weren't turning into a puddle of desperation, I would ensure he didn't last either—it was only fair. But as much as I wanted to stroke him until he unraveled, I wanted him to find the Otherworld while losing himself deep inside of me even more.

Cian twisted to climb off the bed. I was too enraptured by the play of muscles across his shoulders and down his back to question why at first.

A part of me started to panic that one of those awful, hideous cock-blocking cock boots magically appeared in the wagon. I would permanently ban George from desserts, if so, the wee bastard. Then I'd hunt down that fecking leprechaun—

"Glenna," Cian murmured as he untied the old costume skirt at his waist, his eyes fastened to mine. The threadbare satin fell to the floor in ripples of blue. At the heady sight of him, a small canine softly dug into a corner of my bottom lip. He really was so infuriatingly beautiful. His fingers skimmed across the laces of his drawers, the ones hanging low on his hips, then down his straining cock, and I drank in each caress. "I ache to hear you call me your sex god in—"

Groaning, I grabbed a pillow and threw it at him before he could finish that sentence. Cian erupted into laughter. If he were closer, I would have flicked his forehead, the eejit.

"You haven't won that bet, *darlin'*," I scoffed.

He slipped out of my drawers, climbed onto the bed, and began crawling up my body with a boyish, up-to-no-good smile. "Oh, I've already won, *darlin'*."

"I've brought in more sacrifices each night but one."

He cupped a breast, molding it to his hand, and brushed a thumb over my nipple. "I don't need a bet to win, Glennie Lo."

A shiver prickled across my skin. "What are you scheming, Cian Merrick?" The delivery was embarrassingly weak despite my demand and his grin widened.

"The sounds of pleasure confirming what you refuse to say aloud."

He winked then sucked my breast into his mouth and I almost hummed a lilting note of satisfaction. Almost. I would *not* encourage his ego—Holy Mother of Stars! He slipped two fingers inside me—not one to warm me up, no . . . *two*—and the thrumming charge in my body detonated in an explosion of sensation.

"You . . . arse . . ." I could barely get the words out.

He quietly laughed then softly caught the hardened peak of my nipple between his teeth.

I bit back a gasp.

Be strong, lass!

Cian pumped his fingers in and out to the seductive rhythm of his mouth and tongue while *my* fingers clawed into the bedding. Fire was crackling along my burning skin.

Be strong!

My songbird nature wanted to let out every fervent moan crescen-

The Heartbreak Show

doing in my body.

Those delectably cruel fingers of his thrusted deeper, curling inside of me like licking flames.

I turned my head and bit the pillow, refusing to prove him right. Because gods... demi-gods... whatever... I was... I was... *I was...*

No.

I wouldn't let him win.

I gently pushed him away, ready to weep again at the edged torture.

Fear flashed across his eyes. "Glenna—"

"You didn't *finish* your bonus secret," I panted beneath him.

His shoulders relaxed. A baiting smile appeared not even half a heartbeat later. "And?"

"*And*, if you don't *finish* this secret before you *finish* me, I'll make sure you don't *finish* for an entire week." I lifted my chin. "Or longer."

He snorted, far too delighted with himself.

But when his eyes rested on the blood red lips he painted, a look of longing replaced the mischief. Longing and... shyness? Drawing in what sounded like a nervous breath, he wove his fingers with mine and tugged me up, moving me to straddle his hips while he stretched out his legs beneath me.

Cian tucked a strand of hair behind the point of my ear, then cradled my cheek. "To finally rest," he began, "Cian must find his cow *and*," he repeated once more, lowering his voice to a husky whisper, "fall in love harder than he fell for his first. *And*, Glenna Lonan," Cian murmured, "my heart is eternally undone by you."

My mouth parted.

Love me... more?

Cian's and Eithne's fated love was legendary to the fae. My entire Folk kind existed because of Lugh, the son of their union.

My heart is eternally undone by you...

A son who was saved because of their heartbreak.

My trembling hands rested on his chest. We weren't True Mates, not like Rhylen and Filena. Or like Sean and Braelin. But Cian, re-souled or not, was mine. Always and forever *mine*.

Cian buried his face in my neck and kissed my wildly beating pulse.

"I love you, my beautiful ruination," he whispered along my jaw and tears crested my lashes. He was mine, mine, mine. "I love you, my soul's obsession." He seized my hips and slid inside of me in one, slow thrust and I moaned at the heady fullness of him. "I love you . . ." His mouth feathered across mine. "*Mate.*"

I stopped breathing.

He called me his mate.

His mate.

Every wish my aching heart had made was now a glittering mess of tears and laughter at his feet.

He desired to be *my mate*.

Overcome, I slammed my lips onto his.

The firm grasp on my hips tightened.

Then our bodies were moving in a firestorm of emotion. His hips collided with mine. A lightning strike of ecstasy. My fingers dug into his pectorals, deep enough to leave marks. Sliding up the curves of his arms next to sink into his already disheveled hair.

"The tight feel of you," he groaned into our kiss. "Feck, I'm ready to die."

Moonless skies, so was I. This man really did kiss with his whole body and the poetic way he moved was beautiful agony.

A hand cupping my hip drifted lower to grasp my arse—guiding me against him deeper, deeper. His other hand massaged my breast. And I was completely lost in his touch. The slide of fingers on my flushing skin had never felt so divine and yet like torture.

The Heartbreak Show

Gentle and rough simultaneously.

A caress and a branding.

Possessive.

The moans leaving me with every powerful, grinding stroke of his cock . . . they were loud enough to be heard by anyone walking by. But no matter how much we clutched each other close, my soul still fought to be closer. Each beat of my heart demanded to entwine with every beat of his.

Breaking our kiss, he leaned back to drink in my pleasure while slowing his rhythm. Red stained his mouth in a delicious mess. There was something so utterly erotic about smearing the rouge off a man's painted lips. Especially full, swollen lips painted by mine.

"I love you," I whispered to the fevered space between us. My words seemed so plain compared to his honeyed confessions. But I couldn't think straight.

Cian grinned before nipping at my bottom lip. "On your knees."

I didn't hesitate and crawled off him to turn around. He pulled my hips up and . . . *holy gods*, that first thrust would have brought me to my knees if I weren't already on them. He gathered my loose curls in his hands and tugged the strands taut, the rhythm of his hips increasing. A long, deep, throaty sound left him and my body caught fire.

"You are my addiction, Glenna. I hunger endlessly for you."

The arcing strike of his hips was obliterating me.

"Feck, your body . . ."

He circled an arm around my waist, my long, black locks still wrapped around his other hand. He nudged me upright and those skilled fingers of his found my clit. He kissed my shoulder, up the back of my neck. His breath hot along my burning skin.

"I'm yours," he whispered into my ear.

The fingers rubbing me increased their tempo and my head fell back against his. The hold on my tresses relaxed to grasp my waist instead, pressing me flush against him. I could barely drag in air. Goddess save me, he felt so damn good. The throbbing ache for release was building, building, building. The only sound I could form was his name. A fevered prayer my lips pleasured in lifting.

"My body, my heart, my soul," he murmured into kisses along my neck. "All yours."

The gravelly, breathless sound of his voice was my undoing.

A wildfire ripped through me in a gasping cry. I didn't care who heard.

At my unraveling, the rhythm of Cian's thrusts bordered on feral. I reached behind me and gripped his hair while turning my mouth to his. Our kiss was a thunderclap of drunken bliss—slow, deep, heady.

"You're mine," I panted, enraptured by his earthy scent, his possessive touch, his everything. "I choose you, Cian Merrick."

I bit down on his bottom lip with the tip of my canine and tugged.

His body stiffened and he sucked in a shuddering breath.

I released his lip.

"Feeeck," he moaned, long and slow.

Muscles down his body flexed. Fingers splayed across my stomach. In one final stroking thrust, Cian drove deep inside of me and stilled. A soft growl rumbled from his chest. I released his hair and his forehead fell against my back.

For several long seconds, perhaps minutes—maybe a whole eternity—we didn't move. A rhapsodic rush dizzied my head. That same extravagant, intoxicating feeling trickled down each of my limbs too. Cian's ragged breathing stirred strands of my hair in between the gentlest of kisses. The calloused tips of his fingers skimmed along the curves of my waist.

My body was going limp in his strong arms. Instead of collapsing, though, I grabbed Cian's arm and pulled him down to the blankets and pillows beneath me. My gaze locked with his and stars . . . he was so sinful, I was on the verge of fainting at the arresting sight of his swollen, red-stained lips, his blushed skin and messy, just-bedded golden hair, the pleasure still tightening his muscles into definition.

Gods, I could worship him until the end of time.

A corner of his mouth kicked up.

My eyes narrowed. "Did you just read me?"

Cian snorted. "Darlin', the cock struck awe on your face reveals *everything*."

Riddling eejit. "You did read me!"

"I heard you pray in bed, Glenna. *Cian, Cian, Cian* . . ." I froze. A delighted smile flirted across his lips. "While on your knees, before me."

His smile widened.

"I win."

Before I could roll my eyes, make a sound of disgust, crawl off his lap, he tugged me to him and . . . captured my mouth in a sultry kiss that liquified my racing pulse. And I didn't protest. Not even one fraction of a second.

Not when he rolled me over to lie beneath him.

Not when his tongue and lips kissed his surrender across every inch of my body.

And especially not when he worshiped me and I worshiped him, again and again.

Cian Merrick chose me as his mate.

He desired me above all others and the wings of my heart refused to stop flying into the silky moonlight of his affection.

Chapter Fifteen

Cian Merrick

The sun had yet to set behind Caledona Wood. Still, a faint blush of stars streaked the pink and lavender sky.

I tipped yet another sacrificed bottle of whiskey against my lips.

Nothing beat a Caravan winter around a communal fire with friends and family. Might be our last season without work, too. No longer did we need to rest our wagon wheels during the harsher traveling months. Still, to lose this? A right tragedy.

If Rhylen decided to buck this tradition, I would swoon from fatigue in the most dramatic fashion possible—when he looked at me, walked past me, just thought of me. A hundred times if that's what it took for him to get the message.

This lass needed her winter beauty rest.

I studied the fellas beneath lowered lashes. Only Sean had shown signs of elder magic. Still ol' Rhylee Lo considered us each elders. Filena, Glenna, and Braelin too, which ruffled a few feathers. In Caravan history, not one born female had become an elder or chiefess.

A yawn slipped past my lips and Owen side-eyed me with a tipsy smirk.

The Heartbreak Show

Glenna and I decided to postpone our final Heartbreak Show by one night—the last one tied to our bet, that is. The show would continue as long as our tribe needed the revenue. But we hadn't slept much.

Feck, I could drink in her body endlessly. The electric feel of her silky skin beneath my fingers still haunted me hours later.

But nothing, absolutely *nothing*, compared to feeling truly seen for the first time. To have someone I loved more than my own breath know *all* the hidden, strange, scared pieces myself, and then *choose me* as their life partner was life changing.

My gaze tracked Glenna's flurried movements across the fire.

She added seasonings to the wild apple oatmeal she stirred while Mam, on her other side, popped freshly baked berry muffins from their tins.

Glenna's black-as-night eyes flit to mine. A tiny smile curved her gorgeous lips right before she mouthed, "Preening slag."

I snorted and mouthed back, "Loaf trot."

Owen slowly moved into my line of sight from the log he sat on. "He either has an unnatural appetite for porridge—"

"Strong enough to make the oats blush," Corbin interjected.

"Aye, the pot too," Sean added.

"Or," Owen dragged out, "the mortal is elf struck."

"With your ugly mug," I quipped back.

"That's not what you said when you asked me to marry you." Owen snapped my suspenders with a drunken grin.

The ever-present calculating intensity of Kalen's bright blue stare narrowed onto Owen for a moment before Finn nudged his arm with a separate bottle of whiskey.

"For feck's sake." Corbin rolled his eyes. "Time to get over each other."

I slipped a thumb beneath my suspenders. "Not when his vanilla feathered arse fantasizes about whipping me, I can't."

The fellas burst into laughter.

"To Owen's vanilla feathered arse," Sean toasted.

Kalen, Sean, and I lifted our whiskeys, then took a long drink before passing the bottles to the other three fellas.

Rhylen brisked past us toward the outdoor kitchen, not sparing us a single glance. The lad had been overseeing wagon repair inspections and supply audits with two different crews he had assigned last night.

"Lottie?" he called out.

A former felly dipped her head and waited for Rhylen's approach. "Aye, sire?"

"None of the old ways," he reminded with a smile. She peered up and visibly swallowed. "Do the ill need meals tonight?"

"Already delivered, sire. Miss Lonan prepped their food first."

"Do they need anything else?" Rhylen gestured his head toward Glenna and Gran. "Tinctures? Teas?"

Lottie blinked again. "No, sire. The Carrick's and Heffern's mortals are on the mend now."

"Wonderful to hear those *free* mortals are recovering."

He bowed his head at the Raven lass, who didn't know how to take a gov acknowledging her so equally. Never mind that she and Rhylen were the same class until a couple of weeks ago. Or that the idea of govs didn't exist in the same way as before. When she walked away, my brother's smile wobbled a little, but he straightened his shoulders and peered around camp.

Sean started to gesture for Rhylen to join us, but our chieftain moved onto the next task while us eejits sat and drank. In our defense, he refused to let us help with anything tonight. Others in the tribe *did* need to step up and take ownership of various jobs.

Finished with meal prep, the girls, Gran, and Mam eased into our circle while other families began dishing up. Glenna hip bumped me to scoot over. I nearly grabbed her to sit on my lap. My body wouldn't behave, if she did, though. Already I was craving another night with her, this time beneath the stars and whispers of trees.

"Your mate," Gran said to Finn as Mam helped her into a rocking chair.

"Taryn."

"Yer Taryn," she continued with a soft, appreciative pat on Mam's hand, "she doesn't travel with ye, Finn lad?"

"She's a green witch apprentice." Glenna perked up and leaned forward. "Taryn began only a few days ago."

"Who's training her?" Filena asked next.

A corner of Finn's mouth inched up. "Trade secret, love."

"Can your mate bargain?" Glenna asked.

Finn's head tilted. "Ingredients or—"

"Aye, I need a few rare items."

"For?" he asked.

Glenna flashed him a smirk. "Trade secret, love."

Gran chortled a breathy laugh.

"Never introduce them, mate," Kalen warned Finn with a canined grin. The green-haired arse twirled a leaf between his fingers while sizing up Glenna. "Taryn has daggers in her eyes but this one"—Kalen gestured to Glenna with the bottle—"will carve you alive with her smile."

At that, the bladed sass slanting the curl of Glenna's lips sharpened.

Kalen wasn't wrong. Glenna's crowing grins always cut me up into a thousand sighing, panting pieces.

"Put them together?" Kalen shook his head at Finn. "You'll not survive to see the next changing of the leaves, mate."

"Taryn is a wee murderous, aye," Finn said with a delighted shrug.

"Wee?" Kalen repeated with a laugh. "The Black Beak burned

down Stellar Winds Casino in vengeance then practically carried your cursed, dying arse from the wreckage."

Glenna turned to Filena and Braelin. "I adore her."

Braelin's rosy complexion went bloodless. "Vengeance against Ren Cormac?"

Finn nodded, but the movement was guarded.

Owen's gaze shot to Sean's in warning. The lad's fingers were digging into the log he sat on to keep from reacting to his mate's distress.

Primal males were adorable.

But merciful suns, I'd sacrifice George's fashion services for a week to hear Gent of Fem possessively growl at me.

George peered up from his continual thief-struck gaping place at Finn's feet to chitter-gasp at me.

Fine . . . three days.

Satisfied, George returned to his moony-eyed vigil.

Braelin tucked a strand of hair behind the point of her ear. "Does she seek vengeance against all of Clan Cormac?"

"From North Tribe?" Kalen asked.

When Braelin didn't answer, Finn and Kalen both sat up straighter.

"Shite," Kalen whispered. "I thought you had a North Tribe accent."

"Not the whole clan, no," Finn quickly reassured her. "Ren cost Taryn nearly everything."

"Only Ren?" she asked.

"Aye," Finn answered softly. "Only *that* Cormac. Is he your—"

"Second cousin." Braelin squeezed Sean's hand to relax. "Did you know Bale Cormac?"

Bale—her older brother and Ren's righthand on Seren.

Finn and Kalen peered at each other and then shook their heads.

Her shoulders relaxed. "Branwen Cormac?"

Her brother's daughter, who was Filena's age.

The Heartbreak Show

"The Thieves' Guilds didn't operate in the casinos and nightclubs," Finn explained. "We lived on the streets. Slept in old warehouses, we did. Nicked jewels and coin for a stale loaf of bread and moth-eaten blanket." He tossed the leaf he had been fidgeting with into the fire. "There's a kettle pot of fae races on that fecking floating debtor's prison and Raven Folk are the minority."

"Were," Kalen corrected.

"Aye, were."

"Caravan Ravens," Corbin interjected, the most sober of us lads, "are under a bargain to never reveal the Carrion Crime Syndicate's role on Seren to slaves and indentures. The blinding curse can make them appear as other Folk." Both Finn's and Kalen's eye flew wide. "But the Cormacs"—his gaze slid to Braelin—"had governed the City of Stars for fifty years."

Owen pointed at Finn. "Until you set Ravenna Blackwing and her court free."

"All the work of me wee feisty wife again," he said with a crooked smile. "Terrifying lass."

"I want to adopt her," Glenna practically chirped. To Filena and Braelin, she added, "We need another witchy sister, aye?"

I stretched out my legs. "What did *you* do the whole time, then?"

"Pissed her off," Kalen slurred.

"Drove her *mad* with lust." The rascally tilt to Finn's grin turned smug, "She couldn't leave my side." Kalen snorted. "Married me twice, she did."

"Twice?" The furrow between Corbin's brows deepened. "How is that possible?"

Finn winked. "I'm too irresistible to mate bond with *only* once. The magic agreed."

"Gods," Glenna groaned, "no wonder she burned a whole building to the ground."

Kalen barked a loud laugh.

"So," Finn humorously tossed out, "you want to bargain?"

"With. Taryn," Glenna punctuated. "Not with your riddling ways, Finnan Ó Brannon."

"I'm here and she's not."

Glenna considered him a long moment then stood. "Come along, then."

Finn hopped off the log and gestured with his head for Glenna to lead the way. I began reaching for the bottle from Owen when Glenna swooped in and grabbed my hand and yanked.

"You, too, eejit."

"Ask nicely," I drawled. To sweeten the deal, I shook fallen locks of hair from my bleary eyes. The sloshing world tilted for a second. Glenna's brow arched. But I could *see* through her act. Preening my hair was catnip to that sassy hen. "Begging works bes—"

Her free hand whipped out and flicked my forehead.

"Ow!" I hissed. It didn't really hurt, but I lived for those crowing grins. Like the one she was giving me now.

"I can ask more nicely if that wasn't pleasing enough to you, darlin'."

Finn twisted to Kalen and the water spirit dipped his head in a I-told-you-so look.

Glenna yanked me to a stand and began marching off toward the trees. "Hurry up, Finn Brannon," she called out. "Or no bargain."

And the lad listened, like the bargain-addicted fae he was.

I started to laugh under my breath.

Glennie Lo really did have all us males trained on treats.

Chapter Sixteen

Cian Merrick

Finn jogged up to where my langered arse was being dragged into the woods for one of Glenna's ritual sacrifices. Over my shoulder, I drawled, "I can't resist you either, you sexy tree trunk."

"Aye, love," Finn said with a very serious nod of his head. "The only proper reaction to me."

"Since I saw you naked . . ."

Glenna abruptly halted and dropped my hand to spin toward us, making me stumble a step. The forest's edge continued to tilt in my blurry vision but I could still make out Finn's feigned innocence.

"I was quite the vision, wasn't I?"

"A true vision, lad."

Glenna's eyes squinted as her wings faded into visibility. A warning for me to behave while she bargained. Those feathers, especially tipped in soft moonlight, had the opposite effect on me, though. Falling skies, I would do all manner of shady things just to gaze at those wings for an eternity.

Except for when that muffin hag knocked me to the ground.

George patted my leg until our gazes locked.

I sighed.

The wee bastard was right. Even when eating dirt, I would still rob a child for those night-touched feathers.

"Before I bargain for ingredients," Glenna said to Finn, "swear that you have permission to bargain on behalf of the witch who trains your mate."

Fair request. Our camp didn't need to face another curse.

"I swear—"

"I'll tell you what I use the ingredients for," Glenna interrupted, "and you'll name the witch in your oath or no deal."

Finn straightened and whipped his head toward the woods. A second later, he pressed farther into the trees with a tip of his head to follow. We ambled after him, eventually pausing on a well-worn trail. He lifted a pointed ear to the wind, his pale green eyes sweeping the underbrush—then stilled. Flashing us a lopsided smirk, he stepped over the rambling roots of a large oak and placed his palms on the trunk. Faint light trailed around his hands.

I started to gasp and stopped myself.

He had magic?

Since when?

The wild fae younglings lost their magic in the Caravans.

Finn pressed his forehead to the bark and began whispering words I couldn't make out. The tree shook its lower branches, as if nodding one's head. Earth spirits could talk to trees, aye, but this was the first time I had witnessed an actual conversation.

My childhood friend touched an infected area on the trunk. The gnarled, discolored patch of bark glowed beneath Finn's touch and a tiny limb sprouted where burrowing insects had injured the tree. The oak swayed, its branches creaking and groaning, and in a way that sounded like echoes of the wild fae tongue.

The Heartbreak Show

Patting the trunk, like one would a dog or small bairn, Finn stepped away and turned back to us—

My mouth fell open.

Bless me, Finn Brannon was a beautiful male. Always had been—and the elf knew it keenly too. But right now? While soaking up and reflecting back the forest's magic? He was deadly gorgeous. Or my intoxicated brain was playing tricks on me. I glanced at Glenna and her bewildered, enthralled expression mirrored my own. Not the whiskey, then.

Well, this was weird.

"The Maiden," Finn said, all nonchalant, as if he hadn't just made a tree happy dance.

I blinked.

My great aunt was here?

A chill scraped down my spine. I scanned the woods and *that* was a bad decision. Glenna grabbed my arm to steady me.

"She's the witch I work for," Finn continued. "And the one who trains my mate."

Glenna snapped out of her gaping trance. "What?" she whisper-yelled. "I can't bargain with"—she dropped her voice even lower—"a Sisters Three."

Finn lazily pointed my direction. "You bargain with this wee sparkly beam of sunshine, yeah?"

Glenna flashed her canines. "Do *not* use my mate to trick me into bargains."

Oh.

Feck.

Me.

Dizziness rushed my head so fast, my breath caught. The ground warbled beneath my feet. I . . . I was actually swooning.

I fell against the tree at my back and closed my eyes for a long, heart fluttering second.

She growled. For me. Like a protective primal male.

Goddess save me, but I would never recover.

Never.

When I opened my eyes, both Finn and Glenna were watching me with matching did-the-drunk-gobshite-just-pass-out expressions. George left his moony-eyed vigil to wrap his paws around my leg and coo. He was apparently swooning too.

No . . . no, the cuddly little shite was relieved I hadn't sacrificed three days of his fashion services for Glenna to growl over me.

"Not a trick, love." Finn pulled his gaze from George to focus on Glenna once more. "I guarantee no mischief or harm will come to you or yours. Aye, I have permission to bargain under certain stipulations and this counts. I swear all of this to you, Glenna Lonan. And," he continued, a corner of his mouth kicking up, "the oak is sheltering us from listening ears and won't whisper a word to the wind. I bargained for our protection."

Glenna relaxed and lifted her chin. "I create a potion of happiness for my confections."

Finn's brows shot up. "You're a witch?"

"Not truly. I only know how to make the one potion I was entrusted with."

"What rare ingredients do you need?"

Glenna stepped closer and lowered her voice despite the oak's protection. "The nectar of a ruby merry vine. And it *must* be the ruby variety." Finn nodded. "Alpine sweet balm oil, powdered doe-ears"—Finn's eyes rounded slightly—"the plant, not the animal, eejit. Only grows in the eastern bogs. I need the beans of black cat toes, too. Also a plant."

The Heartbreak Show

"How much of each?"

"With two drops per cake, one per batch of cookies . . ." Glenna peered up at the night sky in thought. "Tell your mate I need a double moon crock's nest supply. She'll know what that means."

Finn dipped his head. "And your bargain?"

"Two Raven Folk feathers."

"No deal," he said before she even finished.

My gut sickened. "You'd pluck your own feath—"

Glenna placed a finger to my lips. "One feather and one tear."

I grabbed her wrist and clenched my teeth, but she ignored me.

Unmolted Raven Folk feathers held old magic and were highly prized. But childhood friend or not, I would murder Finn if he agreed to her bargain. What in the hell was she thinking?

"Your tear?" Finn asked.

"Aye, my tear."

A muscle along Finn's jaw ticked. "Still no deal."

"Why?" she fluttered an indignant hand in the air. "It's more than fair."

"I refuse to take your pain and body as payment, lass."

Thank the wishless falling stars. The relief I felt was immediate. I released Glenna's wrist and shot Finn a tight but grateful smile, one he returned.

"The feathers aren't mine," Glenna confessed.

"Whose feathers, then?" he asked.

She shifted on her feet. "Plucked from corpses and saved for bargains."

Finn nodded again, nonplussed by this confession.

My face, however, wanted to twist into equal parts disgust and horror.

The fae scavenged body parts for spellcrafting all the time, I knew this. Carrion bird shifters didn't hold death rites either. Defeathering their own dead wasn't dishonoring—it happened often. Still, my mortal sensibilities clutched her pearls.

Glenna's fathomless eyes darted my way before adding, "All confectioners initiated into food magic are given a personal stash. I never returned mine to West Tribe."

"Then I agree to your bargain of two Raven Folk feathers."

Finn repeated Glenna's order to prove no tricks were involved. Satisfied, she shook his hand.

"Glenna," I gritted out, "if you ever bargain a piece of yourself—"

"Bargain away my beauty?" She laughed with a scoffing flutter of her wings. "Someone has to upstage you."

I cracked a wry smile. "The spotlight loves me, darlin'. I am a *very* beautiful woman."

She stepped closer and hummed her agreement. "Mmm, that you are," she practically purred, leaning in closer. "But," she whispered, nipping at my bottom lip, "not as beautiful as me, *darlin'*."

"True," Finn agreed and I slid him a glare. "But beautiful enough to pass as a woman on Seren."

George released my leg with a happy squeak, startling me, then scampered into a nearby log.

"That was adorable." Glenna pressed two fingers to her lips, holding back her own squeal.

"*That* was the feral sound of unhinged mischief, Glennie Lo. A war cry." I paused for a dramatic beat. "We should all be afraid."

A slender black brow arched. "Are you calling my adopted son *unhinged*?"

"How did he get the cock boots off the dandy, hmm?"

"He saved that man from a fashion crime, he did," she tossed back. "George is a hero."

The Heartbreak Show

Speaking of the hero, George scampered back with a . . . long, blonde-haired wig on a stick? Perhaps it was a wig. Or the—

My eyes bulged.

"George, no!" I croaked.

My gods, *he had a woman's head on a spike?!*

I couldn't breathe. My throat was closing up.

"Feck!" Finn jumped back when the head fell off the spike and rolled over his foot. "Is that . . ." He couldn't finish, gagging when George lifted the head.

George smiled.

He actually smiled.

Glenna rolled her eyes at us both. "What do you have there, wee fella?"

"Don't touch—"

She took the head from George and a thousand screams lodged in my churning gut. I didn't care if my mate was a Raven. Watching Glenna so casually approach a dismembered head clutched in the hands of a fluffy but diabolical ancient raccoon would haunt me long after I was dead.

"This is all your fault," I loudly whispered to Finn.

"Me?" he loudly whispered back. "All I suggested was you'd pass—"

"—Shhh," I hissed. "You'll trigger him—"

". . . as a Lady of Lugh."

George spun toward Finn and squealed again, then dashed back into the log.

The blood drained from Finn's already sickly pale face. "I'll never sleep again if he drags out another body part."

Glenna burst into laughter and then *ripped the hair off the head.*

AND THREW IT AT ME.

"Shite!" I tried to dodge the wad of long, blonde waves but I lost my balance and fell into a pile of leaves at Finn's feet. The hair landed on my face. A violent shiver wracked my body. Swearing every curse word ever invented, I began wildly clawing at the strands while my mate *laughed*.

She fecking laughed.

A wings-spread-wide crowing over me cackling laugh.

I shoved up to sitting, the hair gripped in my fingers. Glenna held out the head and my muscles locked up.

"That's not natural." Finn full body shuddered.

Despite the fresh wave of terror seizing me, my eyes narrowed onto the woman's coy smile. Who lost their head while flirting with . . . with . . . the blade? Her executioner? Death? *Gods* . . .

But something wasn't right besides the obvious.

I dared to lean in a fraction closer. The details of her features were hazy in the dusking light but I couldn't find a single smear of blood, fresh or dried. No stench of decay. Nor did she look real either.

"What the feck is that?" I blurted.

"A wig stand," she chirped in delight. "The eastern city ladies have them fashioned to look like them."

My face grimaced in disgust. "I take back every horrible thing I ever said about the cock boots. *That*"—I pointed at the wig stand—"is an act against the living and the dead."

Glenna grinned. "I'm keeping it!"

"Oh feck no." I violently shook my head. The world around me tipped but whatever blurred that abomination from my sight was welcome. "That fake woman's face of horrors will *not* watch me while I sleep."

"Not fake, eejit. Modeled after a real person."

"That is significantly *not less* disturbing, Glenna Jane Josephine Fecking No Lonan."

Finn barked a loud laugh.

George and Cordelia

The pecker.

"I think she's pretty."

Her eyes sparkled and I knew *that* look.

"Glennie," I growled in warning. If she started collecting those decapitated porcelain mainlanders . . .

Finn laughed louder and wiped away tears.

"Bloody Ravens," I groaned and pushed to my feet just as George scampered back to our circle with a dusty pink dress in his paws.

A *silk* dress.

My jaw dropped. "How long have you had this gown, darlin'?"

George's brown eyes locked with mine and I gasped.

"A month?!"

"Is there . . . a wardrobe in that log?" Finn asked.

"Obviously."

What else would be in a faerie-touched raccoon's lair?

George raised his paws then scampered into the log once again. *Shite.* He often confused my snarky inner-thoughts as actual conversation. The wig stand's porcelain face smiled at me from Glenna's feet and I shuddered. I didn't want to know what other non-clothing pilfered horrors he kept as treasured pets.

I examined the blonde waves spilling through my fingers.

A thrill swooped across my clenching gut.

Glenna plucked the locks from my hand and fit the wig on my head. Her brows slightly puckered while fidgeting with the piece, the corners of her mouth too. But her dark eyes softened.

The weighted feel of soft, thick strands falling to my elbows was strange.

Did I look like a woman? Like Mam?

"Grabbing Kalen, mate," Finn squeezed my upper arm and winked at Glenna, a devilish smile pulling on his mouth. "The lad deserves his revenge against the Ladies of Lugh, yeah?"

"Yeah," I quietly replied.

Glenna and I watched Finn disappear into the trees.

And the ensuing silence began strangling me.

I didn't know what to say or do or be.

Wearing a wig was like slipping into one of Mam's old dresses for the first time all over again and . . . feeling whole. The rightness was indescribable. But a rightness that historically ended in pain.

And my swooping gut began twisting with dread.

"Cian," Glenna whispered.

I furiously blinked back the burning emotion and focused, instead, on the dusty rose silk in my fingers. My mind knew I was loved. That, at camp, I was safe. My bruised heart, though? He still felt every hit. She still heard every word of hate.

"I was wrong."

My eyes snapped to Glenna's and stilled.

"Pink is perfect for your complexion."

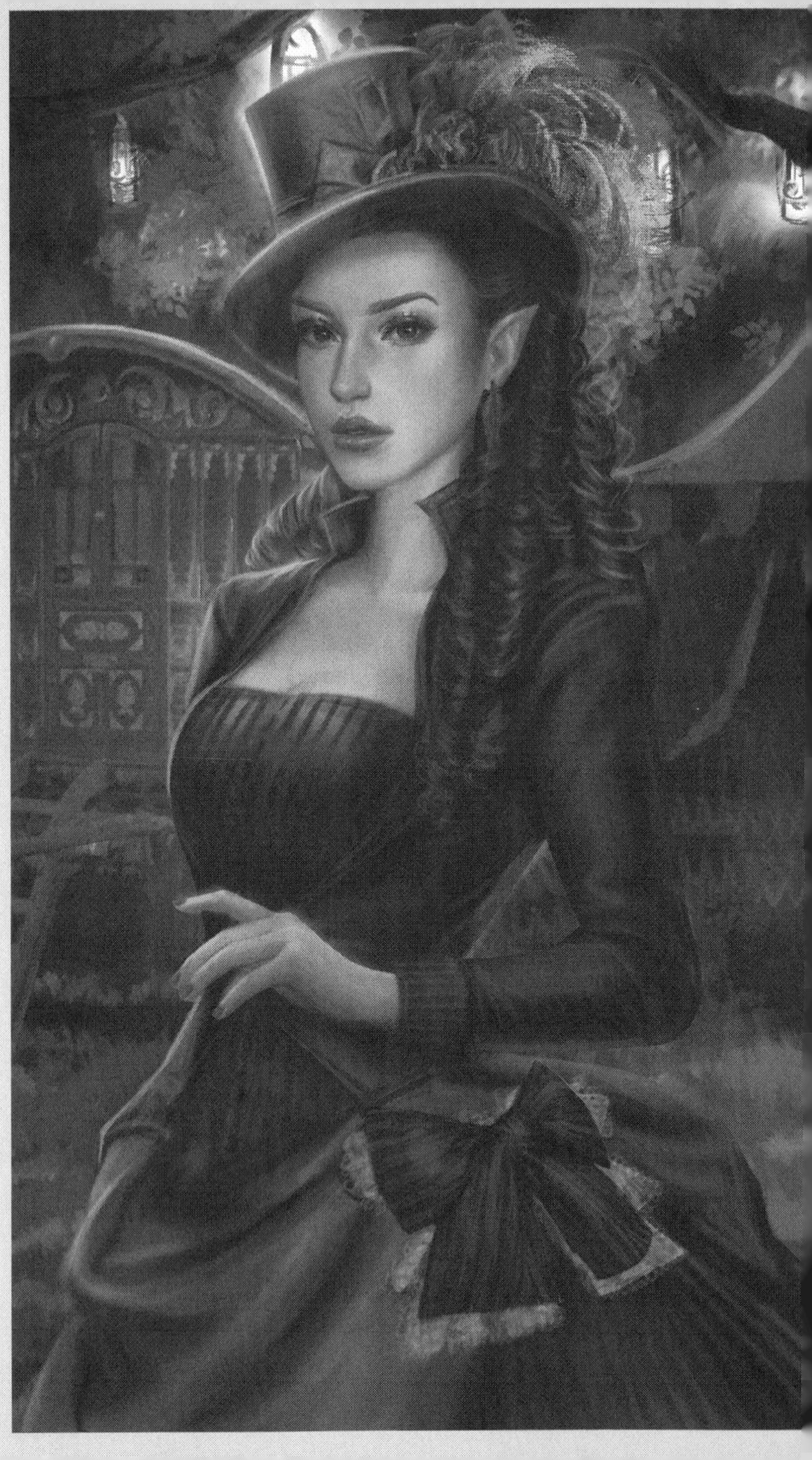

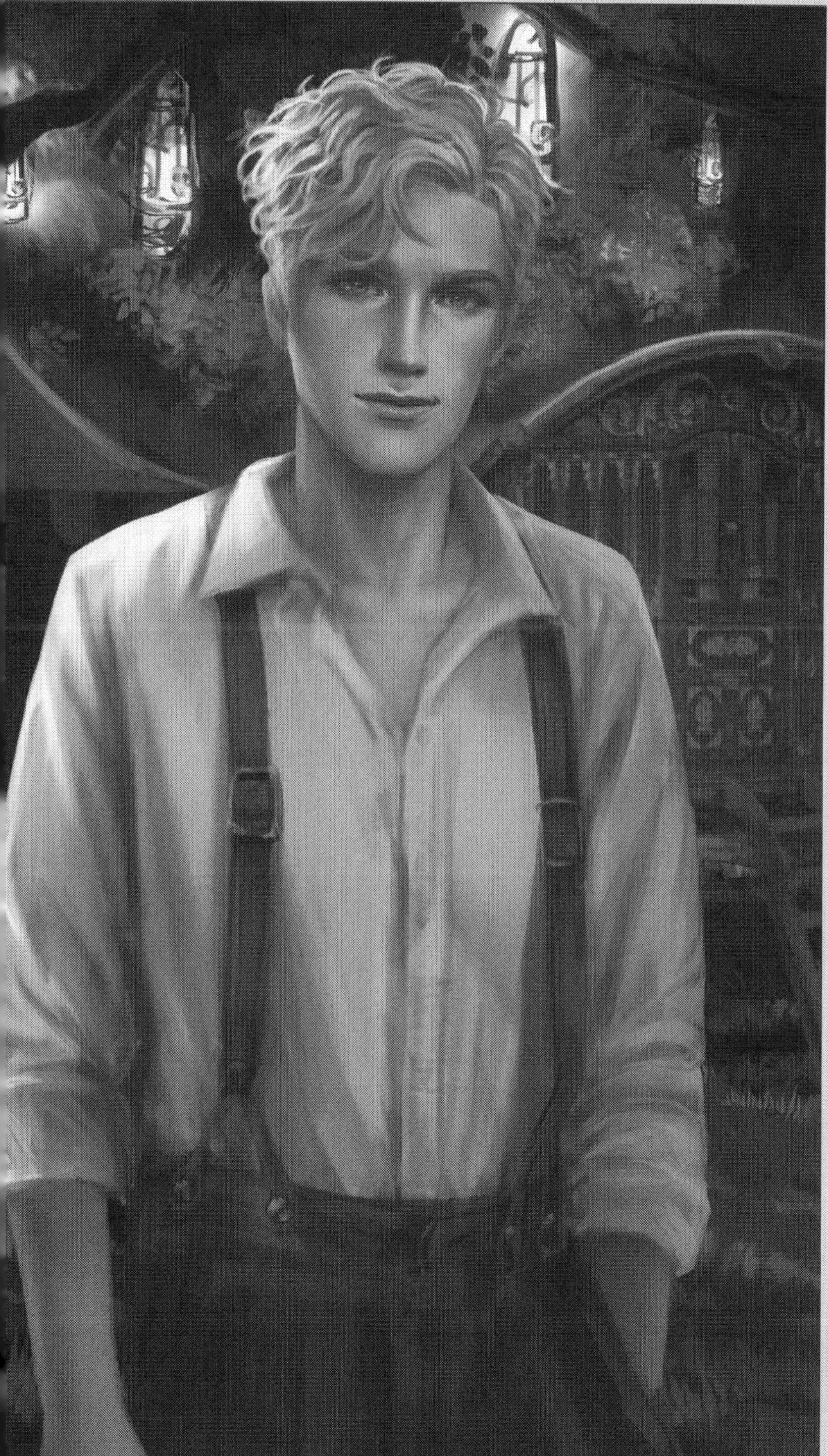

Chapter Seventeen

Glenna Lonan

Cian's lips were a faerie tale. Just the barest hint of his kiss was poison to my already weak-for-him pulse. The honeyed words of love and lust they formed against my skin an enchantment. And oh how the sensual curve of his mouth lit ritual bonfires across my body, each licking flame of his tongue a seductive curl of magic.

I could kiss him for an eternity of eternities.

But, right now, as his trembling lips pressed to mine in a rare, vulnerable search for comfort, I broke for him anew. Stars, I was so angry. Hamish MacCullough better remain behind bars or I might end up there next.

How many times could my heart break for Cian Merrick? And be mended only to break again by his kindness? From his strength and resilience? I was so in love with his illuminating laughter and playfulness after enduring so much darkness, I couldn't stand for the shadows of his past to dampen even a flicker of his light.

Who cared if he wore a dress?

If he enjoyed lace and cosmetics and ribbons?

If he presented as a woman some days and a man most of the others?

The Heartbreak Show

If he responded to she and she responded to him?

Only mortals would decide how the slide of shears across fabric cut from the same bolt decided one's gender. How the stitch of needles assigned one's identity. And how, to be true to oneself, it often required an unsafe public display of wearing the clothing labeled as only male and only female.

The fae didn't give a dying star's arse about any of that nonsense. We were born from nature's magic. And true magic began with one's true nature.

Cian possessed a level of bravery I had never needed to know.

He had remained such a happy, caring soul too.

Despite his fear of becoming what he hated, the only time I had known him to raise a hand was during Bryok's wedding reception, when we had walked from the confectionary wagon to our family's cookfire. Fae from a different tribe were escorting Hamish from the revel and the man was rabid drunk. Recognizing Cian, he had broken free from the middle-ranks gripping him and sprinted toward us. Cian jumped in front of me just as Hamish grabbed his arm, raising his fist . . . but Cian punched him across the jaw first in self-defense.

Knocking him out cold.

The Folk carried that disgusting man's body out of the market, grateful for the dead weight instead of the monster's thrashing.

When his da was no longer in sight, Cian began hyperventilating, his body shaking to the point of clacking teeth. He could barely string together a coherent sentence. My happy-go-lucky, bawdy-tongued, quick to laugh Cian was shattering in my arms. I held him behind the trees as he furiously wiped away tears, my rage building until I thought I would hunt down that man's unconscious body and make it a corpse.

His panic over having to explain himself to others only made his shambling emotions worse. So, I had conjured a story we'd act out when he was calmer, about feeding him cake infused with first kiss magic. And it worked. The others believed his anxiety and tremors were exactly that—from a silly prank.

I didn't know that was his da, then. Only that a mortal had called him Cillian with vile slurs about his personhood while threatening to sell him to Seren.

But that moment cemented our twining hearts.

I was willing to be his comfort, his place of safety, however he needed me—through friendship, sex, a listening ear. Knowing the idea of an "us" was impossible. Believing that he would, in the end, break my pining heart.

I loved him, gods how I loved him.

I gritted my teeth against the memories.

My mate could be kind and playful to those who showed him judgement. But if anyone dared touch him again, I would peck their eyes out to feed to my wood raven cousins in payment to deny their mortal soul passage into the Otherworld.

Cian's hand trailed down the dusty rose silk bodice he now wore. He visibly swallowed.

"You are *so* beautiful." I tapped his chest, just above his heart, and added, "*You*, Cian. All of *you*."

"I feel..." A shaky breath loosened from his chest. "I feel beautiful."

"I'll let you upstage me, but only this once." A corner of his mouth quirked up. I played with a long strand of the wig's blonde hair. Moons above, I couldn't resist preening even his wig's sunny locks. "Georgie Lo?"

Cian play-gasped. "Georgie *Mer*."

The raccoon appeared at my feet, a glove in one hand, a gent's snood in the other.

"Georgie *Lo*, when I win the final bet, I want a similar darted bodice cut but with a squared neckline and slightly larger puffed shoulder seams. Pair the top with a tighter fitted, gored bustle skirt. I prefer padded over caged, too."

"*If* you win," Cian drawled back.

George peered up at Cian.

"Losing tomorrow's show still guarantees my win."

George's head swiveled back toward me.

"*Only* fashion services, Glenna." Those storm cloud eyes of his thinned on me.

"Are you admitting defeat?"

"Feck no. But I *see* your plans, darlin'. No more wig st—"

"Her name is Cordelia."

Cian's face twisted in a mild grimace. Biting back a snort, I pet her bald head, now firmly back onto her pedestal.

"Georgie *Mer*"—Cian began unlacing the garter ribbon I had tied around his wrist the other day—"fetch my parasol, please."

His familiar dashed off.

Cian lifted his heavy skirts and began tying my battle ribbon just above his knee, below the hemline of his silk stocking. He peered up at me through lowered lashes, a flirty tilt to his smile. Heat shot through my core, but I kept my face impassive. Not that it mattered. He would *see* through my mask.

The sound of voices moved through the woods. Owen's laughter and Corbin's swearing the loudest of them all. Why were *they* here for the Ladies of Lugh and cow heist strategizing session? Finn's green head popped around the bend first, Kalen at his side. The pair waltzed up without batting an eyelash Cian's way.

Owen, however, skidded to a tipsy stop, eyes round and mouth agape, making Corbin stumble into him from behind. The lad swore again. But the words died on his tongue when spotting Cian.

"Damn," Owen said with an appreciative whistle and Cian blushed. He actually *blushed* from his friend's approval.

That he feared their rejection so deeply sharpened my talons all over again. Aye, he looked far more like a beautiful woman with a wig than without, but he was still the same person inside and out.

"Always was the prettiest bird of us all, she was," Corbin added.

"Aye," Owen agreed. "A fine looker, our Lady of Man."

Corbin nodded. "Sorry, Glennie Lo, but she'll break more hearts than you dressed like that."

"It's the he-vage." Owen winked at Cian with a slow, playful grin.

"Obviously." Cian puckered his lips at Owen.

One of Kalen's midnight brows arched. "He-vage?"

Cian fluttered a hand in the air. "Male cleavage."

Finn's lips twitched.

"Well, darlin'," Cian said to Kalen, "tonight, is it?"

"Absolutely not," I cut in before Kalen could answer. "You've barely slept and these two eejits are far too scuttered for the train station."

Cian had, at least, sobered considerably. But Owen had a noticeable slur to his words and was swaying slightly on his feet.

Corbin cocked his head. "The train station?"

"Gent of Fem," Cian sighed, "I have two strapping lads, *with wings*, at my disposal."

"You actually trust this fluthered gobshite to carry you to Seren?"

"Aye and carry me like a swooning damsel in distress too."

Owen stretched out his wings with an inviting flex and I ground out an irritated sigh.

Corbin raised a hand. "Why are we going to Seren?"

Cian placed a hand to Corbin's mouth and shushed, never taking his eyes off of Owen. "I've waited my whole life for you, Mr. Delaney." The dramatic arse then jumped into Owen's waiting arms, circling his hands around Owen's neck with a loud, sloppy kiss to his cheek. "Let's fly off into the sunset, you vanilla feathered beast."

For a flicker of a heartbeat, I swore a stricken look flitted across Corbin's expression. But it had to be a trick of shadows. The lad was clearly smiling at the way Cian had dramatically draped himself across Owen's arms.

I rolled my eyes and turned to Finn and Kalen for help, but those two eejits were laughing too. Males were ridiculous. Especially when Cian fluttered around teasing and flirting like the demi-god butterfly of revelry he was.

Well, there were two proven ways to gain a male's captive attention and one of them was not an option here. The other aligned far more with my magic anyway.

I plopped my fists onto my hips. "The plan, you dolts. Or you'll be forced to watch the rest of us feast on desserts all week while you survive on porridge for every meal."

Corbin's eyes flew wide. "Plan for what—"

"Unsalted, unsweetened porridge," I punctuated. "The thick, gummy portion scraped from the bottom of the pot."

Owen dropped Cian and straightened.

"Really?" Cian groaned from the ground. "Greening my gown without any of the fun?"

Owen rolled his bottom lip in to contain another bout of laughter. Wise lad to choose my cookies over Cian's innuendos. I might box the male's ears if he encouraged that prancing strumpet's antics even a fraction of another breath.

I marched in front of the fellas, my glare sharp, my smile sharper, my wings fluffed in warning. Only Kalen met my icy stare and with an appreciative tip of his head.

"Owen"—I pointed a finger in his face and he flinched—"you'll bargain for Cian's safety if the chancer attracts the Carrion Crime Syndicate." That was Cian's specialty—messing around instead of sticking to a plan all the while flirting with the spotlight. "Corbin?"

"Aye," he said quickly, standing straighter.

"Be the voice of reason, please."

He sighed with the weariness of an overworked, sleep-deprived mam with a large brood underfoot. "Aye. So why are we going to—*fecking gods.*" Corbin pointed to the shadows behind me. "Is that an *impaled* head?"

Kalen looked to where Corbin indicated and went deathly still. But, to his credit, he didn't react beyond that. Not like Finn and Cian, who practically clutched each other in primal fear when not gagging.

The strange way Owen studied me, one would think I had turned into a sluagh carrion monster of ancient wild fae lore. "You hid the body from the authorities, aye?"

It was sweet they thought me capable of senseless murder.

"This," I said with delight, "is my new pet, a wig stand gift from George."

"Thank the stars," Owen said, deflating against Corbin. "Rhylen would have *our* heads."

"Not a pet," Cian warned. "That face of horrors stays in the woods. End of discussion."

"Looks like someone is sleeping with the horses," I cooed to Cordelia and kissed her head. "We'll miss the Lady of Man, won't we?"

"Aye, you will." Cian's smile was smug. "Take an extra blanket with you, Gent of Fem."

I sucked in a shocked breath.

A corner of his mouth tilted higher.

My eyes narrowed farther.

"So . . ." Corbin cleared his throat. "What's in Seren?"

The Heartbreak Show

"My cow—"

"—His cow," Cian and I said at the same time.

"And a tacky Lughnasadh's Day hat," I added, "worn by a dozen Ladies of Lugh."

Owen opened his mouth and promptly shut it.

Corbin blinked a few times. "We're risking the Carrion Crime Syndicate's disfavor over a cow and a religious hat? Does Rhylen know of this featherbrained plan?"

"No." Cian sashayed closer. "And here's why."

Chapter Eighteen

Glenna Lonan

For the next few minutes, Cian confessed everything save how he might be a gancanagh. I rubbed my arms in the dewing chill over Caledona Wood while listening. In the distance, the faint blue and purple glow of pixies zipped between the leaves of a maple burnished in golds and oranges.

Nibbling the inside of my lip, I settled my attention onto Cian once more when he began sharing why he didn't want to burden our brother with a quest by the Maiden when Rhylen needed to focus on the tribe. Cian wasn't wrong. Rhylen was struggling to not fall back into old times with friends while helping his tribe move into the new times with him as a gov. Rhylen would become Cian's partner in crime, his protector too and, well . . . he needed to remain neutral with Seren and Ravenna Blackwing.

My brother might peck at us for excluding him. But he was married to someone who could *see* what we were about to do. If Filena *knew*, and I was sure she did, she was also choosing to keep him in the dark.

The boys listened with rapt attention, Kalen seeming the least surprised of the four. That elf's needle point observance was unnerving. He

The Heartbreak Show

seemed far older, too. At least, older than he let on. Had he lied about his age to Carran's military when they killed his clan?

Cian swept his gaze over our group. "Do you pointy-eared peckers agree to remain silent?"

"Is this a bargain?" Corbin asked.

"Aye," Cian replied. "Agree to not speak a word of my birthright or my travels to Seren to Rhylen so long as I request you to keep this a secret."

All four replied with various agreements.

I rubbed at my arms again and peered up at Seren. A heavy stone was sitting in my gut. The dread of his quest was weighing me down more and more with every passing beat of my thudding pulse. I didn't want Cian to go to the City of Stars without me. But I needed to stay here and prep for the next meals of the night. The entire camp was depending on me and my rotating kitchen crew. Not to mention, my brother would know for certain that a Cian scheme was unfolding if I didn't show for work.

"If Cian is re-souled in the Mother's bloodline"—Finn turned to Kalen—"are the Sisters Three then aspects of Danu?"

Danu—the mother of the Tuatha Dé Danann, including Cian.

"Aye, of course," Kalen answered—and paused. "Who did you think the Sisters Three were?"

"The Sisters Three," Cian answered dryly.

Finn comically pointed to Cian in agreement and Cian softly winked back.

Both lads had enough cheek for a second arse, stars above.

Kalen gawked at his best friend with a look bordering on incredulity. One that silently accused, "But you work for the Maiden?!"

Finn lifted a single brow that challenged, "And?" while also saying nothing aloud.

"I fear for the Folk this side of The Wilds," Kalen sighed, rubbing a hand down his face. "Aye, the Sisters Three are the triple goddess Danu. And you, love," he said to Cian, "are not re-souled in birth but in magic. You carry the *soul* of Cian's magic. A generational curse or blessing, as it's called in the Greenwood."

"*Enduring* Ancient One," Cian muttered the translation of his name with a roll of his eyes. "Hilarious."

Kalen grinned. "Cheeky gods."

"Cheeky Moira Merrick, too." Cian drooped against a tree in a puddle of pink silk and heaved a dramatic sigh. "Magic cursed to *endure* until reunited with a fecking faerie cow." Steel eyes locked with mine. "And soul bonds with a love more powerful than the magic of his first."

I allowed him to search my eyes, to know every melting corner of my heart while I sashayed back, "If you're wanting me to say you're the lady man of my dreams—"

"Oh no," Cian cut in, that up-to-no-good grin of his bright and full. "You know what I want to hear, Glennie Lo."

"Good thing you're full of *enduring* magic, Ci-Ci," I tossed back with a crowing grin of my own.

"Mmm," he moaned long and slow. "I can *endure* hours and hours—"

"Alone." I pet Cordelia's bald head and Cian grimaced.

The boys erupted into laughter and I ruffled my wing feathers in preening delight.

Ignoring the smug tilt of my head and sassy pop of my hip, ignoring the fellas too, Cian shoved off the tree and took the parasol George lifted to him.

My thoughts tumbled backward a few seconds.

Did that fluffy, cuddly raccoon just . . . materialize on cue? So Cian could *fashionably* steal the spotlight from me?

George peered at me and moved a paw in a circle over and over. I

The Heartbreak Show

bit the inside of my cheek. He was so adorable, but I had no idea what he was saying to me.

"He moves in mysterious ways, Glenna." Cian popped open the parasol and twirled it behind his shoulder. Of course, he *knew* what I was thinking.

George began slowly walking backward into the shadows, his sweet, blinking gaze locked onto mine. A little giggle left me. "Naturally."

"Obviously."

Corbin cleared his throat to politely gain our attention. I was convinced Corbin Renwick was born a granda in his ancient years half of the month. The other half, he remembered to kick up his heels with the other lads.

"What happens," he began, "when you unite the boots, ribbon, and hat with . . . your cow?"

Cian shrugged then peered at Finn who shrugged in return.

"Grand." Corbin's lips pursed with an ill-humored shake of his head. "What if we can't escape that floating bird cage because of your cow?"

"You think Ravenna Blackwing would lock us up?" Owen asked.

"It's not Ravenna you need to worry about, mate." Finn leaned against the sheltering oak and crossed his arms over his chest. "The entire floating island is an engineered trap. Carran has no jurisdiction of the sky. The kingdom's govs turn a blind eye at the train station, too, for passenger taxes."

"Bastards," Corbin muttered.

"And so," Finn continued, "because Seren can, coercion-infused air is pumped into the ferry cars shortly after undocking."

My jaw dropped. So that really was magic I had seen glimmering in the steam, not an illusion.

"The mortals are under a spell to indulge in their greatest fantasies. And," Finn said with a pause, "they're glamoured to remember little of their indulgences too. You"—he gestured with his head toward Cian—"will need to behave like you're glamoured."

"Everything will humor you," Kalen added. "Pickpocketed? Funniest shite in all three kingdoms. Want to tumble with a street boy behind the warehouses, yeah? Your mum won't remember. Your posh betrothed won't either." The blue-haired elf smirked. "No harm done to your reputation, love."

I couldn't help but smile at that. A clever trick to use on buttoned-up, scandalized-by-everything mortals. I'd sit back and crow over their willing stupidity too.

And this was why Filena and I were soul-knitted sisters.

"Work on your accent." Finn's voice snapped me from my internal ramblings. "You're not a Caravan lass. You're from the eastern cities now. Or at least a wealthy landowning family in Caledona."

Kalen pointed his finger in Cian's face. "And do not, under any circumstances, steal a damn thing. Not even a cigarette from a gent's mouth."

"I'm stealing a cow."

"You're reclaiming *your* stolen property."

"If I do steal—"

Kalen laughed low under his breath. At the haunted sound, humor quickly drained from Cian's face. His hawk-eyed stare on the water spirit intensified. "Rhylen in good with the Syndicate, is he?"

My wings twitched, an involuntary protective response. "My brother has a bar—"

Cian grabbed my hand and yanked me away from the group, to the other side of the oak, saying, "Shield my and Glenna's conversation, pretty tree."

The tree shook its lower branches.

The Heartbreak Show

"Did the oak just agree?" Owen asked. "Cian can talk to trees?"

"You're standing next to a tree spirit, eejit," Corbin replied. "Who is leaning on the *pretty tree*."

"You got your magic back?"

Finn started to speak, but his voice grew muffled while the sounds of the forest grew louder—the tinny melody of tumbling leaves, the creaking groans of branches, the whirring buzz of pixie wings, the bright chirp of insects.

But not anywhere near as loud as the pounding in my ears.

Cian was spooked.

Chapter Nineteen

GLENNA LONAN

Once in the shadows behind the large trunk, Cian spun on me. My stomach dropped. "What's wrong?"

His lips crushed mine in answer. A ravenous, devouring kiss that knocked me off balance. Before I stumbled over, Cian circled an arm around my waist and then walked me backward a couple steps until my back rested against the tree's trunk. Shadows darkened overhead from his parasol and everything, but us, was blocked from sight.

The forest, our friends on the other side of the enormous oak, all fell away. It was only me and him and whatever this crackling desperation was arcing between his parting mouth and mine. The intensity growing brighter, hotter as the dance of our lips grew wilder, as the claiming sweep of our tongues became more fevered.

In the back of my mind, a voice was screaming to ask why the sudden need. We were terrible at openly expressing our fears and vulnerabilities with words, though. Both he and I communicated in physical touch—and why I missed Filena fiercely. Aye, I saw her more these past three weeks than I had all last year, but I no longer held her while we slept. Expressing through touch was also why Cian and I had savored casual relationships to feel more emotionally whole, more balanced. And it dawned on me that he might be panicking. Seren was a weapon used against him by his da and the Fiachnas.

But this kiss, the slow, deep grind of his hips, the twining desire in our panting breaths . . . I was utterly lost in him. Still, we needed to slow down.

As if reading my mind, he pulled away a few inches, his chest heaving against mine.

"My beautiful ruination, my gorgeous Gent of Fem . . . " The words were feather soft against my skin. "I fell in love with you the night I found you teaching Filena how to ward against nightmares."

My pounding heart stilled for a breathless beat.

He tugged me back here, in the middle of a conversation, just to share this?

I blinked as the memories came spilling back.

Filena and I were fourteen. Barry had arrived two weeks earlier, his crusty, sweet-tooth addicted presence signaling to West Tribe that Filena was magical. My blood oath sister grew far too jumpy as a result, suddenly plagued by nightmares again too, terrified anytime a gov wanted to speak to her. I couldn't wing whip the Fiachnas and elders to protect her and so I created a faerie ritual just for my best friend. One I knew would make her feel powerful instead of exposed and helpless.

Stripped down to our thin, fraying underpinnings, with partially plucked daisies woven into our wild tresses and dangling from our wrists and ankles, I hummed melodies while we danced to ask the moon for what our hearts craved most. I had teased that I danced for satin hair ribbons. She declared she danced for a dessert made by the gods. But I suspected, even then, that she had danced for my brother while I had danced for hers.

Hours later, before falling into bed, I made her promise that if the nightmares returned, she would visit the field of moon bright daisies in her mind and dance to the true song in her heart instead of reeling to fear's melody. And she agreed, asking me to hum a tune to her while she drifted to sleep morning after morning and any time she woke from a terror.

Did Rhylen hum melodies to help her sleep now? Did he know?

I blew out a slow breath.

Six years.

Cian had been in love with me for *six years*.

I played with a lock of long blonde hair and slowly met his light gray eyes.

"I loved you," he continued, his voice cracking, "when I believed no one could truly love *me*. I loved you when I believed hope in the impossible was only for fools who wished on stars and that a future with you was a fever dream."

Tears lined my lashes.

"I loved you," he whispered again, "when I couldn't look at you directly because I . . . I would have shattered if I confirmed the slightest whisper of your returned affection."

The heady poetry of those confessing lips lingering on mine dizzied down my body. Was this part of his magic as a gancanagh or—my eyes rounded.

Oh gods . . .

These were goodbyes. In case something happened to him on Seren. These were the kisses and confessions of a lover marching to their death.

"Cian—"

"Marry me, Glenna Lonan," he rushed out. "Right here. With only the stars and this tree as witness."

The gnawing fear in my gut tightened.

Three weeks, the amount of time he had known full freedom in his life. The thought of taking away his hard-won agency sickened me.

"If we speak binding vows," I croaked out, "would the raven mark make you feel like an indentured again?"

His fingers trailed down my cheek in a reverent caress. "I'm a demi-god, darlin'. Do the fae laws about mate binding with a mortal still apply to us?"

"You're enough of a demi-mortal for the Kingdom of Carran and other fae to see you as my property—" I sucked in a sharp breath. "You're afraid of Seren."

"I am yours, Glenna. Feck, Seren. Feck the Carrion Crime Syndicate, my da, and the Kingdom of Carran too." His thumb brushed across my lower lip. "I am yours," he said more softly. "Let those feckers know I belong only to you."

He meant it. He was actually asking me to take away his self-ownership, before both of our races. "Would you later resent me?"

Cian reared back slightly. "You think I want to marry you only for protection?"

"Gods, no. I just worry this is happening too fast. You deserve more than three weeks of self-ownership after a lifetime of none." I drew in a shaky breath. "What if I do something that reminds you of when—"

"Fair." A corner of his mouth quirked up. "Rhylen was a terrifying feathered bastard of a fae master. Gran, though?" He pretended to shudder. "That dirty old hen is a monster."

I hummed my agreement to play along, but mostly to give my heart a moment to settle down. My eyes cinched shut in a long blink, to quiet my nerves. And, in that calming hush, my pulse began fluttering in excitement.

Cian desired to mate bond with me.

And stars above how I ached to bind my life with Cian's until our souls took their last breaths . . .

"As my last act of self-ownership"—he gave a serious dip of his head—"I promise to make you feel guilty about forcing me into this sham marriage of cow heist convenience, but *only* if you bring Cordelia into our wagon."

I sputtered a laugh.

"I also promise to make you feel the shame of owning the sexy, sparkly arse you clearly want to bite and kiss forever, but *only* if you use George to commit fashion crimes against me."

A scoff sassed from my loosening chest. "And waste his time tormenting you when he could be finding fashion treasures for me?"

"What about the orphans in need of clothing, Glenna?" Cian twirled the parasol over his shoulder, the one George thieved to complete Cian's Heartbreak Show outfit. "Do you ever think about the poor, gloveless orphans?"

Arsehole. But two could play this game.

"I'll marry you." Cian's eyes rounded in relief. "But, when I win the most Love-Talker sacrifices tomorrow night, I get George's services for a full month instead of three weeks. And," I lilted, my grin slow and smug, "you'll be my pet in bed for one week. Maybe I'll leash you too."

He burst into laughter. "You win."

I gasped in genuine surprise "You'll sacrifice a whole month of George's fashion services to be my pet—"

"Feck, just for *one* day."

I narrowed my eyes. "Liar."

If I were smart, I would call this bargain. But I knew he was baiting me, to prove that he trusted me.

The boyish tilt to his devilish grin widened and my eyes thinned farther. "It's good to have dreams, darlin'," he cooed with a dainty shrug. "But when I win tomorrow's Heartbreak Show, three different times you will scream in wild ecstasy—"

The Heartbreak Show

"—speaking of dreams—"

"Oh, Cian!"

My eyes flew wide. He actually screamed his name, as if a woman . . . as if climaxing.

"You're my sex go—"

I smothered his mouth. "Shhh, you eejit!" I could barely get the words out from laughing so hard. I was no prude, but if the oak chose to stop protecting our conversation out of secondhand embarrassment, not that I'd blame it, I would prefer to perish where the green earth touched my feet right now than face the fellas ever again. Or my brother.

Cian pulled my hand from his mouth, his laughter matching mine. "And," he said in-between breaths, "I'll marry you."

"You think I will now after that lackluster performance?"

"Be a good little pastry shrew," he murmured, nipping my bottom lip, "and marry this poor brazen heifer."

Brazen heifer?

I wanted to roll my eyes so hard. Except, it was a magnificent insult and I was fecking pissed the riddling eejit upstaged my efforts to outwit and banter him—*again*.

"Just so we're clear, as my property, I would tear the wings off anyone on Seren who dared touch you, Cian *Lonan*."

He softly snorted. "That so, Glenna *Merrick*?"

"Glennie Mer?" I tried on for size.

"Glenna and Cian Lonan-Merrick . . . people will come far and wide to experience heartbreak by the talented Little Glen Blackbirds of Enduring Power."

Now it was my time to throw my head back with a loud laugh. The fae loved a clever riddled name and ours together were storybook perfection.

"Well, Cian Lonan-Merrick"—I sighed for dramatic effect—"I

guess I'll own you for all eternity and, when I win tomorrow, George's exclusive fashion services for one month too."

"Mmm, the way you'll scream my name in gratitude Glenna Lonan-Merrick..."

"Lady of Man," I taunted, "bets."

"Gent of Fem," he drawled back, "bets."

I lifted Cian's hand to my mouth and kissed his fingers. "Life partners?"

"Life partners," Cian confirmed.

We were actually marrying, right here, right now. When we returned to the meeting on the other side of the trunk, it would be as bonded mates.

The air around us thickened in heady anticipation. And I fell into the pools of silver holding mine as our smiles faded into longing.

Then I spoke, the ancient vows light on my tongue.

"I, Glenna Lonan-Merrick, mate bind myself to you, Cian Lonan-Merrick, my chosen mate, for as long as my soul exists. I put you before all others and will protect you with my life." The last part males spoke, but I was his Gent of Fem and couldn't resist. "I belong to you, life partner," I continued, blinking back tears, "for now and for all eternity."

Warmth tingled down my arm and settled on my wrist. The sight of a raven in flight marking my skin soared in my thundering heart. Cian's breath trembled, his muscles tight. This was ownership for him too. I *belonged* to him now.

Per tradition, he lifted the mark on my wrist to his lips, to speak to my pulse.

"I, Cian Lonan-Merrick," he began, pressing a kiss to my raven mark, "mate bind myself to you, Glenna Lonan-Merrick, my heart's obsession, my chosen mate, for as long as my soul exists. I put you before all others and will protect you with my life." He dropped his voice to an intimate whisper. "I belong to you, life partner, for now and for all eternity."

The raven mark appeared on his wrist two beats later and Cian let out a blushed laugh. A sound of pure joy that brightened his entire countenance.

Stars, he was so beautiful, it ached.

"I have never felt so wanted or loved in my life," he confessed, sucking in a tight breath. But a tear fell anyway as he quietly laughed again. "I wore a silk gown on my wedding day."

And, once more, my heart broke for Cian Lonan-Merrick.

"I love you," I whispered into the barest of kisses. "I love you so much it hurts." My mouth trailed along his jaw. "Tomorrow, I will love you even more." I kissed down the column of his throat. "And, when I walk my last"—my tongue flicked the throbbing pulse in his neck—"I will be so full of love for you, I will scream, 'Oh, Cian!'"

"Don't leave out the best part, Glennie Mer."

"*Enduring* One," I chastised, my voice falling flat, "patience. Maybe in another lifetime, if you win, you'll hear the rest."

His eyes squinted.

The corner of my mouth hooked up.

Then Cian moved to kiss me, to prove I'd sing his name. And sexy demi-god before me, did I want to rip the gown from his delicious body and do just that. But, after newly bonding, he'd win. My primal state wouldn't be able to control herself and he *knew* it.

I ducked under his arm and shifted with a cawing laugh.

"Bloody Ravens," he swore as I flew away, the smile in his voice following me around the gigantic trunk to where the lads waited.

I shifted back beside Cordelia, plucking her head from the stand to cradle in my arms.

"So," Owen began, looking over his shoulder, "did you bury the body?"

"Poor lass," Corbin lamented, "slain in her mortal prime."

Still so sweet they thought me capable of murder.

Cian circled into the group a second later, brushing blonde locks from his shoulder and twirling the parasol as if nothing were amiss. Until he saw me, with Cordelia tucked in my arms—my ward against arrogant halflings—and he sputtered a laugh. I tried, and failed, to not grin like an eejit in reply. We were ridiculous.

And so fecking happy we were near to bursting.

Four pairs of eyes darted between us.

Schooling his features, Cian dipped his head to me in greeting. "Tart nag."

"Foppish floozy."

"Well..." Cian turned to Owen and Corbin, like he hadn't abducted me mid-sentence in Caledona Wood to marry in secret—such a fae thing to do, too. "Are you cocks ready to steal back a faerie cow?"

"Aye, I'm still your Mr. Delaney," Owen offered with open arms.

Cian's gaze slid to Corbin's with a pout. "Mr. Renwick?"

Corbin studied Owen a moment, then sighed. "Fine, lass. Let's steal back your birthright, Miss Merrick, and break your generational curse."

"Mrs. Lonan-Merrick to you, sir," Cian replied with a humorous attempt at an eastern cities accent.

Those four pairs of eyes first flickered to Cian's wrist, then mine. The silence that followed was deafening. Then everyone was talking and laughing and grinning and congratulating us all at once.

"Ladies!" Cian eventually hollered, also in a prim but wobbly eastern cities accent. He clapped his hands in a signal to silence. "Hush now so the pretty elf with the stick can talk." He batted his eyes at Kalen and giggled. "Meet me behind the warehouse later, sir?"

Kalen arched a midnight blue brow. "Sure, love. Speaking of warehouses . . ." he gestured for us to study the map he was drawing in the dirt. We gathered around, leaning in closer when he pointed to a circle where I surmised Stellar Winds Casino once stood. "Here's the plan."

Chapter Twenty

CIAN LONAN-MERRICK

"Damn," Owen whispered beside me.

I had never felt so backwoods as I did while peering over the ledged shoulders of a giant to a sea of similarly sized brick monsters. Caledona Wood had textile factories in the large villages, but they were dollhouse furniture in comparison to the warehouse districts on Seren. The chimney stacks alone were intimidating.

Trash lined the alleys below us. Grimy windows on the lower levels were broken, too. A waxing moon hung in the sky, only half-full. Enough light, however, that I could make out the pea soup tint to the air from the many coal furnaces.

Corbin covered his nose. "What's that stench?"

> *"Ye want to dress like a filthy Molly?" Da threw a chair and hit a window. Shattering glass and splinters flew in all directions. I backed into a corner and covered my head. "Then ye can live like one on Seren. Pay fer me lost wages."*

"Despair," I replied, barely above a whisper.

The Heartbreak Show

Caravans had fellys, but Traveler poor was nothing like the decay of living in a trashed, rotting cabin filled with unwashed, starving children and a better-fed drunkard who blacked out in his own piss and, sometimes, vomit.

Like the home of my childhood.

Like the Beggar's Hole district of Seren.

I... I didn't know if I could do this.

My pulse was starting to tremor in rhythm with the fingers gripping the brick ledge.

Blowing out a slow breath, I faced Corbin and Owen. "Ready?"

It didn't surprise me that the Raven Folk govs of Seren were obsessed with magical objects. Raven Folk were collectors by nature. But now I knew why Glas Gaibhnenn was specifically desired after Kalen retold Cian's tale to us.

A Cow of Plenty who appeared during times of famine, whose milk never ran dry.

A good luck charm that brought wealth to its owner.

But her *full* fertility and prosperity magic was bound to Cian of the Tuatha Dé Danann... and I couldn't stop the chills from prickling down my spine again.

"First mission," Corbin reminded us, fixing a wayward strand of my hair, "locate the cow."

Owen unrolled a crude map Kalen drew on a strip of birch bark. "Stellar Winds should be that direction."

We looked across the night-shadowed rooftops toward the illuminated area in the distance. According to Finn, Crescent Street was a road that wound down a park, dotted with trees and benches, with an open market on one end. On either side of the street and lawn were nightclubs, restaurants, shops, casinos, hotels, and other various establishments.

Corbin pointed to a line on the map. "The market is three blocks from here, aye? Let's start there to blend into the crowds."

I was still woozy from flying to Seren in Owen's arms. Angling down alleys and around buildings only soured my stomach further. But I managed to hold onto my delicate eastern cities constitution, even after we landed in the shadows of a nightclub on the fringe of Crescent Street.

"We'll follow at a distance," Corbin said, shifting away his wings.

Traveler Raven Folk didn't stroll around Seren with wealthy mortal women. But representatives from each tribe visited often enough for trade negotiations with the Syndicate that their presence wouldn't raise too many eyebrows.

Owen cupped my face. "If you need to leave, for *any* reason, open your parasol." I nodded my head, not quite meeting his eyes. He kissed my forehead, turned me around, and swatted my arse. "Behave, Mrs. Lonan-Merrick."

"Tsk, tsk, Mr. Delaney," I chastised in an attempt to sound well-bred. Feck, it was awful. Outside of occasional visions when meeting eyes, I really knew nothing of eastern city ways save the conversations I had listened to at Night Markets. Still, lifting my chin, I added, "Lady Glenna warned she would rip the wings off anyone on Seren who dared touch me."

In a swish of silk, I spun on the heel of a cock boot, stepped beneath a flickering gas lamp, and strolled onto the lawn. I kept my head down to save my focus. Familiar sounds warbled in my pounding ears. Hawkers were singing about their wares to the passing crowd. The cloying scent of perfume mixed with meat pies and ale roiled in my already sickened gut the nearer I approached the crowds.

I took another dainty step—

The flickering shadows across the lawn began spinning—spinning faster when I attempted another step.

The Heartbreak Show

My body stiffened.

I gritted my teeth in anticipation of what came next.

Waiting... Waiting...

There.

A discordant buzz hummed in my head.

Voices. Hundreds of voices, speaking from all directions, from within. Soft whispers that quickly crescendoed into shouts for attention. Dark skies, Seren was a noisy roost of chirping birds.

But how I craved this chaos.

My blood was trilling to frolic alongside the multiple intersecting thought threads.

My magic was rooting... rooting... hungry for secrets, to *know* the coerced desires of those nearby. The urge quaked inside of me until I thought I might go mad.

Was there glamoured air on Seren as well? Was the mortal side of me falling prey while the fae side of me was licking its chops? Or was my fight-or-flight just in overdrive?

Pain blossomed behind my eyes.

I sucked in a sharp breath and squeezed my lids shut in a long blink. The buzz in my head was a thousand bees in flight, stinging my concentration over and over.

No.

Not right now.

I peered up to focus my waning cognitive control onto a single star.

One star.

One star.

Only think of one star.

... just one star ...

Not all heroes wear armor, Cillian.

I winced at the rippling, tunneled sound of Mam's voice.

Imogen Murphy, a mortal at camp, has a hidden shrine of small objects belonging to former felly Brandon—

—Why hadn't Owen and Corbin shown signs of elder magic yet?—

Cian, the warrior god who fathered Lugh, wore a dress when he left his known world to chase after his birthright.

My fingers curled into my skir—

The Kingdom of Carran would visit Rhylen within the week.

A moonless sky filled with ravens writhed above the Maiden as smoky wisps of purple whipped around h—

—Fae laws *might* protect me as Glenna's bonded mate.

He met and married his true love in a dress, too.

People rushed by the train station's signalman. He'd never felt more alo—

—Did George have a mate? Children?—

As the sister of a chieftain, Glenna was a princ—

My racing thoughts froze.

I blinked.

My gaze caressed the raven mark on my wrist, peeking out from behind my glove.

Awareness trickled back into my galloping bloodstream.

I was on Seren. As a woman. A *married* woman.

I blinked again.

The Maiden had to know this was my greatest fear. And yet, she asked me to travel by wind to a magic island clouded by mist and fenced in by a tower of glass, dressed as a woman, to slay my enemy and steal back my prosperity.

My birthright.

A low, bitter laugh left me. Of course this was a quest of self-discovery.

To break a generational curse.

To no longer fear the divine parts of who and what I was. To no longer fear my future.

"Miss?" a gent asked beside me. "Are you well, miss?"

Startled, my eyes slammed into his before I could stop myself.

> *A young man lifts a floor plank in a solarium covered in plants. A tear falls into the hole. He reaches for a small box with trembling hands and lifts the lid. An ornate silver key lays atop an ivory silk cushion. Beside the key is a note. "Take care of your mother and sisters."*

"Miss?"

My mind snapped back to reality. A gent in his late twenties, with earthen brown hair that curled just beneath his top hat and rich dark eyes, placed a supportive hand below my elbow.

"Forgive me, sir," I said in a lighter, higher registered voice. "I found myself recalling a painful memory and slipped away. I am well now."

"I'm glad to hear you've recovered." A light crease appeared between his brows. Was it my terrible accent? Could he tell I wasn't female born? Clearing his throat, he offered his arm. "My sisters are waiting for me by the pastry cart. I fear if I do not return soon, they'll purchase the whole shop and all of tomorrow's confections too." Four girls, festooned in the latest fashions, peered our way.

My eyes started to widen.

One was wearing a Lughnasadh's Day hat!

"The youngest, especially, is not to be trusted around confections."

I replied with a dainty laugh, placing my hand atop his arm. "I have a younger sister who is much the same."

"Devilish creatures, younger sisters." He slid me a kind smile.

"Aye, wee imps," I replied then mentally kicked myself for slipping back into my native dialect.

His smile faltered a little. "Ethan Phillips."

Shite. I never considered a female name, for now or for any reason. Everyone just called me the Lady of Man. I opened my mouth to say Eliza, a common name among eastern cities mortals to use today and, instead, croaked out, "Cordelia." A mocking strand of blonde hair fluttered in front of my face in a breeze, as if that creepy porcelain death mask approved. I fought back a grimace and added, "Mrs. Cordelia Merrick."

Fecking stars, I needed a cigarette.

But proper ladies of means didn't smoke. They didn't swear either.

"There you are!" an early teenage girl said to Ethan with a pout. "Another moment and I would have perished from boredom *and* temptation. Have you not looked at these confections, brother? It's criminal to ignore them for so long."

"Eliza," the Lady of Lugh sister chastised. "Manners, please."

Of course, her name was Eliza.

Eliza's face fell flat. "Brother dearest, please look at these confections and, if you love me, even the tiniest pinch, purchase two dozen and with great haste."

The oldest cleared her throat.

"Thank you," Eliza added with a glare at her sister.

The oldest cleared her throat again.

"Nice to meet you, miss," Eliza practically shoved my direction with

The Heartbreak Show

an impatient curtsy. She then grabbed her brother's hand and rounded her eyes, stage whispering, "You shall not ask me to wait one more minute or I will die where I stand. It is truly a dire emergency."

"My apologies for my sister's uncouth behavior," Ethan murmured at me, but he was giving Eliza an indulgent smile. "She's positively wild, that one."

"ETHAN!" Eliza pleaded, tugging his arm.

"Excuse me, Mrs. Merrick," Ethan said with a tip of his hat.

When he and Eliza stepped away, the Lady of Lugh dipped into a small curtsy, followed by her younger two sisters. "Our brother spoils her far too much," she explained.

"Brothers cannot help themselves," I offered in reply. "Especially with the wild ones." I pretended to peer around the market and caught Owen's eye, who raised a brow at me and mouthed, "Cordelia?"

I wanted to shoot him a rude gesture and settled with a mock-glare, instead.

Falling skies, my hands were still trembling. A sheen of sweat dewed my forehead. I would smoke a dozen cigarettes when I got back to camp. No, two dozen.

George, if you can hear me . . . it is truly a dire emergency.

"You have a brother, then?"

"Aye," I answered and flinched. "I'm the eldest of four brothers and two sisters."

"Four brothers!" The middle sister placed a fluttering hand to her chest.

The next youngest tilted her head. "Are you from the North Country?"

What the feck was the North Country?

Was this an eastern term for settlements along The Wilds?

"The accent gave me away, I see." I attempted a smile. "Miss," I said to the Lady of Lugh, "may I ask who designed your exquisite Lughnasadh's Day hat?"

She lowered her eyes in practiced modesty. "Are you a fellow Shaft or part of the Great Seed?"

I bit the inside of my cheek.

"Emeline, do not bore Mrs. Merrick," her sister heaved in a way that suggested it was she who would be bored.

"*Elspeth*," Emeline warned with a tight smile, her cheeks turning a soft pink.

"She did not travel from the North Country to—"

"Actually," I said and leaned forward on the handle of my parasol, as if sharing a secret. "I traveled to Seren to join your . . . your . . ." Stars, what was the word? Congregation? Religious order? Cult?

"You wish to join our Plowed Fields?"

Sweet, merciful goddess, I wasn't meant to be a gent *or* proper lady.

Forcing my face to remain innocent, I hummed a, "Mhmm," not trusting my words.

"We have our Topping Ceremony tonight." Emeline took my gloved hands. "Please say you'll come."

"If I come," I began to ask, my eyes sliding to the fellas, "does that make me part of the Great Seed?"

Owen had to turn around, his entire body shaking.

"Indeed, Mrs. Merrick." She grinned, completely ignorant of these agricultural innuendos or my Raven travel companions. "Your husband approves, then?"

Oh aye, Gent of Fem likes being topped.

"Mr. Merrick is at home," I said with a conspiratorial smile. The girls grinned wider. "Your hat?" I prodded with a dip of my head toward hers. "How would I procure one with . . . well-endowed decor?"

"Oh yes! Once initiated, a lady will top you."

Now Corbin was laughing.

Emeline started to glance their direction.

"I'm curious, Miss Emeline," I rushed out, regaining her fevered-eyed attention, "have you heard of the Cow of Plenty?"

She sucked in an excited, squealing breath and grabbed my hands again with a little jump on the tips of her toes. "We think we located Gloss Gabenonen."

"Glas Gaibhnenn," I gently corrected. She attempted to say it again and fumbled once more over the fae tongue. "Gloss, like a shine." She nodded. "Then Ghav-lyn. Similar to caw—"

"A crow sound?"

"Aye, but gaw ending with a v. Gloss Ghavlyn."

"Estella, she sounds like the faerie boy we met earlier today, does she not?" Elspeth said to the youngest of the three.

"North Country," I replied with a wink. To Emeline, I asked, "Where do the Ladies believe Glas Gaibhnenn is hidden away on Seren? I do love a mystery."

"Well," Emeline began, drawing in closer, the brim of her straw hat nearly touching my forehead, "she is believed to be in Ravenna Blackwing's private chambers at the Palace of Stars, or possibly somewhere in The Crow and Bar, or"—she lowered her voice to a barely audible whisper—"a house of ill-repute."

"How scandalous," I replied.

Emeline's eyes darted toward her sisters, then her brother and Eliza, who were still picking out treats. Heat crept up Emeline's cheeks once more. Blinking back her nerves, she leaned forward and whispered in my ear, "A brothel of males for males named *Beau Fine*."

I stilled.

"Sounds like *bovine*, yes?" She leaned back. "We always suspected the Cow of the Milky Way was on the City of Stars. Part of why the

Ladies visit here each dawning winter."

Everything inside of me just froze.

My heart. My muscles. The blood in my veins.

"But it wasn't until Glass Gavanonon was spotted shortly after the fires. Terrible accident, that fire."

Did the Maiden honestly believe I would willingly enter a Molly house?

Emeline's lips pinched at the corners. "Do you need a seat, Mrs. Merrick? You look peaked. Mrs. Daniels needed a lie down upon hearing—"

"No, no, I . . . I . . ."

My throat ached. The air in my lungs constricted tighter. My fingers itched to open the parasol and flee this island. But fury was quickly replacing the fear and searing the edges of my clearing thoughts. Hamish's voice had lived in my head long enough. The lads would never let anything happen to me either.

"Just shocked," I forced out.

"Indeed."

"Miss Phillips." An older lady in a black dress, pearl earrings dangling from her lobes, and pewter gray hair piled high in curls, slowed before our circle.

"Priestess." Emeline quickly straightened and lowered her head. "I have a Seed for our Plowed Field."

"Well done." The older woman considered me. "Your name, miss?"

"Mrs. Cordelia Merrick." I dipped into a shallow, wobbly curtsy. Thankfully, neither of the women present seemed to notice my lack of practice in the art of etiquette.

"Your husband approves of our society, Mrs. Merrick?"

"Mr. Merrick is a modern man and doesn't interfere with my choices."

The Heartbreak Show

The woman's mouth lifted ever so slightly. "Then, ladies"—she gestured toward a tree at the far end of the lawn—"it is time."

Chapter Twenty-One

CIAN LONAN-MERRICK

It is time...

Was that a coincidence?

I rolled a wine-soaked, reconstituted bilberry in my now gloveless palm. Three other Great Seeds stood with their backs to mine, starry-eyed and grinning like scuttered eejits. Except, they were drunk on magically heightened religious fervor—similar to the small handful of women in straw hats across from me.

Me? Horror had long seized my pulse and was now bleeding into my expression.

This would be my first *and* last cult ritual, dying stars above. I would blame the Carrion Crime Syndicate's glamour, but these mainlanders performed this shite without being coerced to indulge their greatest fantasies.

> *A woman scratches feverishly in a journal, her cheeks flushed. A man calls for her. She startles to a stand and gently calls back, "On my way, darling!" She blots the ink and blows on the pages, then quickly covers her scandalous words with a la-*

dy's magazine and leaves. My mind steps forward and sees past the obstacles to a titillating romance she penned between her and Lugh and his large, shining—

My mind snapped back to reality.

Naughty Lady of Lugh, I wanted to applaud. I hadn't meant to meet her eyes but . . .

Wait.

Shining?

My nose wrinkled. Did the illumination enhance his performance? Her pleasure? Or was that merely a decorative fantasy?

Where was that delightfully unladylike Lady? Was she the brunette or redhead? I needed to *know* the rest and—and that would not be happening.

The ladies started circle-dancing around us initiates while passionately singing a plucky ditty about planting seeds to honor Lugh's foster mother, Tailtiu, the Goddess of Harvests, who had *painfully* died in the labor throes of turning forests into farm fields.

I blinked.

A happy song . . . about dying *painfully* . . . to seed plowed fields.

These were city women, not farmers' daughters. They had cooks who baked their bread and prepared their vegetables. Brothers who spoiled them with excessive treats at a market designed for kings and queens, not rag quilt peasants like me. What did they know about surviving off the land? Of having to consider tree bark flour and milking wild deer to not feel the hollowed pains of hunger?

It was . . . disturbing.

Apparently, every day was Lughnasadh to these wealthy women too. Throughout the year, they traveled to different gods-blessed locations to worship Lugh and his family as well as to harvest more Seeds for their Plowed Fields. Seren was their early winter stop.

"She died for the shaft!" A collective breath was taken. "Of wheaaaat!"

The muscles of my mouth strained to remain neutral.

There was far too long a pause between those lines.

Through the blur of grinning, singing faces moving by, I caught Corbin peering my way. I expected to see delight twisting his lips at my suffering—mine sure would if roles were reversed. Instead, they were pressed into a straight line. I angled my head to peer over another set of shoulders and fruit-topped heads bobbing past and . . . two Raven Folk lads were in conversation with him and Owen by the Palace of Stars, near the center of Crescent Street on the Beggar's Hole side of Seren.

Carrion Crime Syndicate Ravens.

Something light hit my face and I reared back. A ball of cotton plopped onto the ground in front of me. I had just registered the object when I was hit again. The ladies were bouncing on the balls of their feet and throwing cotton balls and petals at us while crying out, "The seed! The seed! The seed!"

What.

Was.

Happening.

"Great Seeds," the priestess intoned and the Ladies quieted. "Show us your berries swollen with life's vigor!"

I lifted my palm, eyes round and mouth clamped tight. The blue ball rolled toward my fingers with the movement; I started to sputter and caught myself. One look from the fellas and I would crack.

Emeline, who was now positioned across from me, grinned and bunched her shoulders in excitement.

I found myself smiling back. The feminine part of me relished the girlishness of this moment. Men didn't dance and sing around each other

The Heartbreak Show

to welcome new acquaintances into their circle of friendship. Aye, the weirdly intense worship of Lugh was on an alarming, laughable level, their rituals were silly too. But their sisterhood and celebration of each other was beautiful.

"Repeat our sacred oaths," the priestess intoned once more. "I, a handmaiden of Lugh."

I murmured the words, a warmness blooming in my chest.

"A descendant in heart and spirit to the attendants once bound to Eithne's care."

That was an unexpected plot twist. They honored both of Lugh's mothers then.

The priestess lifted her own berry for all to see. "I promise to uphold the ancient vows to honor the gods and cherish each other."

I pretended to speak the lines, skipping the word "promise" and mouthing others. As a halfling, I wouldn't risk the possibility of a magically binding bargain.

"And promise to not share our secrets outside of our Plowed Fields."

Once more, I maneuvered around the bargain.

"By eating this berry, the fruit of Tailtiu, I will preserve the legacy of Lugh and his family."

That part was easy enough.

The ladies placed the berries to their lips and, once finishing their repeated line, plopped it into their mouths.

We gathered these blueberry cousins in the hilly heaths around the northeastern villages when rolling through late summer. Usually, we added them to porridge. But wine-plumped, reconstituted bilberries were delicious, holy stars . . .

"Sponsors come forward."

Emeline stepped toward me and I arched a brow.

"Top your Lady."

Dying suns save me . . .

I compressed my lips together as tight as possible.

Pulling on the ribbon beneath her chin, Emeline untied the bow and my pulse kicked up. Ohhhh . . . *gifting* me her straw hat was the Topping Ceremony.

Well, shite.

Standing on her tip toes, she gently placed the elaborately decorated hat on my head.

Magic slammed into me. My muscles stiffened. A bright, effervescent sensation began pulsing in my veins.

Emeline kissed my cheek, then kissed the other.

She pulled away quickly, her dainty brows drawing close together. "Mrs. Merrick?" She jumped back and clapped a hand over her mouth.

Light was shimmering along my skin.

"A child of Lugh!" a woman shouted.

Terror ripped the breath from my lungs. I . . . I was glowing.

Soft wonder pinked Emeline's cheeks. "I kissed the face of a goddess."

One by one, the Ladies of Lugh fell to their knees before me. A few were weeping.

"A goddess walks among our Plowed Field," the priestess said, practically panting in her excitement. "A daughter of Lugh."

At the commotion, Owen and Corbin turned toward me and gaped—the Syndicate lads no longer in sight. I could make out Owen's mouth forming, "Feck. Me."

Hands touched the pink silk of my skirt and Ladies whispered, "Cordelia," in reverence. My face started to grimace at the mention of that decapitated mainlander head of horrors. But, in a way, I supposed I was a Cordelia—a mold of the real women before me. I wasn't a well-bred lady of upper-class eastern society. I was a backwoods Caravan lass who drank straight from the bottle, smoked cigarettes, and shamelessly walked around the train station in a strapless corset.

"Bless us, True Lady of Lugh," the priestess beseeched me.

Magic shimmered down my body at the prayer.

"Daughters of Man . . ." I said before I realized I was speaking, and in my native dialect too. "You are all cows of plenty. Turn your Plowed Fields into a great harvest for those who hunger." The words were light on my tongue. "Share from your tables the food Tailtiu sacrificed her life to provide for *all* instead of hoarding her provisions. Make this an act of worship to Lugh, who generously shared from his table in memory of his foster mother."

"I swear it to you," the priestess cried out. "We will share Tailtiu's bounty and provide a Lughnasadh feast for those who hunger. We will become cows of plenty."

"May the blessing of your prosperity also be theirs."

The magic rushed from me. I wobbled on my feet, my head spinning, but miraculously remained upright.

What . . . that . . . *Holy Mother of Stars*, I answered a prayer! As a living, breathing fae deity!

The weeping around me increased.

Fanatical joy shone in Emeline's round eyes.

Panic, however, was bubbling inside of me again and ready to hit a full boil at the feel of their pawing hands and whispered praises. Eventually they'd snap out of their goddess struck fervor. Or claw me to death in their glamoured-heightened states. I was the closest to touching Lugh they'd ever know.

Raising my skirts the barest inch, not wanting to flash cock boots in their faces, I attempted a step. A ripple of alarm moved through the Ladies.

"Don't leave us!" a voice cried out, followed by equally as agitated agreements.

Frenzied fingers gripped my skirt.

Oh feck no.

I grabbed the parasol hanging off my arm and, locking onto Owen, popped open the umbrella.

He jumped into the air the moment he saw what I was about to do.

But fight-or-flight demanded I run—NOW.

The hands holding onto my skirts tugged. But I was in a full panic at this point and barreled forward. The ties for both my dress skirt and petticoats ripped. I tripped over the falling silk, dropping the parasol, yet managed to hop out of the pools of fabric without losing my balance. Then I was sprinting across the lawn in a bodice, drawers, stockings, my cock boots on full display, and while gripping the straw hat in my fingers.

Pleas and shouts were far too close for how fast I was running.

I glanced over my shoulder and nearly fainted.

Those fecking unhinged Ladies of Lugh were chasing after me!

Chapter Twenty-Two
CIAN LONAN-MERRICK

Owen cut behind me in a sharp landing. The women skidded to a stop as I spun to face him. Wind from his wings whipped at their skirts and blew hats from their heads. Scooping me up—like the damsel in distress I really now was—he flew back toward Corbin, who was waiting in the air.

"Primry Green!" I shouted over the thundering whoosh of his wings. "Ground level."

I was too dizzy from magic loss to stand that high above the streets.

We flew over rooftops, to throw off the Ladies, before angling down alleys. A familiar twinge of knowing nipped at my gut when we turned a corner. A persistent feeling that grew as we angled deeper into the alley. I tapped on Owen's arm and pointed to a space near a gas lamp. After nearly being mauled, I didn't want to face thieves in the shadows too.

I sprang from Owen's hold the moment we landed and began retching.

My entire body was shaking from shock, my head woozy from magic drain. Moons above, this was wretched. I'd rather be hungover from drinking too much. Was this how Filena felt?

Gentle hands scooped back the long strands of my wig. "I can't marry you now, love bug."

I started laughing, appreciating Owen's call back. Stars, I needed something to break the tension inside of me. Slowly, I straightened, pressing a hand to my still churning middle, and took in our surroundings.

A brick building stood at my back with two servant entries. A nightclub, I believed. Boisterous piano music was spilling out of the partially open windows a story above us. The flicker of lamplight warmed the space around us, though we stayed in its darker patches. Across the alleyway was another brick building, but its atmosphere seemed more relaxed. A casino, perhaps? Or a sit-down restaurant?

"So," Corbin awkwardly drawled, gesturing at me, "you glow."

I erupted into laughter all over again at his comment; I couldn't help it. All I could think about was that delightfully lewd romance about Lugh and his shining cock.

"I apparently have a goddess form," I said, wiping tears from my eyes. "And she's . . . she's a sassy bitch"—I started laughing once more—"The priestess had the audacity to ask for a blessing. And I . . . the goddess me . . . she called them all cows"—I fell into another round of laughter—"called them cows and . . . and . . . told them to share their plenty."

I was on the verge of wheezing at this point. That whole ceremony was the most deranged thing I'd participated in and I enjoyed all kinds of kinks. I blew out a slow breath. My chest was heaving from laughing so hard. I wiped at more tears, the fellas too.

Gods, it felt good to laugh like this.

I had been dying inside since the first agricultural innuendo.

"Speaking of cows," I said, exhaling another slow, measured breath, "mine is in a Molly house named *Beau Fine*."

The fellas immediately sobered.

"The Syndicate stopped you?" I asked next.

"Aye," Corbin answered, "to ask what our business is on their nest."

Owen added, "Establishing connections with a few bosses for Rhylen, we told them."

"Then they saw the Ladies of Lugh and flew away faster than the wind." Corbin studied me. "Not even a second later, you began to shine."

I fell against the brick wall behind me and peered up at the stars to gather my thoughts. I had glowed.

Glowed.

"You're sure your cow is in a male brothel?" Owen asked.

I rolled my head toward the lads. "Emeline mentioned two other places, the Palace of Stars and a nightclub named *The Crow and Bar*." Owen pulled a face of disgust. Aye, it was a terrible name.

"*Beau Fine* makes the most sense," Corbin agreed.

Almost every village had a brothel. But it was illegal to entertain the same sex and gender on the mainland. A male house of ill-repute would be the last place a lady would tread. Not even half-crazed, zealous ones.

I paused.

Actually, nothing would surprise me about that lot of women. Maybe the Syndicate underestimated them.

I sighed. "*Beau Fine* rhymes with 'bovine.'"

Owen snorted.

"I'm too indecent for polite society." I gestured to my drawers. "The Ladies of Lugh will immediately recognize my shiny arse too."

"I'll take the Beggar's Hole strip," Corbin said to Owen and I relaxed. It would be much faster for them to hunt for *Beau Fine*.

Owen nodded, then considered me. "You'll be fine here by yourself?"

"If trouble finds me"—I patted the brick building I leaned against—"I'll slip into this fine establishment." I shooed them away with my gloveless hand. The glove I had removed for the berry was probably in the skirts I also left behind.

I expected them to leave with that last reassurance.

Instead, the lads, for the first time since landing in this alley, took me in, their grins crooked and eyes crinkled in humor. I looked ridiculous. Opportunistic strumpet that I was, I declared, "Goddess pose," then stuck my arse out, touched my gloved hand to my lips in a flirty smile, and kicked up a leg behind me to show off a cock boot.

My brothers both laughed, shaking their heads.

"Only you, *Cordelia*," Owen teased.

"Do *not* tell Glenna—"

"Oh darlin'," Owen drawled with a mischievous grin, "no bargain." Then he shifted into a raven and flew off.

Corbin chuckled and then shifted into the air next.

Feathered peckers.

I fell against the stone wall once more and heaved a sigh. The music changed above me to a rollicky tune and a cheer went up followed by whistles. Maybe someone outside had a smoke. I desperately needed something to ease my frayed nerves.

Placing the Lughnasadh's Day hat to my crotch, I inched into the warm lamplight. At the corner, I pressed myself to the cool bricks and peered around the bend. A smattering of small parties strolled along the lawn, too engaged in conversation to notice me. The sidewalks, thankfully, were relatively thin compared to the bustling activity a block away. I appeared to be at the far end of Crescent Street, on the opposite side of the market. And not a Lady of Lugh in sight.

Encouraged, I stepped more around the bend and froze.

Another insistent knowing pinch twisted in my gut—and I stilled.

My gaze slid to the sign above the door.

Bó Finne

The Heartbreak Show

The White Cow.

A brothel of males for males named Beau Fine . . .

Oh dear, sweet Emeline—no. It was pronounced *fin-nuh*, not "fine." The White Cow was a magical faerie tale creature whose milk never ran dry and whose path formed *Bealach na Bó Finne*—the Milky Way. I didn't know many old tales, but all fae knew this one and, thus, their mortal pets.

A delighted part of me wanted to double over in laughter. Gods was *Bó Finne* a cleverly lewd tongue-in-cheek name for a male brothel on the City of Stars.

But I was starting to panic again.

This was why my Sight insisted we land here.

My faerie cow, whose magic milk apparently also never ran dry, had to be hidden in this establishment.

I started to step back into the shadows when a servant's door pushed open to a flushed, giggling middle-aged woman in a silk gown. A well-sculpted man, perhaps my age, leaned against the doorframe, shirtless and in tight, unlaced breeches that hung low on his hips. His auburn hair was falling out of the corded tie at the nape of his neck. A sultry smile teased his rouge-stained lips.

Ah, so the men serviced more than males and these doors were discreet exits.

"Work for me," the woman pleaded. "A footman, perhaps. Then we can—"

"Mrs. Halifax," he murmured, "I wouldn't dare ruin our time among the stars—"

She leaned up on her tiptoes and kissed him with a grunting, sloppy desperation that would be humorous if it didn't look like she was trying to claw her way into his skin. Gently, the man cupped her by the shoulders and eased her away with a wink. The woman took a few steps backward and, upon seeing me, squealed. Then she erupted into another fit of giggles before dashing past me and out of the alley.

I flashed the man an are-you-all-right look. But he didn't notice. His gaze was falling down my body in a slow perusal of my state of disrepair, lingering on the hideous red monstrosities on my feet.

"The goddess!" a woman screeched.

My head whipped back toward Crescent Street. The galloping heart in my chest spurred faster.

"Feck," I hissed. "Feck! Feck! Feeeeeck!"

"I see her shining face!"

I was glowing—again? I studied my hands and nearly deflated into a puddle on the cobbled street. Just the gas lamp glow.

I pivoted back toward the alley entrance and could weep. The male prostitute was still here, peering around me to the six Ladies of Lugh dashing our way.

"I need you to hide me."

"Ladies of Lugh are not welcome in this establishment anymore."

My brows shot up. *Anymore*? There was a whole story here that I was dying to know. But this wasn't the time. The man pointed at the Lughnasadh's hat in my hand. *Oh*. "No," I said with a wild shake of my head. "I'm not one of them. Not really. I faked the . . ."

The dimple appearing on his right cheek stole the words right off my tongue. I knew that dimple. The sultry way his lips curled in invitation despite rejecting my plea was oddly familiar too. It was the cinnamon brown eyes sweeping across my disheveled state, however, that silenced the pounding blood in my ears.

"Drew Barclay?"

He went preternaturally still. "Where did you hear that na—" He gasped, his features sharpening. "Cian?"

"I'm hurt you believe someone this beautiful would be anyone else."

He genuinely smiled then. "Damn, but you do get prettier every year."

"Daughter of Lugh!" the priestess shouted, raising my pink silk skirt above her head. Silver moons above, she was spry for an older woman. Or compelled by magicked fervor.

Drew started laughing under his breath. "What have you gotten yourself into now, Cian Merrick?" With another chuckle, he tipped his head to follow him.

I jumped into the low-lit service hallway and slammed the door behind me. My fingers were shaking, but I slid the bolt into place and then slowly spun toward my former Autumn Night Market lover from South Tribe.

Chapter Twenty-Three
CIAN LONAN-MERRICK

The threat of being sold into prostitution was a living fear I carried most of my life. Three weeks ago, that was almost my reality, too. At The Wild Hunt, after being arrested and before Rhylen arrived, I had willingly traded myself in a bargain with Bram Fiachna to pay for reparations in Glenna's stead. And, since I couldn't easily look those arseholes in the eyes when they faced me, not without putting Rhylen at risk of paying for my insubordination, I hadn't *seen* their intended trick.

My fingers curled into fists.

I would have agreed to anything to spare her.

Glenna didn't know of my bargain, though. I made Rhylen, Filena, and the lads promise to keep silent. I never wanted Glenna to feel she owed me a favor simply for loving her. Plus, she had her own wounds to bury and I . . . I had mine.

An ache squeezed inside of me until it hurt to breathe. I needed my Glenna. I needed her sharp wit to calm my chaos and her physical touch to comfort the ghost pains still bruising my body. Gods how I loved that sassy hen to distraction, and I felt her absence keenly.

Drew grabbed a loose linen shirt from a pile on the floor and threw

The Heartbreak Show

it over his head.

I blinked. "South Tribe sold you?"

"I only had a ten-year contract. Moved to Seren over the summer."

I took Drew in again, from the rings gracing his long fingers to the antiquated style of breeches he wore. We were Autumn Night Market dalliances since the age of nineteen, though I had known him since we were sixteen. Both runaways taken in by the Caravan fae. Both attracted to all genders, sexes, and races. But I hadn't seen him this past year and figured he had either been sold or he had moved on from our annual affairs.

"Farris Leith." A corner of his mouth kicked up. "My new name."

I snorted. That was a bloody brilliant name. One that translated to "vigorous, wet, dripping male" ... my smile started to slip as my thoughts caught up to me. It was a consort's name.

Farris moved toward me, each step sensual and calculated. "Why is a poor Caravan indentured being chased by the Ladies of Lugh while wearing"—he pointed to my one glove, the drawers still tied around my waist, the cocks boots, then said—"a silk bodice from this year's Vanderbilt Leeson catalogue?"

I was wearing *what*?! I could almost hear George chuffing, the wee bastard.

What was this stars damned Vanderbilt Leeson catalogue? Were they a dress designer on Seren?

No, not important. Not right now.

My heart rate was a hummingbird's wings. My breath trembled in short, uneven pants. "You're now a—"

"A Molly. Mary-Ann. Rent boy, aye."

I lowered my voice. "Were you forced?"

He chuckled low, a bitter, humorless sound. "Poor village slum lads like you and me have few options outside of the Caravans."

Farris leaned his shoulder on the brick wall adjacent to the door I rested against.

"The consorts . . ." He pointed behind him and said more softly, "We're a family."

And poor village slum lads like us didn't have families or communities who wanted us. The fae saw us as their pets, too. Not their equals.

His eyes dipped to my mouth. "Why are you in Seren, Cian?"

I sighed. I looked unhinged; I might as well sound mad too. "I'm looking for my faerie cow."

Farris moved closer to me, his eyes still fixed on my lips. "You lost a *crodh sidh* on Seren?"

I forgot that Farris was part fae himself, the bastard son of a backwoods mortal woman and a wild fae male from the Greenwood. His mam was thrown out of the village for her affair with a tree spirit. Farris was raised in a brothel until he ran away when he aged out of the brothel's protection.

"Aye," I confirmed. "The cash cow Ren Cormac hid in Stellar Winds Casino is my birthright."

His gaze flicked back up to mine, but I focused on the space between his brows.

"That's *your* cow?" He started softly laughing, like I was a few marbles short of a sound mind and he found that adorable.

Loud banging shook the back-alley door I leaned against and I startled, jumping away.

"Do not harbor a daughter of Lugh!" a woman shouted from the other side.

Farris's autumn leaf eyes flew wide.

Muffled shouts sounded from the front before he could ask me what they meant.

"Mrs. Cordelia Merrick entered your debased establishment," a stern voice declared and I swore under my breath. The priestess.

"Your kind are not welcome here," a man with a strong brogue answered.

Farris grabbed my arm and yanked me down the hallway. "Mortal women still have few rights on Seren."

"Mrs. Merrick belongs to us," the priestess snapped back.

He tugged me up a narrow flight of stairs toward the loud piano music.

"If she invokes Mr. Merrick's name, Seren will have no choice but to comply since you are legally *his* property." He paused on the stairs. "Is there a Mr. Merrick?"

"I'm married to the Caravan princess beneath Seren," I rushed out. "Chieftain Rhylen Lonan's sister."

His jaw slackened. "You're mate bonded to a Raven Folk gov?"

"Aye—"

"Mr. Merrick will not take kindly to his wife being coerced into debauchery by one of your harlots."

"Fecking Ladies of Lugh," I muttered.

Farris tugged me up the stairs and down another low-lit hallway. The lively piano music, jeers, and laughter muffled the sounds of pleasure and creaking beds coming from behind the doors we passed.

Nausea gripped my middle.

I enjoyed sex. No—I *loved* sex, but . . . I would have been trafficked into prostitution, by my own da, by the Caravan fae.

"Please tell me you consented to this," I whispered to Farris, on the verge of retching again. He was right, there were few options for poor village lads like us. But this wasn't the only one. "Please tell me this work is what you wanted."

He peered over his shoulder. "Aye, I wanted this."

My muscles relaxed.

"Mainlanders think a Molly house is a brothel." He glanced at me over his shoulder. "Aye, there is sex work but it's far more than that. Men also want a safe space to find companionship. They spend an evening with other men talking, laughing, lifting drinks. Nothing more. Some men hire a consort to just hold them, fully clothed. *That* is their greatest fantasy, to be held."

Tears pricked my eyes. I knew that heartache intimately. Until Rhylen, I hadn't experienced the kind touch of another male. Only cruelty. My brother embraced me often and had since we were young teens. Told me he loved me too.

"Decent pay," Farris continued, "a warm, soft bed, my own room, three meals a day, a family."

Honestly, those amenities sounded dreamy after the village slums and indentured Caravan life.

"The dom is a decent fella?"

"A good male." Farris pulled me into a room and quickly closed the door. "He takes care of us lads."

I brushed away a tear. "Then I'm happy for you."

Farris dipped his head at a half-dressed man wearing heavy cosmetics who angled past us. Another man followed quickly behind him, throwing me a faint smile before disappearing into the hallway.

Why were there men in . . .

Feck. Me.

The room pulled into sharp focus and a giggle bubbled in my chest. George would swoon. Hell, I was swooning.

An entire room of dresses and suits and costumes and cosmetics and—WINGS!

I would rob a blind old lady and her husband's grave for those shimmering black wings.

Shite. No. I needed to focus.

The Heartbreak Show

My cow. I was here to break a generational curse, not do shady things for a pair of wings.

I released Farris's hand, gaining his attention. My gaze swept around the large room. Confirming we were alone, I whispered, "Where's the cash cow?"

"I'll tell you," Farris whispered back, "if you'll deliver a letter with wages to me mam in Ballycarraig."

"Aye, I accept your bargain."

"She's ill," he continued. "I don't trust the post leaving Seren."

My stomach sank. Seren was a greedy nest. "I'll find her a healer too and ensure she's warm and fed."

Farris swallowed thickly and nodded his head. "I'll find a few lads to sneak your cow out of *Bó Finne* without the Syndicate catching wind."

I sucked in a quiet breath. "Why would they help me?"

"Pissing off the Seren govs is what we lads live for."

I nearly searched his eyes, but I was still feeling a wee dizzy from magic loss. The slight shudder following his words said it all, though. Delight danced in my thrumming pulse. I hoped my creepy arse cow made Glenna shiver, too. The sadistic cake witch enjoyed my reactions to Cordelia far too much.

"Two Traveler Folk are with me." His brows bent low. I was clearly alone in the alley when he found me. "They're returning here."

"We need a distraction." He tilted his head while studying me again and more strands of auburn hair fell from his loose tie. "A show for the dance hall."

Goosebumps fleshed across my skin. "What if the dom decides I can't leave—"

"Guests put on shows from time-to-time."

I bit the inside of my cheek and peered around the room.

"And," Farris continued, "the dom is at the Palace of Stars. Dinner with our new Corvus Rook. Only a couple of boss underlings in charge tonight."

Cosmetics cluttered the lamplit vanities. Jewelry hung from pegs on the wall and spilled out of cases. Wigs rested on solid stands, not creepy death masks. My gaze rested on a familiar object and I drew in a trembling breath—a gancanagh's dudeen.

At the sight, multiple thought strands hit me all at once.

The room tilted. Whispers tickled my mind. The voices were growing louder and louder with each tight breath too.

No.

I gritted my teeth.

I didn't have energy to spare for this. Still, in the strange upside-down clarity defogging my head, the magic's message faded into bright visibility. My Sight was trying to tell me this was the right path. All the other times it acted like this too.

And I *knew* the perfect distraction.

"Can you ask two men to make 'fire' behind me with those scarves?" I pointed to the yellow and red chiffon hanging from pegs on the far wall. Farris dipped his head. Walking farther into the room, I murmured, "I'll need tobacco. A pair of men's trousers with lady's drawer's underneath. No wig." I strode toward one of the closets and rummaged through the garments until my fingers touched ribbed boning and ivory damask. "This lacy corset for a top."

I was already salivating just thinking of the delicious curves of Glenna's waist and breasts in this gorgeous piece. The color, the style . . . it was perfect for her. And now to claim a souvenir for me. A grin alighted across my face as I spun on my heel and pointed to the wall.

"And those wings."

Chapter Twenty-Four
GLENNA LONAN-MERRICK

I blew a wayward strand of hair from my eyes. A light sheen of sweat dewed my face from cooking over the fires while simultaneously rushing back-and-forth during our midnight meal prep. The sourdough starters weren't quite ready yet, so I baked over a dozen rustic loaves with the little yeast I had left. Without a dedicated, enclosed kitchen, it was growing harder to regulate proofing in the cooler night temperatures too.

Moira and Braelin lined up pots of roasted vegetables beside the bread I was slicing. After a quick fork test and extra pinch of salt, Braelin began mashing the cooked vegetables into a savory spread. Gran hummed a tune while sprinkling a light dusting of cinnamon over the wild apples Moira had sliced earlier in the evening.

I could moan with the smells swirling around me. Tonight, we had meat for our bean and barley soup, a rare indulgence my brother wanted to gift his tribe. My mouth had been watering since browning the cubes of beef in lard and wild garlic.

Finally finished, I wiped my hands on my apron and moved away from the table for the children, elderly, and expectant mothers to serve themselves first. I couldn't recall the last time I had known such food riches. I might weep in joy over the cramps from eating so much.

When I wasn't sick with worry, that is.

I peered up at Seren and swallowed. Since Cian left, I had been on edge. It wasn't normal for bonded mates to separate minutes after exchanging vows. My primal state wanted to tear apart Caledona Wood until he was irritating me with his nonsensical schemes again.

That man truly had far too much energy.

When he turned that boundless energy on me, though? I no longer cared about anything save the possessive crush of his lips, the claiming touch of his hands as he gripped my hips, the teasing caress of his fingers sliding down my body, the deliciously whispered confessions against my throbbing pulse.

Sex with Cian was a religious exp—

I groaned. That preening doxy wouldn't get me to confess that he was a god in bed. Not even in my private thoughts. No matter how much my primal state frothed at the mouth to take him in every way imaginable from moonrise to sunset. Stars, if I didn't calm down, I would embarrass myself in front of the camp the moment his sparkly arse appeared with that up-to-no-good grin of his.

My family and friends sat at their usual spots around the communal fire, laughing. Braelin and Sean cozied up close, their heads pressed together as he cupped her face while speaking low near her ear. Her blushing smile warmed my heart. The soft way he kissed her cheek too. They were the cutest lovebirds.

I blew out a slow breath and looked around for Filena. But seeing her gray eyes would make me think of Cian and . . . I clenched my jaw and shifted on my feet. Maybe George would keep me company? We could trade Cian stories, to roll our eyes over his antics and innuendos. Aye, I was getting so twitchy, I might march into the woods and demand that

Cake Witch Raven

the fluffy lad cuddle with me.

Kalen's piercing gaze tracked me across the fire for a second before turning back to Finn. Had Cian asked him to keep an eye on me? Or was my agitation that obvious?

"Glennie?"

I jumped and turned toward my brother, eyes wide. "Is everything well?"

"Oh aye." Rhylen studied my face. "You look distressed, though."

Shite. I forced myself to unclench my jaw and uncurl my fists. Rhylen peered out into the dark edges of the forest toward our wagons. "Where's Cian?"

"He . . . went to the train station."

A broody line creased between Rhylen's brows. "The trains stopped running hours ago."

Cian owed me for this secrecy.

I looped my arm through my brother's and tugged him into a walk. "Where is my sister hiding?" I needed to change the subject away from Cian. A self-satisfied corner of Rhylen's mouth perked up and I grimaced. "I just threw up a little."

He erupted into laughter and I melted. Seeing my brother so happy was the sweetest icing on the richest cake. I nuzzled in closer and leaned the side of my head on his upper arm as we ambled aimlessly around center camp.

"You'd tell me if you were troubled, aye?" he slowed to face me, taking my hands in his. "Or Gran, at least."

"Aye."

He waited a few seconds for me to elaborate. When I didn't, he gently squeezed my fingers. "There isn't anything I wouldn't do for you, Glennie Lo," he whispered. "I love you—"

Rhylen froze, his gaze riveted to my wrist.

The Heartbreak Show

To the raven mark soaring across my skin.

"When?" he rushed out.

I couldn't tell by the rough, deep timbre of his voice if he was angry or elated. But when his smiling eyes lifted to mine, my heart skipped a happy beat.

"Early this evening."

He pulled me into a tight embrace. "If he hurts you in any way—"

"I'll peck his mind to insanity."

"Good."

I pushed back enough to meet my brother's eyes. "You believe Cian would hurt me?"

"No," he said quickly with a little shake of his head. "He would cleave his soul from his body with a dull, bent spoon before ever hurting you. But," he added with a rascally smile, "amuse me."

"Well, then, *protective* older brother"—his mischievous smile grew—"I'd peck his mind to insanity, then bind him to a tree for the Wee Folk to find."

A single, dark brow peaked. "The . . . Wee Folk?"

"All those little hands and feet crawling all over him with no way to itch."

Rhylen threw his head back with a loud laugh. "I'm not sure who is more terrifying, you or Filena?"

A smug grin settled on my lips. "Break Filena's heart gently, darlin'."

My brother's conspiratorial smile filled my night sky with warm sunlight. Filena could curse in this physical mortal plane. But, as cousins to the wood ravens who guided souls into the Otherworld, Raven Folk could deny a soul entry by pecking out the physical eyes to feed to the old fae, thus damning that soul to the Underworld.

"Now," Rhylen said, narrowing his dark purple eyes on me—eyes so much like Gran's. "Why did Cian leave his newly bonded mate behind at camp?"

I was going to growl at Cian for putting me in this position.

I opened my mouth, hoping, praying that something clever and witty fell off my tongue. I had made a bargain with my mate and wouldn't betray his trust no matter what.

"Rhylen!" Sean hollered, saving me from conjuring up an excuse for the gobshite.

My brother's gaze darted over my head, that furrow between his brows appearing once more as he loosened his embrace.

"A flyer from West Tribe," Sean said when reaching us. "News for the chieftain."

Rhylen kissed my forehead before taking my hand in his and pulling me toward center camp with him and Sean. "Don't think we're done talking," he whispered to me while walking. "I know you, Glennie Lo, and you're covering for Cian."

"Why would I cover for that eejit?" I playfully snapped back.

Rhylen just chuckled.

A couple of minutes later, we paused in front of a middle-rank male from West Tribe. Filena moved through the gathering to stand beside Rhylen with a side-long glance my way. She tapped the raven mark on her wrist and mouthed, "Wild Onions." Of course, she *knew*. I playfully glared and mouthed, "Buttons lover."

Rhylen quietly cleared his throat and both me and Filena straightened.

"Sire," the male began and my brother flinched. It was barely noticeable. Rhylen continually struggled with his new position of power despite his smiles and calm command. To be respectfully acknowledged as a gov by someone at West Tribe, though? It was strange for me to hear too. "A new head elder was elected in West Tribe."

People around us shared curious looks and gathered in closer.

The Heartbreak Show

Rhylen tipped his head for the messenger to continue.

"Skye Fiachna-Brannon, Chiefess of West Tribe."

I quietly gasped. Shocked whispers murmured around camp. A female? West Tribe had a *female* top gov? And Rhylen thought he had ruffled feathers by electing female elders onto his council. Wild fae in the Greenwood had female leaders, though, including war chiefs. Yet the gods had chosen only males to govern the Caravans . . . until now.

My wings begged to appear and fluff in approval.

Bryok's first cousin was the only decent Fiachna in that whole greedy, shady lot. But hadn't Rhylen banished the Fiachnas from West Tribe? Clearly, the elders had disagreed after Rhylen's gov status was revoked.

Finn leaned close to Kalen. "Brannon?"

Hearing Finn, Sean answered, "Kev Brannon most likely."

Finn's jaw slackened. Kev was Finn's foster brother, the youngest son of the famed Ó Brannon family who trained wild fae orphans for Seren's Thieves' Guilds. But . . . Skye had rejected him before exchanging vows beneath the Truth Telling Tree a few years ago, scandalizing both families.

Falling moons, the gods sure were busy dismantling and remaking West Tribe.

"Pass on our congratulatory wishes to Chiefess Fiachna-Brannon," Rhylen said to the messenger. "She's welcome at our table any time and has my full support."

"Our chiefess invites your family and elders to a feast in seven days."

Rhylen bowed his head. "We would be honored." The messenger gaped at my brother's equalizing gesture. Straightening a beat later, Rhylen gestured to our food. "Sit with us a spell before returning?"

The male nodded, shaking Rhylen's hand.

Was I dreaming? In what world would a middle-rank from West

Tribe desire Rhylen's hospitality? Filena didn't seem surprised, though. That lass was full of secrets, just like Cian.

The muscles in my gut clenched. My gaze roamed to Seren and I drew in a shaky breath. Was he in trouble? I huffed a laugh under my breath. No, that brazen heifer was causing trouble. Or the center of it. He was wily enough to riddle himself out of any situation though—I hoped. How I wished I could see his feminine side prance and flounce across the City of Stars in that beautiful pink gown. I would endlessly swoon at the sight.

But if anyone touched *my* mate, flirted with him, tipped their hat at her, I would destroy their arses and without remorse. The pretty eejit was *mine*.

"We had a change in the elder council too."

The messenger's voice snapped me out of my spiraling thoughts. I swallowed back the tightening nerves knotting in my throat. Maybe I should start making a dessert. Something to keep my hands and mind busy.

My brother walked our guest over to the table and handed him a wooden bowl the fellas had carved. Sean followed after them, leaving Braelin with me and Filena.

One of Filena's auburn brows kicked up. "So, darlin'," she practically purred in delight, "you married before he went to Seren, did you?"

"Shhh," I quickly hushed, placing my fingers to her lips. "I made a bargain."

I expected Filena to *know*. But Braelin?

Speaking of the lass, she nervously nibbled on her bottom lip. "Finn told us to distract Rhylen and why. Then he grabbed Owen and Corbin."

I stilled. Wasn't that breaking his . . . I pushed out a slow breath. No, that was before Cian's bargain. Plus, the bargain only stated to keep Cian's birthright and trip to Seren a secret from Rhylen.

"We've separated Rhylen from Sean at times too," Braelin continued. "One less person to interrogate, aye?" I dropped my hand from Filena's face. Oh fine . . . I supposed Braelin could know my and Cian's secret wedding. "We've been keeping both lads busy as much as possible."

Filena pulled a piece of moss from her hair, flicking me an innocent smile.

I snorted. "A terrible burden, pet."

"Aye, we have suffered greatly," Filena confirmed with a straight expression. "Pity us."

We were quiet for only two seconds before the three of us burst into laughter.

Relaxing my shoulders, I loosed a dramatic sigh, then linked my arms with theirs. My stomach grumbled for the delicious scents behind me. But I'd wait until Rhylen and Sean had moved on to other tasks this evening. "Want to meet Cordelia?"

"Who?" Braelin asked.

"My new pet. Cian loathes the sight of her."

Filena grinned. "Cian repellent is a gift from the gods."

I giggled. "George needs to find us each a Cordelia to prop in front of our wagon windows. Falling stars, his face! I would molt feathers from laughing so hard."

We moved away from the fire toward the wagons, laughing and gossiping and planning other practical jokes against Cian. Before disappearing into the woods, Filena peered over her shoulder at Rhylen and flashed him a wicked smile. My brother wouldn't interrupt us, he respected our space, but he would fixate on what that smile meant . . . and not think of Cian.

Gods, I loved my sisters.

Chapter Twenty-Five
CIAN LONAN-MERRICK

Owen and Corbin ambled into the dance hall on the second floor of *Bó Finne*, frantically peering around the room for me. I poked my head farther around the velvet stage curtain and discreetly wiggled my fingers. Corbin spotted me first and mouthed, "What are you doing?"

"Farris," I whispered, twisting to face my old lover. "Those Traveler lads in the audience are with me."

"Want them to watch you or participate in *other* White Cow activities?"

I bit back a snort despite my dizzying fear. The wrong ears were everywhere, though, so I played along. "Those fellas need to lift their skirts and ride a *Bó Finne* into the night." The Lughnasadh's Day hat was bundled in a dark sheet in Farris's hands. "Give this to the looker with the longer hair. He likes roleplay."

Winking at me, Farris disappeared behind the stage to move toward Owen and Corbin without drawing attention. A moment later, the curtain ties were released and the stage plunged into darkness. Two shirtless, muscled men knelt opposite each other, holding an end to the red and yellow scarves. Taking their cue, I ambled onto center stage and

The Heartbreak Show

positioned with my back to the dance hall.

I was so lightheaded, I had to focus on breathing.

This felt wrong without Glenna. The patrons here, however, were no different than those who attended the annual mating ritual at the Autumn Night Market explicitly to appreciate the male form and for the high of arousal—myself included.

But gods, when I told Rhylen I would show my ankles and shake my arse as much as it took to not eat termite flour bread, I didn't think it would come to *this*.

My cursed cow better bring prosperity to Rhylen's tribe or—

I blinked.

That didn't make sense.

How could something that would bring me prosperity . . . also be my curse?

Kalen's words faded back into memory. *You carry the soul of Cian's magic. A generational curse or blessing, as it's called in the Greenwood.*

I blinked again.

"Sir," I said to one of the shirtless men. A dark brow kicked up in reply. "Is a magical cow birthright a curse or a blessing?"

"Uh . . ." He exchanged a nervous look with his friend. "A blessing?"

"Godsdammit," I hissed under my breath. "All this fecking time." I pointed at the other man. "She's giving me an opportunity." Both men slowly nodded.

The fear knotting in my chest loosed to a breathy laugh.

This fecking faerie cow *wasn't a curse*.

I . . . I wasn't a curse.

The Maiden's quest to reclaim my birthright began at the train station, when I created a coin beggar's show to reverse our tribe's destitution and protect Rhylen from spiraling in his grief. I had declared that I would do *anything* for my brother, one of the great loves of my life.

And Glas Gaibhnenn, according to Kalen, was a faerie cow that appeared in times of famine.

Lifting my chin, I gritted my teeth. Gods, I was terrified. My entire body was shaking, my heart pumping so fast I thought it might rip past my ribs. But I had to believe the Maiden had protections in place. I *was* her favorite re-souling, after all.

A smile trembled on my lips.

"Gents," the dance hall host shouted from the other side of the stage. "We have an impromptu boylesque *After Midnight Act* for you." A round of applause echoed in the small space.

Boylesque?

"A gancanagh to *wet* your desire and break your *hard, throbbing* hearts." I bounced on the tips of the cock boots as men whistled and cheered. "Music! Lights!"

From behind the velvet drapes, shadows darkened as oil lamps were turned down. The piano started up, a sultry song.

"Glenna," I whispered, "I dance for you."

The curtain started to slowly open and, after inhaling deeply, exhaling slowly, I began pulsing my hips to the melody. Wings covered most of my backside. But not my trouser-clad arse. More whistles, jeers, and cheers went up. The shirtless men in front of me waved the scarves in an up and down motion.

Closing my eyes for a few seconds, I formed an image of Glenna in my mind. The spill of her black, rag-curled hair across our pillow. Her crowing smiles and laughs—feck, how I loved her taunts. I swooned over the glee in her eyes when winning our verbal foreplay and humorous bets, too. The softness of her gorgeous breasts made me weak in the knees...

I shut off *that* image.

The Heartbreak Show

If I didn't rein in my thoughts, the lads here would get the wrong idea.

"Beware," I projected, needing the distraction. "For he will break your heart."

Sinking my fingers into my hair, to flex my bicep, I peered over the black feathers fastened to my shoulders and flashed my ash-rimmed eyes at the room—promptly locking onto Owen and Corbin, who gaped at me. But not in horror. The humor cracking across their wide-eyed faces at me in a pair of wings while performing a Fire Dance doused my racing nerves. I puckered a flirty kiss at Owen who rolled his bottom lip in to hold back a laugh.

"One touch," I sang out, "and he'll own your body."

I turned to face the audience, arcing my hips to the carnal beat as the fingers once in my hair slid down my chest, and across the front of the corset I wore. But when reaching just below my navel, I halted my descent with a dramatic wink at everyone and drawled, "Hello, boys."

The room thundered with cheers.

A door slammed open in the back of the room. Heads turned as the priestess charged in, barely sparing me a glance. I was in tight-fitting breeches, my disheveled hair reaching the elven-prosthetic jewelry tips of my ears, with my male figure on display. I was speaking my native dialect in a lower registered voice too.

Farris tapped on Owen's shoulder, handing him my covered-up hat while whispering in his ear. Nodding, Owen tugged on Corbin's sleeve then followed Farris out of the dance hall.

A doorman angled past the fellas into the room and skidded to a stop before the priestess. Fecking stars above, that woman was bolder than brass. What on the Mother's green earth gave that Lady the notion that she could boss around a goddess? What would she do to me, if caught? I shuddered at the thought.

"Debauchers," the priestess shouted over the audience. The piano faltered. "Hand over Cordelia Merrick. She must be delivered to her husband."

Men booed but she didn't back down.

I snapped and pointed for more light. The only person allowed to upstage me was my mate. But I'd also lean into this disruption for our needed distraction. A couple men moved along the edge of the stage, turning up oil lamps. As I hoped, the room turned their attention back onto the flirty swing of my hips and flex of my muscles.

"His honeyed tongue"—I suggestively licked my lips—"will ruin you for anyone else."

The burly doorman took the priestess by the elbow and the crazed older woman yanked herself out of his reach.

"If the goddess is sullied by—"

"Lads," I called out and lifted the gancanagh's pipe to my mouth. "Who has a match?"

The men twisted on their seats to face me, several jumping to their feet with match books in hand. I slinked toward a younger man, biting my lower lip at those who brushed the feathers of my large wings as I preened by them. Unlike the Heartbreak Show, however, I wouldn't touch anyone, not without Glenna here, not without her permission.

A part of me was grateful she wasn't here, though. An epiphany was blooming in the dark corners of my most vulnerable memories. The Ladies of Lugh aside, performing a boylesque in a Molly house was strangely . . . healing.

My whole life, people had judged me, abused me, spit on me for having more than one gender, for being attracted to more than one sex. But in this room? In all my exchanges with the consorts? I was embraced. Aye, the patrons here were lusting after me too—that was the point of this little side-show. Still, I had never felt so safe and free to openly be .

The Heartbreak Show

. . *me.*

And so did others in this room, like Farris had shared.

A delighted, vindicative laugh was building inside my chest.

Feck you, Hamish!

The chosen audience member struck a match. I rested my foot on the edge of the table to display the large cock boot, earning a laugh from those around me. Glenna would be rolling her eyes so hard at me right now, especially as I stroked the hideous phallic footwear while leaning in for the lucky lad to light the tobacco. The men roared in approval.

I puffed on the pipe and . . . *dying suns* . . .

A surge of magic moved down my body, different than my goddess form. A power that flexed my muscles and sharpened my senses. The fast flutter of heart rates filled my ears. Across from me, the young man's pupils dilated; a soft breath passed his parting lips.

Oh feck.

W—what just happened?

Was . . . I actually a Love-Talker?

I lowered my leg and pivoted away from the young man, careful not to meet eyes as I made my way back to the stage, internally swearing.

Just grand.

Fecking brilliant.

It was a Topping Ceremony all over again and just when I was starting to have fun.

My stomach sank as another bolt of magic pulsed through me. I could hear the continued acceleration of heartbeats, the quickening of breaths. Blood pumped hard in the veins bulging down my arms. My muscles were more defined and noticeably rippled with each step.

I handed the pipe to a random gent before climbing the steps back onto the stage. More magic equaled a larger drain and I was already teetering on the cusp of that dangerous line. Still, the show must go on. Farris would return for me when it was time to pull the curtain.

The silky piano melody glided over my flushing skin. I ran a hand down my arm and across my chest in a provocative touch the crowd devoured.

Feck it.

"If he speaks," I sang out in sultry tones, "he talks only of love."

I would champion them in a social and political war that left bruises soul deep.

"And when he desires *you* . . ."

I met the eyes of a man near the front. Information, secrets, fears rapidly flooded my spinning head.

A heart that craves romance and companionship over sex.

"He will watch the stars with you and share your dreams."

Another pair of eyes.

Dread that the one he loves is embarrassed by him.

"There'll be no shame in your relationship."

More eyes and more reassurances spoken directly to their fears and longings.

The room soaked up my Love-Talker infused words. The piano music had stopped a few minutes earlier, stripping the room vulnerable in the deafening silence. Heart rates around me beat even faster, louder.

I could feel a growing desperation lapping against my waning energy.

Like the Ladies of Lugh, they fevered to capture a piece of me.

Power crept over me at that realization. A knowing that I could harm every person in this room. It was sickening in its building intensity.

The Heartbreak Show

Seductive in its dominance. But I would *not* abuse my magic to break the hearts now beating in the palms of my hands.

I would not become . . . *him*.

Farris crept into the dance hall the exact moment the magic tethering me to the audience snapped. Men blinked in confusion. I stumbled back a step. The hall tilted, then rolled the other direction.

A charged stillness settled on the room.

An uncomfortable kind of quiet that skittered across my skin and burrowed into my heightened animal awareness.

Two Seren Raven Folk moved into the room and locked onto me. The boss underlings? They didn't move, though. Almost as if they were too stunned to . . . do what exactly? No one was misbehaving.

The moment that thought scrolled across my mind, the room erupted.

Chapter Twenty-Six
CIAN LONAN-MERRICK

Men stood from their chairs with pleading shouts to continue. A few approached the stage and fell to their knees.

Why were they bowing before *me*?

I blinked back the haze.

My knees started to give out and I grabbed the velvet curtains.

Damn, wings were heavy. They might be the reason I toppled over in the rapid energy loss hitting me right now. But I'd still rob a bottle from a baby for these gorgeous feathers—

"Cian!" Farris cut through the clamoring gathering toward me.

The priestess shrieked a gasp at hearing my name.

Fecking hell, she was still here?!

The burly doorman, who had apparently been under my spell, realized that, aye, the maniacal zealot was, indeed, still here and swiped for her. The priestess was quick on her feet, though, and maneuvered out of his grasp to push toward the stage.

The two Syndicate boys shifted into ravens, flew across the room, and landed in their elven forms in front of the stage, wings out. They were protecting me from the crowd? A third appeared from backstage

The Heartbreak Show

and began blowing out the stage lamps while shooting me curious looks. Ah, not me, then. They were protecting the building.

But it didn't get darker. The stage remained illuminated.

I glanced down and . . . *oh gods*.

A faint, strange light glimmered along my skin.

I was glowing . . . *again*.

Not as bright as my goddess light, but that didn't matter when there was close to a hundred eyes taking in my fading god form. Was a gancanagh a god? Or was I also manifesting the masculine demi-god side of myself?

"Cian, father of Lugh!" The priestess cried out. "In the splendor of his son's ravens!"

I heaved a sigh. This was getting old.

Still, guilt began gnawing at the edges of each intersecting thought thread racing through my mind. I didn't mean to bewitch the audience. Or trigger the Ladies of Lugh into a religious frenzy. Seren's coercion magic was intense. Thank the moonless skies they'd all forget about their strange encounter with the gods when leaving the City of Stars.

What a ridiculous night.

But . . . of course, I had a magic pipe that enthralled men . . . *at a male brothel*.

Of course, I had a magic cow with milk that never ran dry . . . *at a male brothel*.

And, of course, for my demi-god forms to appear, I needed to don magical cock boots.

A laugh spurted past my compressed lips.

My great-aunt knew my raunchy brand of humor well.

This whole night, she also ensured I held power over Seren instead of the reverse, like I had long feared—a twist of fate I was still trying to wrap my head around. I understood the underlying message, though. No one could own my power *or* my personhood but me—not Hamish, not the Syndicate, Carran, or the Caravans. And I now believed this from the marrow of my soul.

If I could, I'd fluff my wings in happiness. Damn, I loved these feathers.

Farris jumped onto the stage, whispering into the ear of one of the Seren Ravens before circling an arm around my waist. "The Syndicate showed up as protection. Over a dozen Ladies of Lugh have gathered around the entrance demanding we free their goddess, Cordelia Merrick. One started knocking on chamber doors." He pushed us backstage and into the connecting hallway. "The Syndicate believes you're one of our new consorts."

"Not after my *illuminating* performance, they don't."

Farris chuckled. "Never a dull moment with you, Cian Merrick."

We angled down narrow stairs to a large storage room. Farris plucked a shirt from another pile of spares and handed it to me. I unshouldered the wings to slip the tunic-styled shirt on.

"A Traveler Folk glamoured your skin in additional payment for services. That's what the Syndicate lads were told."

"You're not asking me, though," I murmured, shimming the wings' straps back onto my shoulders.

"Your sister has magic. Why wouldn't you?" Farris slid a sly smile my way. "You're a walking spotlight, love. Not surprising."

I barked a laugh at that. Stars above, I really was a shameless hussy, down to my core magic.

My amusement sobered quickly, though.

A strange brewing sensation was vibrating in my chest the farther we strode across the room. The percolating feeling almost unbearable when Farris unbolted a metal door and swung it open. A blast of cool night air bit at the skin of my neck and face. Owen leapt forward and

The Heartbreak Show

pulled me through the door and—I dug in my heels.

In the middle of the alley was a partially charred, black-spotted taxidermized dairy cow forever captured in a bug-eyed, crazed moo.

"The feck is *that*?!"

"Behold," Owen said with a full-body shiver, "your birthright."

Three consorts by the cow stepped away, providing me a better view.

This beast wore four red ladies dress boots. The front ones were nearly burned beyond recognition. Wax fruit had dripped off a blackened straw hat—my face twisted in a grimace—and in a horrifying way that made it look like the flesh was melting off her face. I took a tentative step closer. Was that the singed remains of a garter ribbon on her hind leg?

Gods, was this a joke?

The vibrating sensation in my chest, however, was urging me to touch that monstrosity. No, this was real. The magic was unmistakable. But stars above, this cow looked like she had survived an apocalypse, not a building fire.

She also wasn't green, like her name suggested, but a dappled white and black. Perhaps the green related to her luck and prosperity magic?

"Do you think she glows too?" Corbin asked.

I scrubbed a weary hand down my face and groaned—then stilled. "Did you hear that?"

Corbin pivoted toward the alley adjoining this one and hissed, "Shite."

"We need to go. NOW." Owen moved me closer to my cow. "Jump onto the back."

"Are you mad?" I shot back. "What if I fall off?"

The clomp of shoes echoed on the cobbled street and brick buildings.

"Goddess!" a woman pleaded. "Do not abandon your Plowed Field!"

"Daughter of Lugh!" another shouted.

Farris tipped his head at the consorts. "Distract them."

The men sprang into a run toward the approaching mob. Before rounding the bend, they slid to a stop. Fear flashed across their faces. Then they started wildly gesturing for us to hurry before dashing back. That didn't bode well.

Owen tugged on my arm but I twisted to Farris and kissed his cheek. "Take care of yourself, friend."

A soft smile stole over his lips. "Visit us lads, aye?"

"Aye," I agreed. "I promised to personally deliver a letter." His russet eyes rounded slightly at the reminder of our bargain. "I'll bring my mate—"

"Cian," Owen gritted between clenched teeth.

With one last look at Farris, I stepped onto the brace Owen formed with his hands and swung my leg over my cow as if she were a horse. But the wings knocked me back. Corbin swore and held the wings up while I mounted again. Then, with a humored roll of his eyes, arranged them on either side of where I perched.

A dizzy spell hit me. The alley spun. I began sliding away from the fellas.

There was no mane to grip, no saddle with stirrups.

I was going die.

We hadn't moved yet and I could barely stay on the back of this charred heifer—

My hands involuntarily darted out to clasp what felt like leather strips in my curling fingers, but there was nothing there but air . . . *oh*. A bridle faded into visibility. Was it bound to me? It had controlled my body.

The Heartbreak Show

"Thank the wishless falling stars," Owen muttered as he grabbed the lead rope and quickly looped it around my waist and tied it tight to the back of the bridle, forcing my body to practically embrace my cow's upper back.

The clatter of boots and voices grew closer.

I peered over my shoulder and . . . the blood rapidly drained from my head. Men and women were now running toward me.

Owen removed the sheet around my Lughnasadh's Day hat, not wanting the fabric to catch wind and blow it away. I adjusted my position for him to stuff the lumpy, fruity piece beneath my chest, then I pressed closer to Glas Gaibhnenn's spine. Magic whooshed through me at the contact. A bright, fiery sensation that danced across my skin.

"Hold on," Owen shouted to me over the stampede.

Wind from his wings whipped my hair around my face while the wing gusts from Corbin lashed at my back. Owen wrapped his arms around my cow's neck. I couldn't see Corbin. But a second later we were lifting off the ground. A little wobbly at first.

My stomach rolled.

The vibrating sensation in my chest intensified. Why was it growing stronger? If this taxidermized nightmare transformed into a real beast mid-flight, we were in a steaming heap of sparkly shite.

The alley below became smaller and smaller the higher we ascended. The mob of men and women settled beneath us. Emeline grinned and waved. Did she know I was the same person? I smiled back. That lass was too sweet for that lot of Ladies.

"The Cow of the Milky Way!" a woman shouted. "She lights a path across our sky!"

My eyes squinted. Then I burst into laughter. I hadn't noticed, too consumed with escaping Seren without being torn to pieces, being captured by the Syndicate, or falling to my death.

Well, Corbin, you have your answer.

My fecking faerie cow was blazing brighter than a shooting star.

We cleared the protective glass wall and began descending toward Caledona Wood. This scorched, glowing bovine of prosperity was, officially, the weirdest thing I'd brought to a gathering.

If we made it to camp, that is.

My pulse stuttered to a stop. A conspiracy of Ravens crested over the wall and cawed.

The Carrion Crime Syndicate was fast on our tail.

Chapter Twenty-Seven
GLENNA LONAN-MERRICK

"Sit with me, lass." Gran patted the stump beside her rocking chair.

I slowed my pacing.

Sitting sounded like torture right now. But when Gran arched a make-no-fuss browed look at me, I plopped down onto the log, a growl lodged deep in my chest. I was either wound so tight I could march across Caledona Wood, tearing up trees and tossing them into the sky for days, or deflate until I was a tattered, fraying cotton mound of listless, wasting-away sighs in the grass.

I now had far more respect for growly, primal male problems because good gods this was intense and annoying.

A weary sigh loosened from my tightening throat.

Filena left to oversee the washing between meals and Braelin disappeared to . . . actually, I didn't know. She was a solitary one sometimes, that lass.

My knee bounced and I twisted a strand of hair around my finger.

Gran chuckled. "That boy has driven ye mad fer years."

"That boy is chaos incarnate," I mumbled.

"Oh aye." Gran plucked the hand fidgeting with a loose bow on my dress and tugged me closer. "Ancient wisdom for ye, lass," she whispered.

The territorial anxiety crawling just beneath my skin tensed.

Smiling softly, Gran lifted her hand and—flicked my forehead!

"Stars, Gran!" I reared back. I thought she was going to tuck my hair behind my ear, or some other tender, grandmotherly gesture.

"Ye're an eejit, Glennie Mer," she said on a delighted cackle.

"That's it? That's your ancient wisdom?"

"How long have ye been fae?" She wiped away tears.

I opened my mouth—and froze. She had called me Glennie *Mer*.

The old hen continued to laugh at my suffering. I probably did look a sight. Now that I thought of it, the Folk at camp had been giving me a wide berth all evening. Aye, separating immediately after bonding was *not* done, let alone minutes afterward.

"I panicked," I confessed, pushing back the stinging tears I willed not to fall. "He wanted protection and I couldn't refuse the gobshite in the end."

"Ye crave the chaos he stirs in yer well-measured life, ye do." She chuckled again. "I know ye, my wee Glennie girl. Ye love being driven mad by him."

The knotted muscles in my shoulders bunched higher.

Familiar, repetitive routines soothed me, organized spaces and supplies too.

She was right, though. My life was a mixing bowl of well-measured ingredients.

My competitive, refuse-to-back down nature, however, craved the challenge of Cian's flirty rivalry, wrangling his drunken butterfly tendencies, too. And goddess save him, but that lad needed someone to help keep him anchored to the ground or . . .

My brows pushed together.

The Heartbreak Show

What was that light in the sky?

"Gran." I pointed to Seren. "Can you see—" My hands clapped over my mouth in a sharp gasp. I jumped to my feet. That light was . . . cow shaped.

He did it!

He actually found Glas Gaibhnenn!

"Rhylen!" Where was my brother? I turned in a circle, hunting for his familiar silhouette amongst the bustling camp. "Rhylen!"

A faint chorus of caws sounded from above. My head snapped up. Ravens flocked around the glowing light, avoiding the fella's flapping wings.

I turned around to shout my brother's name and nearly jumped out of my skin when he was suddenly there at my side, Sean, Finn, and Kalen on his other. When had they crept up beside me?

The lines of Rhylen's mouth curved down. A scowl darkened between his brows. "Is that a . . . cow?"

Finn shuddered.

"Aye," Sean confirmed, his voice as uncertain as my brother's. "Owen and Corbie too."

Rhylen slowly turned his intensity on me. "The train station?"

My fingers curled into my palms. Not sure what to tell my brother, I just shrugged, which was the wrong answer.

"Glenna Merrick," he stressed in a low voice, "did Cian cattle raid the Carrion Crime Syndicate?"

That pretty eejit owed me many, *many* favors after this.

"Well, thank the stars Cian is almost here to tell you himself, Rhylen Lonan, since I was on the mainland with *you*."

Kalen huffed a quiet laugh.

My brother's lips wanted to twitch into a smile at my sass—my riddling too—but *Chieftain* Rhylen kept his mouth in a firm line. A twinge of guilt hit my middle. Placing one more stone onto the responsibilities he shouldered wasn't very sisterly of me.

Softening my voice, I added, "Cian traveled to the Underworld for you, brother. For all of us. A course he didn't initiate and one that would have burdened you more than you feel this moment if shared sooner."

At that, the crease between Rhylen's brows deepened. "I believe you." He held my gaze for one more long, worrisome beat then angled his head toward the night sky once more.

The Syndicate flew away from the fellas and toward us. Four males in black silk vests, sleeves rolled up, and wearing felted low top hats on their ear-length or shorter hair shifted beside two females in matching crimson and black striped bustled corset gowns, both with rosettes in their curled and coiffed hair.

"Her Ladyship will arrive momentarily," one of the males said.

A warning hint of canine was Rhylen's reply, his eyes darkening, but he dipped his head. My brother was a gooey cinnamon roll center until his family was threatened. He'd fight all of Seren for Cian.

Our six Seren cousins, in unison, turned to watch the boys land.

My hammering heart was in my throat. I searched for Cian but the faerie cow's shine was blinding. Where was that troublemaking eejit? Was he still on Seren? Tears pricked the back of my eyes right as a roll of anger thundered down my tightening muscles. I would snap every wing on Seren if they refused me my mate.

A hand slipped into mine and I tensed. "Look closer, darlin'," Filena whispered.

Straightening my shoulders, I studied Owen and Corbin right before they touched ground, my eyes hunting once more for the silk pink gown and the messy golden hair that drove me wild. Poor Corbin, the lad's face was practically pressed to the cow's glowing arse.

I stilled.

The Heartbreak Show

Why was there a third pair of wings? On the cow's back?

My gaze trailed the slope of the ruffling mound of black feathers to—I sucked in a sharp breath . . .

. . . And instinct took over.

I began running.

I heard my name being called, but I was a stretchy band pulled tight and released at the sight of my mate. Tears streamed down my cheeks. Angry, joyous tears. I wanted to shake that man and kiss him senseless.

At the same time, Ravenna Blackwing shifted by her lackeys right as the faerie cow began shaking. I registered this, even as I ran by the former Raven queen, especially as I approached Cian's trembling familiar, but my primal state was too driven to reunite with my mate to consider anything else.

Until a loud bellowing moo echoed through the woods, that is. Glas Gaibhnenn bucked her hind legs. Cian unknotted a rope around his waist and fell off his cow in an unceremonious thwump, scrabbling away on hands and knees. The moment Cian hit the ground, the cow stilled. A bright flash of light illuminated Caledona Wood. I skidded to a stop, throwing an arm up to shield my eyes. When the night returned, I lowered my hands and gaped.

Glas Gaibhnenn was frozen into a spelled taxidermized state. Like witch-cursed skunk ornaments. And seven moons, she was hideous. The poor beastie appeared like she had survived a Samhain sacrifice to Lugh and vowed her revenge.

Cian groaned as he fumbled to a stand on wobbly legs in large wings, cock boots, tight trousers that hugged the curves of his legs, an old-fashioned faerie tale styled tunic—similar to Finn's and Kalen's shirts—his hair wind-tousled in a just-bedded mess, ash heavily lining his gray eyes, and . . . were those fake elven ears?

Our eyes locked.

His chest heaved, as if the sight of me took his breath away.

I couldn't breathe either. He was so Otherworldly gorgeous, especially dressed as he was, a blush warmed my neck and face. Stars help me, I was about to swoon.

Behind me, the camp roared with humor, Filena's cackling loudest of them all. A laugh spurted past my compressed lips too. Only Cian would fashionably arrive late to a gathering by riding a vengeful, glowing cow across the sky, led by two strapping winged lads, as if he were Lugh with his two magical ravens.

As if he were . . . a deity.

But he was.

The barest hint of light touched his skin, almost unnoticeable. Almost.

At my warming cheeks, the sensuous lines of his far too-pretty mouth curved higher. He was enjoying my lovestruck stupor far too much.

Fisting a hand on my hip, I cocked my head. "Cow eat your dre—"

In one step, he cupped my face and slammed his lips onto mine.

A storm erupted in my chest at the crushing feel of his perfect mouth. Only half a night gone, but my heart was keening from our separation. Even now, he was still too far away. Clawing my hands into his hair, I twisted the strands around my fingers and yanked him closer, deepening our kiss. He moaned, low and raspy. And sweet goddess, I could devour him this moment. Those sounds of pleasure only heightening the primal desire flaming through me.

In the background, suggestive, teasing hoots and cheers bled through my Cian-drugged possession, and he slowed our kiss. Reluctantly, he pulled away and I could weep. More, more, I was desperate for so much more. Our panting breaths tangled together in a sultry dance. I was melting away in his arms.

Lowering his mouth to my ear, he whispered, "A dozen women ripped the skirt from my body while worshiping me."

"Mmm," I replied in a heady daze. So, the cow did eat his dress. She was an angry thing. Cian straightened as his lips inched up in a delighted smile that was pure mischief. Why was he looking at . . . his words pushed through the fog. Baring my canines, I shoved him back. "What?!"

His grin widened.

A growl rumbled from my chest. I would kill them. All of them.

The arse bit a corner of his mouth in a flirty taunt. "Like my wings, darlin'?"

No, change of plans. First, I would tie him to a tree for the Wee Folk to torture, then I would pluck the eyes out of each woman who dared touch my mate.

He winked, grabbing my hand. "Rhylen gets to torture me first."

Chapter Twenty-Eight
CIAN LONAN-MERRICK

"You read me?"

"Gent of Fem," I murmured, "the murder in your heart is written all over your cock-struck face."

"Full-blooded gods save me from this eejit," she groaned.

Several other smart replies teetered on the edge of her tongue—they always did. But she remained quiet.

I tugged her toward the gathering. Rhylen and Ravenna watched our approach. My brother shifted on his feet, several emotions flitting across his features. Relief. Humor. Love. Frustration.

Letting go of Glenna's hand, I marched past Ravenna without a single acknowledgement and pulled Rhylen into an embrace.

My brother tensed. A spark of panic at my intentional rudeness toward the former Raven queen. Yet, no matter how nonsensical my behavior seemed, Rhylen rarely questioned my deliberate choices. He knew me the way Glenna knew Filena—soul deep.

A heartbeat later, Rhylen wrapped his arms around my waist, beneath the wings, and tightened his hold. "I trust you," he whispered. "No matter what you did or didn't do, I always have your back." Then, loud enough for others to hear, he scoffed, "It wouldn't have come to milking deer, eejit."

"Rhylee Lo," I drawled in reply, "you'd give Gran caterpillar milk if she asked for it." The cheeky old hen winked at me.

"Gods, Cian, if you—"

"'Darlin', it's . . . *God* Cian."

At that, Rhylen quietly laughed. "You're the fecking worst."

I leaned back to grab Rhylen's face, slightly squishing his cheeks, and my brother started chuckling under his breath again. We had shown each other playful affection this way since we were children.

"Tell me I'm *divinely* pretty, Rhy-Rhy."

"Feck off," Rhylen replied, full-on laughing now.

I grinned, then kissed him on the cheek, whispering, "Love you," before turning toward Ravenna.

My body was still slightly shaking from flying down from Seren with just a flimsy rope and magical bridle keeping me aloft. Feck, that was terrifying. Especially as I swore the cow would shift mid-flight.

"My lady," I eventually greeted and narrowed my eyes.

The Maiden's friend she might be, but I didn't trust the former queen and her trickster line. Nor would I allow her to harm my family. Locking onto her gaze, I focused. A surging wave of information crashed into my magic-exhausted state.

> *A Raven male, with feathery black hair that fell across dark purple eyes, walked Ravenna up against a wall. Anxiety flickered across her face, but she quickly reined in her fear.*
>
> *"Marry me," he pressed against her lips.*
>
> *"You know I can't," she whispered back.*

He grabbed her hands and pinned them above her head and she sucked in a tight breath. "I see through your riddles, love," he sneered.

She laughed, an ill-humored sound that shivered down my spine.

"I am bound to a bargain older than you, Ren Cormac."

Ren Cormac? I nearly snapped out of my vision from shock. Instead, my Sight peered into her memory's eyes to root around for this secret . . . and new images began rapidly fluttering across my mind's eye.

A bargain with the Mother, the Maiden, and the Crone to hide ancient fae artifacts from the Kingdom of Carran. Without wings, there was no way to access Seren. Not even the Sisters Three could unless flown up.

I didn't see an agreement to abstain from mate bonding, though.

Ren cocked his head, pulling me back to the first memory. "And our bargain, love?"

The blood quickly drained from Ravenna's face.

My Sight dug into her memories again and—my heart dropped to my stomach.

She had bargained with Ren, granting him a favor at his time and choosing, for his agreement to build Seren's factory districts. She needed a way for Raven Folk to have leverage with the Kingdom of Carran's colonizing mortal leaders. A way for her Folk to make an income to survive, too, after money had been introduced.

My mind, once more, returned to the scene unfolding before me.

> *Gritting her teeth, Ravenna hissed, "You choose to incur the wrath of Danu?"*
>
> *"Ravenna Blackwing," Ren practically sang in smug delight, "I call in my favor owed."*

Holy gods, she was bonded to Ren Cormac. That was how he had tricked her. And why my Cow of Plenty ended up in Stellar Winds Casino. What other treasures had he used to satisfy his greed?

"Cian Merrick—"

"Lonan-Merrick," I interrupted. Regardless of her service to the gods, she would *not* make me or Rhylen pay for the chaos Seren's coercion magic had, ultimately, wrought.

Shocked whispers rippled through the gathering at my dominating behavior.

The former queen, however, bowed her head, unruffled.

As my great aunt's friend, she was no doubt well-aware of who and what I was. Aye, I was part mortal, but the other part of me topped the govs in Raven Folk pecking order.

"Cian Lonan-Merrick," she began again, "several guests are being escorted to the mainland this night for the safety and returned enjoyment of all."

"Those zealous Ladies were unwelcome in establishments *before* I arrived."

Rhylen's brows shot up.

At the mention of those women, the adorable, murderous scowl on Glenna's face deepened and I could giggle in delight. Stars, how I would have fun poking at her primal state over the next few days.

Ravenna lifted her chin. "You took an artifact from *my* family."

Took, not steal. Until tonight, she was the guardian of my faerie cow.

"*Your* family?"

The cow belonged to my kin.

"Old bargains, *Cian*."

She knew I carried the soul of Cian's magic. Her bargain to protect this specific artifact for the Sister's Three was now fulfilled.

I snorted, to keep up pretense. "Even bairns know better than to separate familiars from their magically bonded owners. Or"—I flashed her a devilish grin—"to cross the will of the gods."

A sly smile darkened Ravenna's rouge-painted lips.

As the Corvus Rook of Seren, the head of the Carrion Crime Syndicate, she had to confront me after tonight's insanity and cow heist to not look weak. Everyone knew to cross the will of the gods earned curses and bad luck, a convincing enough argument for her attendants.

The former queen's gaze drifted to Mam, who studied the ground under the former queen's acute inspection. Edna chirped her greeting from Mam's shoulder and Ravenna dipped her head at Mam's red cardinal.

"You have done well, *fáidhbhean*."

"I have done little, my lady."

"You sacrificed your heart for Folk kind and the Tuatha Dé Danann." Ravenna placed a single finger beneath Mam's chin and lifted her head. "A *Mother* among mortals."

Moira's green eyes flew up and squinted with a familiar sharpness. I almost laughed aloud. How had I missed her intense seer's stare when younger?

The Heartbreak Show

Ravenna's attention returned to me. "I'm terribly vexed with you."

"Terribly," I agreed.

Despite the scowl darkening her elegant brows, a faint curl of satisfaction ghosted across her lips.

"Chieftain Lonan of *Blackwing* Tribe," she said loud enough for all to hear, "your brother will require your company when visiting Seren next."

Rhylen blinked back the shock at hearing his tribe's name.

"An honor, my Lady," he replied with a bow.

Ravenna Blackwing, who would still be our Raven Queen if not for the Kingdom of Carran's cruel dismantling of each fae court, had given Rhylen the protection of her name.

A name that still held power among Raven Folk, including the Caravans.

With one final glance my way, Ravenna and her Syndicate lackeys shifted into Ravens and flew back toward the City of Stars. Good. I was done with Seren this night. I would return to Farris later this week, however, to fulfill my bargain.

My tumbling thoughts paused. Was Ravenna's graciousness from Glas Gaibhnenn's abundance and good fortune magic? Now that she was reunited with Cian's re-souled magic? Or had my great aunt informed Ravenna of my quest?

A little paw tapped my leg. Feck, I could swoon in relief. On the ground before my feet lay a case, one I knew was filled with smokes and a book of matches.

I dropped to one knee and gathered George in my arms for a cuddle. "You heard my dire emergency."

My familiar quietly chittered.

"You want to ride my cow through clotheslines?" George chittered again and I snorted. "She's not a getaway cow, you wee, fluffy imp."

George patted my cheek, a think-about-it gesture, then climbed down my lap to place the metal case in my palms. Winking at the cheeky fella, I rose to find the entire camp staring at me with wide, expectant eyes.

I couldn't blame them. My entrance *was* glorious. But, also, my faerie cow was, indeed, the weirdest thing I'd brought to any gathering. There was no hiding my magic after tonight, either. Well, not *all* of my magic. I would take my Sight's ability to the grave.

Rhylen swept a you're-dismissed look around camp and the crowd began reluctantly dispersing, talking low amongst themselves while shooting me curious glances.

Stars and moons, I was ready to pass on the spotlight to someone else for a spell. This shameless hussy needed a break. And two dozen cigarettes in a row.

Giddy over that latter prospect, I lit a smoke and moaned with the first puff. At the exact same moment, Barry huffed a disgruntled groan. My raccoon was petting the cock boots still on my feet, cooing—and I grimaced.

Filena was the first to crack, followed by Gran.

Narrowing my eyes at my sister, I rolled my shoulders to make the knee length wings strapped to my back flutter and she cackled louder.

"I give you one night without duties," Rhylen said, trying and failing to keep a straight face.

"Well, darlin', you were taking too long to name your tribe. I had to do something."

He shook his head. "Cock boots. A Lughnasadh's Hat"—he pointed at the tacky head accessory on the ground—"Riding a glowing cow across the sky to camp. In wings and fake elven ears."

"While named Cordelia," Owen added with a smirk my way.

"And," Corbin added, "chased by dozens of men and women in fanatical love with his shiny arse."

Finn and Kalen burst into laughter, the pointy-eared bastards.

"Cordelia?" Glenna grinned, her dark-as-night eyes glittering with glee.

I shot Owen a rude gesture and the shitehawk giggled. The male actually fecking giggled.

"I swore that cow would shift before we landed," Corbin said.

I thought about that for a moment. "Probably because the boots and hat touched her hide, but not the garter ribbon."

Finn looked at Kalen and, with a shiver, groaned, "Forever weeping."

"A garter ribbon to shift?" Rhylen asked. When I nodded, the whites of my brother's eyes comically rounded. "How much did you drink?!"

A fair question. Most of my chaotic mischief happened when I was drunk.

"That's Glas Gaibhnenn, Rhylee Lo," Gran said with awe in her eyes. "Yer brother brought ye a gift of prosperity, he did."

Rhylen's brows pushed together. "The faerie tale cow?"

"Aye, lad. Sister of Bó Finne."

"Of the Milky Way," Rhylen muttered. It was a statement, not a question. "Of course, she is."

Well, shite. I didn't see that coming.

Coming. I bit back a delighted smile. The Maiden had a filthy riddling mind for being . . . a maiden. I had clearly inherited more than her seer magic.

I dragged on my cigarette then pointed it at my cow. "Ol' Ghavie Mer here is my birthright."

Rhylen rubbed his temples and closed his eyes in a long blink. "How many of you knew?"

Everyone raised their hands. Even Braelin.

Rhylen threw his head back and laughed. "Arseholes."

Finn winked at me and I puckered a mock-flirty kiss back. The rascally lad had ensured everyone kept Rhylen distracted while I was about the Maiden's business.

I tossed the butt of my cigarette into the fire and dramatically sighed. "Help me secure my faerie cow," I said to Rhylen, "and I'll tell you everything."

Finn clapped my back, cutting off Rhylen before he could reply. "Been too long since my wee feisty forest cat has seen my pretty face."

Kalen snorted. "Taryn is probably setting up wards to keep your fine, devilish good looks out."

"I'm too skilled, mate. It's why she married me *again*."

Glenna groaned. "Bring her back when you deliver my ingredients. The poor lass needs a slice of cake with a bite of happiness and a stiff drink."

Both Finn and I lifted slow, crooked smiles at Glenna who groaned again. "Not that kind of stiff drink, eejits."

I pulled Finn into an embrace and whispered, "Pass along a message to my great aunt. 'You're a very naughty lass and need to bring a sacrifice to the temple after all those bawdy milk cow and Love-Talker pipe jokes.'"

After also making me suffer through those agricultural innuendos.

These phallic boots of nightmares too.

Finn arched a humored brow. "Will do, love." My childhood friend gently squeezed me and I kissed him on the cheek, earning a grin. Then he strode toward my brother.

Kalen shook my hand while Finn said his goodbyes to Rhylen and the other fellas. Not caring that I saw, or fearing my response, the water spirit slid an appreciative sidelong glance at my Glenna one last time before turning away to whisper in Owen's ear. The two shook hands a beat later and the intuitive nudge in my gut twisted. I already *knew* what was coming, but my heart stumbled a beat at the confirmation.

My best friend would be joining Kalen in the Greenwood, as his bargaining agent.

Why Owen hadn't shown signs of elder magic now made sense. Maybe when he finished aiding Kalen, he would.

Corbin shifted on his feet, drawing in a tight breath, catching my attention. Beneath lowered lashes, a crushed look stole over his eyes while watching Kalen and Owen—

My mouth parted.

This wasn't the look of disappointment over losing a friend while he went on an adventure without them. The grief sloping his shoulders, the downcast tilt of his head . . .

How had I missed this? His seemingly playful annoyance over my and Owen's joke about getting married was . . . his attempt to laugh off the hurt. How long had he been in love with his best friend? Did Owen realize this too?

I was grateful my Sight hadn't picked up on this sooner than my non-Sighted realization.

Not wanting to invade Corbin's privacy further, I returned my focus back onto Finn and Kalen as they walked backward with one final wave. A beat later, the two wild fae elves disappeared into the shadows of Caledona Wood, George fast on their heels. I cracked a smile. That wee bastard was so thief struck, hearts were practically shooting out of his moony eyes.

Seven dancing suns above, what a ridiculous night.

Rhylen met my eyes and gestured with his head toward my cow. I nodded and he focused back on the lads while waiting for me.

A hand softly knotted with mine just as I was about to stride over, and I turned toward Glenna. Heat raced just beneath my skin at the sight of my life partner. She was absolute perfection.

And all mine.

I kissed her fingers. "Cupcake vixen."

"Pluming doxy."

I bit my bottom lip. "You *do* like my wings."

"Wings or not, I'll still win our final bet tomorrow night."

My grin widened. "Darlin', I have a Cow of Plenty. Forfeit and accept your losses."

Her laugh was low and unyielding. "I'd rather lose to a faerie cow than hand you an easy win."

I smirked. "Either way I win."

She rolled her eyes.

"Just admit it, Glennie Mer," I crooned in sultry tones, "you love me in feathers."

"*Cordelia*," she purred, "no treats from me until you explain what happened on Seren."

Oh she wanted to play dirty?

Flashing her a sensual smile, I lowered my lips to her ear and whispered, rough and wanting, "*Darlin'*, by the end of this night, you'll be worshiping me."

Her breath fluttered, her chest rising and falling deeply.

My thumb traced the shape of her breast. "My obsession," I softly moaned in her ear. "My ruination."

The fingers resting on my chest began digging into my shirt.

I nibbled on the lobe of her ear. "You'll beg me for relief and I'll deny you until you cry out that I'm your—"

She scoffed and shoved me back.

"Trust me, you will."

"Trust me," she sassed back, "you'll be weeping in your pillow

The Heartbreak Show

when George is mine for the next month."

"Gent of Fem, bets."

She leaned close, her lips brushing mine. "Lady of Man . . . bets."

And with that, her fists curled at her sides, she marched off toward her brother and I laughed. The flirty glare she shot over her shoulder was a thing of beauty. A promise to punish me and feck, I couldn't wait.

Tugging on Rhylen's sleeve, she pulled him toward my faerie cow. The fellas, Filena, and Braelin jogged after them.

I began trailing my brothers and sisters when I caught the flicker of firelight off Mam's gold hair, and I slowed my steps. The tresses appeared bright, as if shining, and I swallowed thickly. My gaze flitted over my new familiar then back to Mam. Before catching up with my family, I felt words burning in my chest for the woman who burned them into mine first.

Mam peered my way as I approached her, a small smile softening the corners of her mouth.

"Me brave, beautiful son."

Kneeling before her, I took her hand and pressed her fingers to my cheek. "I . . . I became a gancanagh on Seren. Male faeries from the Mother's line become Love-Talkers, aye?"

She nodded and I swallowed thickly. "Not all male kin, but many are."

"Pulses pounded in my ears," I continued. "I could have broken every heart in that room, Mam. It would have been so easy."

"But ye didn't, aye? Ye chose kindness and love."

"Because you were right," I said with a kiss to her palm. "I'd *never* be him."

Tears glistened on her lashes. "Ye, me wee Cian, have a strong, wise heart made to speak only love."

I closed my eyes in a long blink and soaked up her affection. "Not all heroes wear armor," I murmured. Taking in her newer skirt and bodice, the shiny black ribbon in her long golden hair, I whispered, "Some wear dresses."

A tear fell down her cheek.

"I love you as big as the endless, blue sky, Mam."

Kissing her hand, then her cheek, I stood and walked toward my birthright, no longer afraid of the divine parts of who and what I was.

No longer afraid of my future.

Chapter Twenty - Nine
GLENNA LONAN-MERRICK

The gobshite won our bet.

And not just by a little either. His designated pot for gold cock boot overflowed with coins, jewels, and other tradeable trinkets.

The memory of the smug curve of his flirty smile pooled liquid heat in my core all over again.

My primal state right now was, annoyingly, turned on by every mundane thing he did, too. The way his lips closed over a spoon while eating? My pulse blushed. When bending over to pick up firewood? I struggled to breathe. The easy stride of his walk, the slight tilt to his head when listening to another talk, the goading flash of his eyes as we ambled back to camp? I could push him up against a wall and take him before removing all our clothes.

Gods, I was so stars damned pissed that I lost.

But I also wasn't, not when so many benefited from Cian's win.

The entire tribe lifted a cheer at the wealth Cian dumped onto my kitchen worktable. Musicians struck up their instruments soon after and we'd been celebrating ever since, passing around wine and whiskey, removing our shoes and dancing with abandon. A true faerie revel.

That poor beastie of his, though, the one that gave us plenty, needed a sudsy bath and massaging brush down. It was the least we could do.

Glas Gaibhnenn was still in the storage wagon, locked up. Though reunited with Cian, she remained in a spelled taxidermized-like state so long as the new hat, boots, and garter, to replace the charred ones, didn't touch her.

My nose wrinkled.

The Crone had horrible fashion taste. Why a Wishing Tree garter ribbon, hideous red boots, and a tacky arse Lughnasadh's Day hat on a milking cow to reanimate her when Cian was present? The poor lad, and George, would be lamenting her fashion challenged getup all their days.

Unless the Crone changed her mind.

But I doubted she would. If I were honest, it was also pretty funny.

Cian surmised the Crone turned his cow into a witch's ornament while hidden by Ravenna—no grain or land was needed to keep her alive this way. But, regardless of if Glas Gaibhnenn was reanimated or spelled, her magic pulsed. She was too powerful.

The lads would begin building a small barn and fenced in corral for her tomorrow, for the other livestock we could now buy too.

Filena hadn't spellcrafted an object yet but, as a *cailleach*, she had powers from the Crone. Once Cian's cow could safely be returned to her natural state, Filena would attempt transmutating a normal lead rope into one with protection spells, to ensure the faerie cow couldn't be stolen—again.

Speaking of my witchy sister, Filena sighed and leaned her head against my shoulder.

Across the fire, Cian, who was still wearing my skirt and fraying corset from tonight's show, danced with Owen and Corbin, the three of them laughing at each other's antics. The song changed a measure later and Cian let go of Owen's and Corbin's hands to grab Rhylen's and pulled my brother into a slow dance.

"Look at those eejits," Filena murmured with a yawn. "They're half-drunk with happiness."

Cian, with his back to Corbin, playfully kicked Corbin in the arse, knocking him into Owen's arms.

Filena yawned again.

I suspected why Filena drooped against me. I should be tired for the same reason. Stars, I barely slept last night. I was a little sore today too and, yet, I was ready to drag Cian into the woods and make him moan all over again.

Except, I lost our final bet.

I cringed just thinking about it.

As if reading my thoughts, Cian peered my way and . . . I knew that heated look. A jolt of excitement shivered down my traitorous body.

Whispering into Rhylen's ear, my brother nodded his head, then my mate broke away and strode toward me in a swish of skirts, the muscles of his arms and shoulders painted in firelight.

He was so pretty, I sighed.

Filena snickered.

I poked her in the side. "Go back to sleep," I teased.

Cian slowed before us and I lifted a brow.

"Sister dear"—he crouched before her and brushed a strand of hair from her face—"need me to walk you to your wagon?"

Filena pushed up from my shoulder and shook her head. "Rhylen will leave the revel too early."

My brother was now guiding Gran in a slow dance beside Owen and Corbin, next to Sean and Braelin.

Plucking Sheila from her pocket, Filena snuggled her wee hedgehog against her cheek. Lloyd rolled over in her lap with a twitch of his tail, his little feet up. Smiling, she reassured her brother with a quiet, "I'll manage."

Cian stood and kissed the top of her head. "I'm stealing your pillow."

He then tugged me off the log and pulled me into a slow dance away from listening ears. I happily fell into his arms, the ones circling me and holding me close.

Cian buried his face in my hair as we swayed to the music. "I ache for you, Glennie Mer."

"It's terrible to want."

He quietly laughed, a low, gravelly sound. "I *want* your back arching when I touch you," he murmured into my ear and my eyes fluttered closed. Stars, the erotic things that came out of that man's mouth. Just one sentence, one spoken confession and I was already growing listless. "I *want* your legs wrapped around me," he continued. "I *want* your mouth to send me to the Otherworld."

"That's not what you *really* want." The words were feisty. The delivery, to my will-not-back-down shame, was embarrassingly breathy.

He smiled against my skin. "Darlin'," he lilted in a rough whisper, "the filthy things I want to do to you are too numerous to name. So," he drawled, a waggish glint to his voice, "tell me, what is it I *really* want."

I barked a laugh at his attempt to seduce me into saying what he *really* wanted. I might have lost our final bet, but I wouldn't make things easy for him.

"Meet me in a candlemark," he murmured, pretending like he hadn't just tried to trick me.

"What scheme is brewing in that big mortal head of yours?"

Instead of answering me, he cupped the back of my neck, then captured my lips in a soft, reverent kiss. A promise of the slow, sweet torture to come. My lips followed his as he stepped away, an extra rascally glint to his self-satisfied smile. The smile of a boy who knew he was magic.

The Heartbreak Show

I playfully narrowed my eyes.

He blinked innocently at me.

Then the eejit left me to pine for him.

I almost flew after Cian, to see what mischief he was up to. But I waited, watching a candle melt in a lantern for what seemed like the longest fifteen minutes of my life. When the final drip slipped down the tallow, marking that time was up, I alighted into the air in my Raven form.

When I shifted in front of our wagon, he wasn't outside, not that I could see, at least. I climbed the steps and entered. It, too, was Cian-less save a single candle lit by our bed. A creamy white object was laid out across our covers and—

I sucked in an excited breath.

Where did he get this? How?

I darted over to our bed and slid a finger across the beautiful damask corset with satin stays in the back and silver clasps in the front. Beside it was a pretty set of drawers with satin ties and lace trim on the hems.

Giggling, I quickly undressed from one of his shirts and his back-up trousers and donned the new undergarments. For a final touch, I tied thigh-high stockings with old ribbons just above my knees. I trailed a hand down the front of the corset when finished, enjoying how it tightly fastened around my breasts, waist, and over the top of my new drawers.

I dashed outside, not caring who might see me, and rounded the wagon.

Cian was leaning against the back, watching the stars. Slowly he turned his head and his chest rose in a soft breath. I wasn't normally shy, but this man had given me *everything*—companionship when I was dying of loneliness, supplies to bake again, my own kitchen, revenue so my brother could provide for his flock, these pretty underpinnings... *him*.

"Thank you," I whispered, too overcome to speak.

His eyes widened. Aye, I had indebted myself to him. He opened his mouth to protest, but I put a hand up and stopped him. No words needed to be spoken. What was done was done.

Stepping toward my mate, I took him in for the first time. The old-fashioned breeches he arrived in hugged the curves of his legs and arse once more, while still barefoot from the revelry. His nicest button-down shirt lay mostly open, the sleeves rolled to his elbows, revealing a tantalizing stretch of skin. His hair fell across his forehead to the tips of his ears in golden waves. And . . . the wings he had always wanted were strapped to his back.

I really did find him mouth-wateringly irresistible in those wings.

"You are . . ." his voice caught and he drew in another ragged breath. "Feck, I can't think around your beauty."

A blush warmed my cheeks at the way his gray eyes worshiped every inch of me. I truly did feel enchanting. "Where did these come from?"

He pushed off the wagon and closed the distance between us. "Boylesque dancing for a roomful of men."

Anger instantly hit my pulse and I bared my canines. "You did what?!"

He quietly laughed at my territorial reaction, taking my hand and leading me to a mossy log on the edge of the forest. It was then I noticed a series of lit lanterns positioned in a half-circle. On the log was a shawl. A smile wobbled on my lips. He really did think of everything, including the night's chill.

A drumbeat started up, a sensual rhythm. My brows pushed together. I peered toward center camp through the forest. What was going on? Were the lads putting on an impromptu Fire Dance?

I turned back to Cian and my mouth slackened.

Noticing my attention, he began rolling his hips to the slow, pulsing beat.

The Heartbreak Show

Sweet goddess . . .

He was . . . dancing for me? I grinned, tears lining my lashes. This was the one courting ritual I hadn't yet experienced with anyone—with *him*.

Fingers suggestively dragged down his bottom lip as ash-lined eyes flashed to mine. He was going to torment me this night. And moons above, did I embrace this torture.

Rings, gracing two fingers and his thumb, glinted in the warm light, adornments he must have borrowed from the fellas. Tilting his head back, his hand slid down his throat to trace the defined lines of his pectorals, his hips still moving in a grinding rhythm.

The tips of his fingers paused their descent at the unbuttoned portion of his shirt. He bit a corner of his lower lip and slipped one button open, followed by the rest, then pushed his shirt open. The breeches he wore hung low on his hips. My gaze lingered on the black feathers draping down this back, on the salivating flex of his abs . . .

Gods . . . stars . . . my blood ignited into a wildfire.

I was consumed. Burning. Always burning for this man.

Sunlight throbbed low in my belly when he wore corsets and dresses, when rouge painted his sultry lips. I deeply loved the feminine side of him. And when his masculine beauty was on display explicitly for my pleasure? My heart ceased to beat.

Lantern light gilded his magnificent wings and flickered across the ridges of his abdomen and the vee of his hips in a tantalizing dance of ambers and shadows. His ring adorned hand played with the ties of his breeches, before brushing his hardening bulge in the lightest of caresses. Before grinding against his palm. The muscles of his chest tightened with the touch, his mouth parting in an aroused breath.

I gripped the log and shifted to find relief. But there was none.

And I couldn't take another second of his arcing hips, the beautiful lines of his body not pressed to the curves of mine.

Letting the shawl fall back to the log, I stood and he paused only long enough to say, "My soul's obsession, ruin me."

In two steps, I grabbed the laces on his pants and yanked his hips flush to mine. He bent back at the waist, my fingers still gripping his laces, and continued moving to the sensual drumbeat against me.

I was dying, my pulse electric at the teasing friction of his body.

And something wild inside of me snapped to life.

My nails scraped across the hardened peaks of his nipples, down the ridges of his abdomen. A claiming touch. The moan that left him was deep and slow. Then his lips were on mine. Hungry, demanding. My head spun in raw, animalistic want. He tasted of sunshine, laughter, and every silken, forbidden desire I possessed.

And skies help me, the way this man kissed with his whole body was intoxicating.

He dug his fingers into my upper thighs, lifting me up. I wrapped my legs around his waist, our lips claiming the other's in bruising sweeps. He walked us into the forest, gently lowering me to a blanket he had prepared.

I pushed his shirt down his shoulders and arms, the wings too. He tossed them to the side and unlaced his pants, just as impatient as me. My hand wrapped around the hardened length of him and his head fell back in a shuddering breath. But only for a beat. His mouth dropped to the base of my throat, kissing fire along the pushed-up swells of my breasts as I stroked him.

"Corset and stockings only," he rasped, slowly tugging my drawers down while trailing the tips of his fingers over my clit. I bucked, chasing after his touch, and he, with a rakish smile, placed a hand on my hip to hold me down. The next breath, he lowered himself to his stomach and buried his face between my legs, groaning at the first taste of me.

The Heartbreak Show

I twisted my fingers into his hair, dizzy at the feel of his hot breath. I could writhe in heady agony with each curling lick. My fingers held him closer. My head tilted back as I dragged cool air into my feverishly panting lungs. I was growing shamelessly desperate for the wicked flick of his tongue, the cruel way he drew me into his mouth, and ground against his face for more, more, more. And holy gods, did he devour me. My eyes drifted closed for a long moment at the exquisite sensations thrumming in my core.

But no matter how much I wanted to shatter apart right now, I was impatient for *him*.

Always in tune with me, Cian leaned back on his knees and peered at me through messy blond strands while prowling up my body in a flurry of kisses along my corseted stomach. A breathtaking show of muscle danced across his shoulders and arms. At the beguiling sight, another flush of arousal stirred hot in my rushing blood. The heat of his body covered me, the ragged pulse of his breath searing my skin. And gods, that man's tongue . . . I might faint at the feel of him tasting the singing beat of my pounding heart fluttering in my neck. As if marking me.

"I crave you to the point of madness," he whispered.

A single finger glided down the length of my arm, circling around my wrist. Capturing my lips with his, he pinned my hand above my head. His other possessively gripped my hip.

In one dominating push of his hips, he drove into me.

I sucked in a sharp breath; my back arched.

The seductive roll of tribal drumbeats filled the forest, a rhythm that took over the sensual, languidly arcing lines of his body.

"You're mine," he said, his thrusts deep and unyielding. "Say it."

My chest heaved with the delicious fullness stretching me. "I belong only to you."

"Mine," he repeated, breathless. "Fecking mine."

Those roaming fingers of his left my hip to tease circles around my clit.

"I'm drunk on the sinful feel of you."

Flames licked my tightening skin. My breathing trembled with swelling anguish. The grinding roll of his hips bordered on obscene, the carnal sight liquefying fire in my thrumming core. Dying suns, he felt so fecking good, I might actually lose my mind.

He released my hand and I buried my nails into his forearms. I was on the edge of splintering apart. The heat swelling inside of me was throbbing hotter with every relentless stroke. My eyes cinched shut. Oh gods . . . I wasn't . . . I was—

He abruptly stopped.

Why wasn't he moving? Fecking hell, I was so close.

My eyes flew open to his smug smile.

"What do I *really* want, Glenna?"

I squirmed, too delirious with need, and he pulled out of me, delighted at my suffering.

Narrowing my eyes, I drawled, "To finish this night."

His taunting grin widened. "I can finish without you."

I growled, the emptiness practically whimpering for relief. Well, I could finish without him too. I lowered my hand to myself with a challenging snap of my eyes and he grabbed my wrist and pinned it above my head once more.

"What do I *really* want, darlin'?" he asked, slowly, emphatically.

I clenched my jaw. A bargain was a bargain. I had never broken one, but petting his ego would only feed his vanity. The arse, though, promised to bring me to the edge of release and deny me unless . . .

Fine.

I'd get this over with.

Rolling my eyes I, as quietly as possible, muttered, "You're my sex god."

"Bargains, Glenna." He pushed my legs wider with his knees and teased my entrance with the tip of his cock and I . . . I . . . damn him.

"You're my sex god," I said louder, but as humorously lackluster as possible.

The hard length of him slid across my clit next and I bit back yet another whimper.

"In ecstasy, Gent of Fem."

A sassy reply begged for release. But no matter how much he riled me up, I was completely weak for that boyish, devilishly mischievous grin and the fall of golden locks down his pleasure-flushed face. Cian Lonan-Merrick possessed a kind of beauty so devastating it ached.

Most of all, though, he had one of the most beautiful souls I had ever known.

Aye, he had given me *everything*.

My competitive nature refused to acknowledge my loss. But I was so wildly in love, I couldn't resist him, bargains be damned.

"On your back," I ordered and that saucy grin of his turned feral.

He *knew*.

I would give him what he *really* wanted. The only reason he rolled us over until I straddled him. Moaning when I sank onto his cock.

Gripping my arse, he rocked me against him, long and slow. The stockings tied to my thighs creased into my skin with the movement. My breasts strained against my new corset with every heaving breath. My long hair swayed across my arms. Cian fisted a handful and gently tugged me toward him, the fingers of one hand still biting into my soft flesh.

Our lips collided in a fevered kiss.

Stars above, I could kiss him until my soul's final breath.

"I'm obsessively in love with you," he whispered against my mouth. "An eternity together is heartbreakingly short."

"I love you," I said on an unraveling gasp. "I love you . . . I love you . . ."

I came undone in a lush starburst of sensations. My nails dragged along the smooth, sculpted lines of his chest. Still drowning in him, in this, my hips rode him deeper, faster through my release. When muscles down his body tightened, gripped in pleasure, when his breathing ended in sharp moans and the sweetest agony flushed across his face, I threw my head back and cried out, "Cian . . . oh god, Cian . . . you're my sex god!"

He broke into laughter before I finished, his still flexing muscles now quaking.

Hooting and cheers erupted from camp and I slapped a hand over my mouth. When had the drums ended?

Cian laughed harder at my mortified horror, practically wheezing for breath. Tears began pooling in his eyes.

"Really?"

He blew out a slow breath, trying to calm his delight.

And started laughing again.

Aye, torture by Wee Folk, it was. Followed by waking in bed to Cordelia staring at him.

But, Holy Mother of Stars, the joy shining from his smile alone was almost blinding in its beauty, a brilliant light that radiated from every part of his being.

"Ask me," he murmured, still trying to rein in his humor.

"Ask you *what*?"

That up-to-no grin of his slowly inched up his face. "If light radiates from *every* part of my being."

"You read me?!"

He grabbed my hands and rolled us over. Before I could protest, he buried his face in my neck, burning a trail of embered kisses down my throat while cupping my corseted breast. I was quickly melting into

The Heartbreak Show

moonlight. I could take my final breath in his arms like this.

But I couldn't let him win.

"Darlin'," I drolled, albeit breathlessly, "your shiny, sparkly arse can go—"

"Wrong part."

Wrong . . . a laugh burst from me.

Cian lowered and captured my happiness in a playful kiss, both of us unable to stop our laughter. As our kisses grew more drunken, endlessly heady, I found myself lost in the wonder of this past week. We had started in poverty and ended in riches. And all because of this gorgeous, kind, rascally man. Cian Lonan-Merrick was pure sunshine and chaos, my whole heart, the bawdy half of my soul.

And sexy demi-god before me, how I loved this shameless hussy.

Epilogue
11 years, 6 months, 9 days later

CIAN LONAN-MERRICK

I gazed up at the stars, enjoying the warmer night air. Behind me, Blackwing Tribe's Night Market had been open for a couple of hours now. The murmuring sound of crowds moved through this side of Caledona Wood. Hawkers sang about their wares, drowned out by the distant whistle of the occasional train.

Normally, Glenna and I would have a Heartbreak Show performance . . . but not these past couple of months. Not for a few months more either.

My three-week-old daughter made a tiny mewling sound while adjusting her head. Pressed to the bare skin of my chest, to the steady thump of my heart, she settled back to sleep. I wrapped my partially unbuttoned shirt tighter around her and nuzzled my cheek against her downy head.

Ferelith Lonan-Merrick owned me heart and soul.

She was breathtakingly beautiful, with wispy black hair, tiny, pointed ears, and the most adorable trembling cry. I was so in love with her, with parenthood, life before my daughter seemed almost a hazy dream . . .

The Heartbreak Show

My eyes jumped to the forest, my brows pushed together.

A strange clomping noise was coming from the woods.

Were those boots?

George chittered not too far away. I glanced over at the fluffy lad—and my mouth dropped open.

The wee imp was riding on the back of ol' Ghavie Mer down the forest trail toward me. Lloyd was behind him. Of course, Lloyd was involved. I didn't expect to see Edna also riding on the back of my faerie cow, though. She chirped at me and I snorted.

"George," I drawled, "you can't steal my cow."

He met my eyes and I sighed.

"There are other ways to deliver Ferelie Mer a sock—"

Edna alighted into the air, the small pink wool sock in her beak. Cheeky lad. Mam's cardinal laid the sock on my shoulder and returned to the back of Glas Gaibhnenn as the cow slowed before me.

Ghavie licked my fingers as I was making slow, caressing circles on Ferelith's back. She had taken quickly to our daughter and was, at times, protective of her.

"Thank you, darlin'," I said to Ghavie, trying not to grimace at the feel of her sticky saliva on the back of my hand. "Come, lass. You know the rules. No roaming when the market is open."

Holding Ferelith to me with one hand, I took the lead rope and turned Ghavie around.

She made a huffing sound.

"Aye, even if George promises you earrings."

The vain heifer was as shameless as me.

A few minutes later, I handed my faerie cow to Farren, who was on mucking duty. He rolled his eyes at George, who had handed the eleven-year-old lad a lady's glove before scampering off. Moons above, Farren Lonan looked so much like Rhylen at that age.

Farren was just a year younger than Rhylen when I met my brother. My first friend. The first person around my age to stick up for me. The first male to touch me with affection, not cruelty.

I tucked my daughter closer to my heart. I couldn't imagine how a parent could hate their own child. Beat them. Say heartbreaking things to them.

Four years ago, Hamish was released from jail. Two weeks later, he was found dead in an alley, stabbed in the gut. The constable didn't investigate long. It was concluded Hamish MacCullough of Kilkerry had gambled with the wrong house of cards and dice.

I kissed my daughter's head and began wandering back home.

Glenna was waiting for us, sitting on our wagon steps in her chemise, her long, black hair spilling down her back. Gods, she was gorgeous. She had been napping after being up most of the day with our wee one.

She ambled over and reached for our daughter. "Here, let me—"

I twisted away with a scandalized gasp. "Get your own baby."

"Oh aye?" She plopped a fist onto her hip.

"Aye," I confirmed. "Grab one of Rhylen's and Filena's million children."

Glenna spurted a laugh.

"Is that a . . . pink sock on your shoulder?"

"Pink is a perfect color for Ferelie's complexion, obviously."

"Naturally." Glenna lifted a black, elegant brow. Then yawned. The skin around her starless night eyes was still far too puffy.

Taking her hand, I kissed her fingers, then tugged her back into the wagon. She had just woken from a nap, but she needed to rest longer. She missed our daughter as much as I did when she wasn't in my arms.

With an encouraging nudge, Glenna crawled back beneath the covers. Ferelith let out a little sleepy cry when I moved her away from the

Glas Gaibhnenn

warmth of my chest to the much cooler bed linens beside her mam. Glenna began quietly singing an old lullaby and I could swoon. The vision they made together was too much for one heart to take in.

Deciding to join them, I began unbuttoning my shirt. Glenna's gaze drifted down my torso. I smirked, making her roll her eyes. I continued undressing down to my drawers, then dipped onto the bed and settled beside my lasses.

Flashing my mate a mischievous smile, I slowly scooped an arm around Ferelith and scooted her closer to me. "My baby."

Glenna adjusted her head closer to mine on our pillow. "Ferelith's complexion clearly looks best in emerald green."

"How dare you insult George's fashion expertise," I said in feigned outrage. "Take it back."

"Maybe cornflower blue too."

"May Georgie Dirty Paws never bring you mismatched shoes again."

Glenna quietly laughed and I leaned over and kissed her forehead.

I kissed Ferelith's next, before rolling to my back and placing our daughter on my chest again, where she belonged.

"Stars above, you're a cuddle strumpet like George."

"Get. Your. Own. Baby."

I expected a witty reply, but she was oddly quiet. And . . . blushing. Her eyes traveled down my arms, my chest, my stomach, before settling on our daughter.

A slow, flirty smile played across my lips.

Glenna loosed a sound that was a cross between a sigh and a scoff. But the heat in her gaze was unmistakable.

I rolled my head to be closer to hers and a lock of blond hair fell across my eyes. Glenna pressed her lips together. That sassy hen was addicted to preening me, but she didn't want to pet my ego either.

The Heartbreak Show

"Glenna, darlin'," I lilted, "you either get to stare at my bare chest or preen my hair, but not both."

"Our daughter is on your chest, eejit."

"Mhmm," I playfully agreed. "And you're swooning over my hevage."

"Full-blooded gods save me—"

"Get over here, Gent of Fem."

I opened my arm. Glenna Lonan-Merrick could never resist me. It was cute how she tried to be strong. But it only took a couple seconds before she was scooting over to rest her head on my chest beside our little love. Once my mate was settled, I wrapped my arm around her back and held her close.

"Ready?" she murmured.

"One," I whispered back. "Two. Three."

We both kissed Ferelith's head at the same time, a ritual we started the very day she was born. Glenna softly giggled, trailing a finger down our daughter's arm to her small hand. The wee lass wrapped her tiny fingers around a single one of her mam's and I drew in a tight breath.

That act of trust was small, but it broke my heart. From the moment she drew breath, she trusted us to care for her every need.

My da failed me. But I wouldn't fail her.

My little girl would always know she was loved . . . and accepted.

She was perfectly made.

I caressed her other hand with my finger and grinned when she curled her tiny ones around mine as well.

Aye, the gods don't make mistakes.

The End

But also not *not* the end.

(keep flipping, you'll see what I mean)

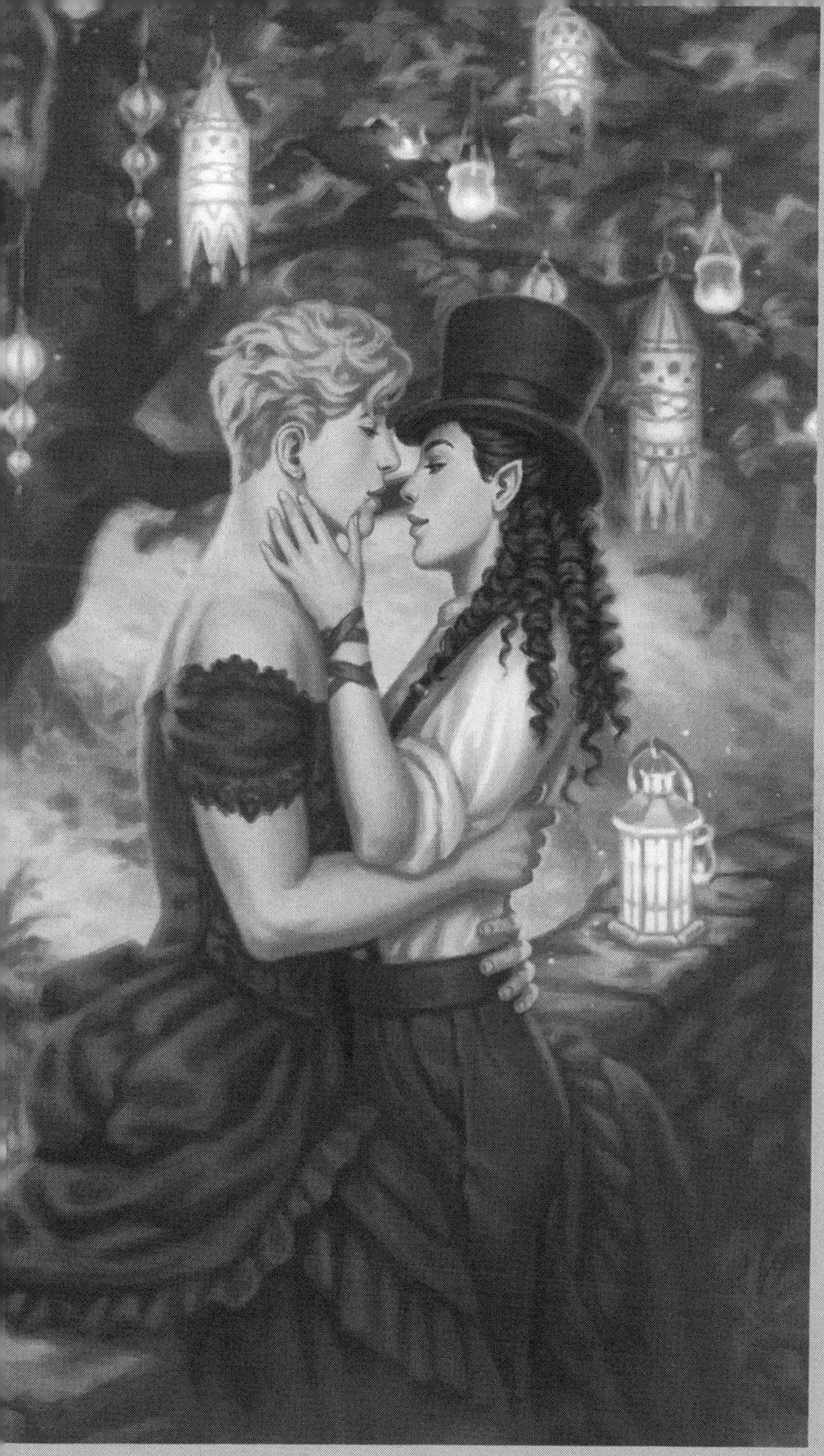

Thank You Readers

Thank you, my wee faerie reader, for adventuring across the pages with Cian and Glenna. I hope you enjoyed their flirty rivals-to-lovers romance. I will forever be your fangirl if you took a few seconds to leave a 1-2 sentence review. It doesn't have to be fancy. But every review helps me (and other readers too). Thank you!

Want more from the Bound by Ravens world? Of course you do!

Up next is Kalen Kelly's adventure, LAST GREENWOOD WILDS. And like the title suggests, Kalen will be adventuring into The Wilds to save the wild fae from Carran's military by bootlegging them across the border into a neighboring kingdom and while searching for his sister. Of course, no story about Kalen would be complete without his best mate, Finn Brannon, who will make an appearance or two or three. Or complete without a faerie cat and a stowaway tavern girl who may prove to be more a master of disguise than Georgie Dirty Paws.

Also, as mentioned in THE HEARTBREAK SHOW, Owen Delaney will be joining Kalen into the Greenwood. We might see a wee bit more of Corbin too.

After LAST GREENWOOD WILDS, will be Farris Leith's story with a mob boss's daughter on Seren.

Aaaaaand . . . I have a spin-off in the works for all the children mentioned in the main series epilogues: Annie Ó Dair (Brannon), Kieran Ó Dair (Brannon), Farren Lonan, Brenlea Lonan, Ferelith Lonan-Merrick, as well as a few more yet to make your epilogue acquaintance * winks *

To keep up to date with my stories, releases, and more, be sure to:

1) sign up for my newsletter, MoonTree Books

2) join my reader group, Jesikah's Forest Faeries

Thank You Friends

This bawdy song and dance of a book wouldn't be possible without sacrifices to the Love-Talker . . . ahem, Yours Truly, the romantasy writer.

MYLES SUNDIN

Love of my life, thank you for the endless cups of coffee, grilled cheeses, and working out story problems with me while walking in the wood, finding cool rocks on the beach, and while snuggling on the couch.
Also for entertaining my readers at conventions with "the husband synopsis."
Cheers to 30 years together. Cheers to 30 more!

THE MOO CREW

Andra Prewett, Jessica Maass, Jill Bridgeman, Kelly Stepp, Kim Gerstenschlager, Lana Ringoot, Michelle Downing, Sarah Jordan, Tyffany Hackett, and Victoria Cascarelli: darlin's, thank you for the kindness of sharing with me your time, energy, memes, feedback, grammar hunts, reels, encouragements, recipes, personal stories, potato humor . . . is there anything you Raven Folk sisters don't do?? Your reactions when Finn showed up AND you learned Cian would be stealing the cash cow . . . was #MooCrew magic. I adore you all exceedingly *ugs all my alpha/beta readers*

MY DUBLIN FRIEND

Faerie kisses to my Dublin friend, Deirdre Reidy, for double-checking my wobbly *Gaeilge* (aka Irish). Any and all errors in the *Bound by Ravens* series are mine. *Go raibh maith agat!*

KELLY STEPP

You are a gift sent from the bookish gods. I can't ever adequately thank you enough for the support you've given me these past couple of years. The best personal assistant an author could want. A treasured friend too.

KATE ANDERSON

Thank you for always swooping in and editing my stories with a fine-toothed comb. Also, when you editing-comment-cackled over the Shaft and Great Seed Ladies of Lugh innuendos, I felt my gutter-humor dark soul restored.

NIC PAGE

Darlin', thank you for proofing Cian's and Glenna's chaos . . . ahem . . . *my* chaos. Your constant support and love of my characters and stories means so to much me.

MY BELOVED MOONTREE FOREST HOs

Alisha Klapheke, Melanie Karsak, Elle Madison, and Robin D. Mahle . . . A lass couldn't ask for better work wives. And dearest friends. And co-admins. But good bookish gods set on top shelf high, who knew Romantasy Books (Facebook) would explode like it has. Or that predictive text answers would be our Prozac in this crazy industry. Love you as big as the endless blue sky, I do.

BELOVED AUTHOR FRIENDS

My other work wives (aye, I have a harem of you, haha), Heather Renee, Tyffany Hackett, and Hanna Sandvig . . . you make my heart sing. I look forward to another year of conventions and writerly shenanigans with you! Also, to my community of writer friends who are too numerous to list here . . . THANK YOU. I couldn't do any of this without you.

MY ARTISTS

Lauren Richelieu, Ellie Northwood (Mageonduty), Chicklen.doodle, and Alexandra Curte . . . I am in awe of your magic and weep whenever you bring my characters and worlds to painted life. My eternal gratitude * blows kisses *

STEWART CRANK AND KIRSTY GEDDES

You two became instant celebrities and household names among my readers. A million thanks for lending my characters and their stories your magic and voice acting talents. *hands you both cake infused with a bite of happiness*

JESIKAH'S FAERIE ARC READERS

My magical faerie forest tribe . . . reviews and social media recs are an author's bread and butter. I can't express my gratitude enough for loving on my books and for sharing them with the world. Truly. May George always bring you mismatched socks, one glove, and wig stands named Cordelia.

MY READERS

You wee darlin's . . . this author is your forever fangirl. Thank you for celebrating my stories and characters. I am continually humbled and moved by your support. Your comments and shares and reviews and cards you send me are everything. There will never be enough words to share how grateful I am to you.

More Books
by Jesikah Sundin

A BOUND BY RAVENS NOVEL
STANDALONE FAE ROMANTASIES

Stories about thieves, bootleggers, caravans, faerie markets, and mob bosses, all run by the Raven Folk.

BOUND BY RAVENS
THE NIGHT MARKET
THE HEARTBREAK SHOW
LAST GREENWOOD WILDS

THE BIODOME CHRONICLES
ECO-DYSOTOPIAN FAERIE TALE

She is locked inside an experimental world.
He has never met the girl who haunts his dreams.
A chilling secret forever binds their lives together.

LEGACY
ELEMENTS
TRANSITIONS
GAMEMASTER

THE EALDSPELL CYCLE

STANDALONE EPIC FAERIE TALES WITH A HISTORICAL TWIST

Dreams are dangerous . . .
Unless she unlocks the powers of her mind.
He fights his Otherworld shadow self.
And with only fae magic to re-spin their tales.

OF DREAMS AND SHADOWS

OF HEART AND STONE

OF THORNS AND CURSES

THE KNIGHTS OF CAERLEON

AN ARTHURIAN LEGEND REVERSE HAREM FANTASY

Under J. Sundin

Four cursed knights. One warrior princess.
A faerie sword that binds their lives together.

THE FIFTH KNIGHT

THE THIRD CURSE

THE FIRST GWENEVERE

A HARTWOOD FALLS ROMANCE

CONTEMPORARY ROMANCES

Under Jae Dawson

MOONLIGHT AND BELLADONNA

HEARTBEATS AND ROSES

SNOWFLAKES AND HOLLY

Etsy Shop

A dash of moon magic. A pinch of tree laughter. Stories whispered on the wind.

Hello Etsy wayfarers! Welcome to my bookish shop. When not slouched behind a computer, cursing the keyboard gods, you can find me frolicking through the woods with a camera around my neck or on the Comic Con circuit as MoonTree Books. Have fun poking around at my wares.

BOOKISH WARES FOR SALE

- Signed Paperbacks
- Limited Edition hardbacks
- Book Swag
- Book Boxes
- Custom Character Candles

Scan the QR code to visit my store.

Have questions? Message me on Etsy and we'll figure out your next fantasy adventure together.

JESIKAH SUNDIN is a multi-award winning Fae Romantasy, Dystopian Punk Lit, and Historical Fantasy writer, a mom of three nerdlets, a faeriecore and elfpunk folklorist, tree hugger, enchanted forest photographer, and a helpless romantic who married her insta-love high school sweetheart.

In addition to her family, she shares her home in Seattle, Washington with a rambunctious husky-chi and a collection of Doc Martens boots (including a pair from the early 90s). She is addicted to coffee, GIFs, memes, smutty innuendos, potatoes, cheese, kilts, mossy forests, eyeliner on men, lists, and artsy indie alt rock.

www.jesikahsundin.com

Made in the USA
Columbia, SC
21 June 2025